About the authors

Belinda is single. She writes poetry and paints in her spare time and enjoys walking in the countryside and local woodlands with her dog.

Felix, also single, took an active part in Formula Ford racing in his youth and is now interested in unusual cars, watching football and rugby, going to the movies and visiting art galleries.

PASSIONATE INTENTION

Belinda Vale
and
Felix Foreman

PASSIONATE INTENTION

Vanguard Press

A CIP catalogue record for this title is available from the British
Library.

ISBN: 9781784656 911

Vanguard Press is an imprint of
Pegasus Elliot MacKenzie Publishers Ltd.
www.pegasuspublishers.com

First Published in 2020

Vanguard Press
Sheraton House Castle Park
Cambridge England

Printed & Bound in Great Britain

Dedication

This book is dedicated to Felix's sisters,
Susan and Alison.

Acknowledgements

Sincere thanks to Julie and Louise, our bookworm friends who read the book and provided useful feedback during its creation.

Chapter 1
(July 1988)

Belting out the latest Shakin' Stevens number at ear-splitting volume, the battered old blue van braked sharply, barely stopping long enough for its passenger to jump out onto the scorching pavement.

'Thanks, mate, see you Monday! Have a good one!'

As the vehicle drove off, leaving a wall of acrid smoke in its wake, the figure – male; mid-twenties, average height – hesitated for a moment, undecided whether to walk straight home or call in his local for a pint first. It was a no-brainer really, the heat had been relentless all day and even now, at six p.m., the sun was still blazing down from a cloudless sky. A long, cold pint would lubricate his dusty throat nicely.

As he turned, an approaching woman stopped dead in her tracks, stared at him, pulled a face and walked out into the road as she passed, quickening her pace. Then a couple came along behind her, breaking off their conversation at the sight of him, also staring and giving him a wide berth. He turned to look at them. They stood close together, watching him.

Strange, he thought. Okay, so he was a bit dusty and dishevelled after a day's hard work, especially in this heat;

it went with the job, but he didn't look like a tramp or a mugger. Some people could be very intolerant.

'Out!' the publican shouted, as he entered the bar.

'I just wa—'

'Out, I said. Vagrants are not welcome here!'

'But…'

Herbert Holloway, the licensee, flipped up the hinged bar top. Six foot three in his socks, and a former middleweight boxer, removing this unwanted guest posed no problem to him. Still displaying some nifty footwork, he crossed the bar, empty at this hour but for an elderly regular who watched the proceedings from a window seat as he glanced through the evening paper.

Bert stood in front of the heap of filthy, black clothes from which an equally filthy, sweat-smudged face emerged. A trickle of blood from a cut had congealed on its cheek; the whites of its eyes flickered wildly from beneath charcoal lids.

'Nah then, do I 'ave to use force, or are yer goin' ter leave quietly?'

'Bert! Stop mucking about; I'm gasping for a drink here!'

Recognising the voice now, particularly the northern accent, Bert gasped, genuinely shocked at the appearance of Robbie Munro, one of his regulars. Screwing up his eyes, he stooped towards him, trying to get a better look.

'Gawd love us! Robbie Munro… what the 'ell's 'appened? Yer been in a fire or summink, son?'

'Eh? No, I just finished work—'

'What, down the bleedin' mines now, are yer? What are yer like? Get yourself in the gents and clean yerself up, mate, then I might just think about serving yer... and don't leave the place lookin' like a chimney sweeps' feast day, neither!'

Robbie could hardly believe his eyes when he saw his own image staring back at him from the mirror in the gents; it was scary. No wonder people were giving him looks of disapproval. How come those two buggers – his mates, allegedly – had left him to walk the streets looking like Dick van Dyke's understudy?

Having apologised profusely and cleaned himself up sufficiently for Bert to allow him a pint of ESB as long as he downed it and made himself scarce, Robbie drank up and left, playing over in his mind what he was going to say to those two on Monday and already bracing himself for the Sooty and Sweep jokes. He turned into his tree-lined road, relieved to be nearly home after a demanding day's work at the site of a Victorian house that was being restored as part of a heritage project. His task had been to carefully dismantle the period fireplace and then restore the chimney breast and flue before cleaning and rebuilding the fireplace. It had been very cramped, and he was hot, tired, hungry, slightly humiliated and desperate to take a shower.

He wondered how his mother, Fiona, had been spending her time. The doctor had advised her to get out in the fresh air every day, adding that the exercise and being around other people would help with her recovery.

Robbie hoped she'd had a good day. Though not especially close to his mother in the past, he wanted her to overcome her pernicious dependency and was doing all he could to be supportive, at the same time encouraging her to help herself, for she was the only person who could do it. The whole family had done their best; now it was up to her.

Reaching his home, he walked past the oddly-shaped tarpaulin-covered vehicle parked outside, and up the path of the semi-detached house, letting himself in through the front door, intending to have his much-needed shower and a meal before going out again later. About to call to his mother that he was home, he was instead lost for words as there, before him in the hallway, stood a vision of loveliness. His jaw dropped open and for a moment he thought he was in the wrong house except that Lucy, his Labrador, came bouncing up to him with her usual boisterous welcome. A stunningly attractive young lady was standing there right in front of him, his mother at her side, showing her a family photograph on the hall table.

'Och, there y'are, Robbie,' his mother said, 'I want to introduce ye to Anna…' she paused for a moment, '… Sarri?' she queried.

She was answered with a nod and a smile.

'Sarri,' Fiona repeated, pleased with herself for getting it right first time. 'Anna, this is ma son, Robbie…' she broke off, looking her son up and down and frowning before adding, 'aye, and will ye just look at the state o' him!' She peered up into his face. 'An how did ye come by that?' pointing to the cut under his left eye.

Anna had strikingly blue eyes that lit up as she smiled and said hello to Robbie.

'Robbie!' his mother scolded. 'Ye look like a *gangrel*, laddie! Ye'd best go and take a shower or hae yoursel' a bath!'

Huh, good job you didn't see me half an hour ago, Robbie thought.

He smiled awkwardly at Anna. 'Yes, sorry, I am in a bit of a mess... I won't shake hands. Er, excuse me won't you, if I go and get cleaned up.'

He dashed up the stairs, threw off his sooty garments, selected a clean shirt and jeans, shut himself in the bathroom and turned on the shower.

When he came down for tea, his mother explained Anna's presence. Fiona had been walking in Richmond Park, where Anna had been sitting on a bench, writing. She sat down next to her and Anna moved along, making more room. They made polite conversation, both commenting on the warm sunshine and how lovely the park was with its trees in full leaf and the brightly coloured shrubberies. The bees hummed a lazy tune as they searched for nectar and butterflies danced around them, others settling and just warming their wings in the sun.

'Don't let me interrupt yer writing, hen,' Fiona said, patting her arm. 'I'll just sit here quietly and take in the view while I rest ma legs... that's if ye doan't mind having me here alongside ye, of course?'

Anna smiled warmly, inwardly struggling a little bit to understand Fiona's broad Lanarkshire accent.

'No, please, I do not mind,' she assured Fiona. 'I am just writing to my parents in Switzerland. My father, he asked me to find a headlamp for his classic Daimler, but I'm afraid I am not having any luck so far.'

'Och, are ye frae Switzerland? Aye, an' I did wonder about your accent.'

'Yes, my home is in Basel. I am here working as an au pair for a family in Barnes and also studying English at Richmond College.' She spoke in a warm tone, with a slightly husky voice.

'Ye speak the language very well, lassie, Fiona told her. 'Better than ma Scottish-English, I dare say – why, ye'll be one of their star students, I'm sure.' She took in Anna's light blue jeans and crisp white shirt, a gold necklace glinting in the sunlight. She had an honest and open face framed by fair hair that curled and tumbled carelessly around her shoulders. She sat relaxed on the wooden bench, legs crossed at the ankles, her white peep-toe sandals completing her outfit. They had chatted for a while and then Fiona asked her if she would like to go back with her for a cup of tea.

'Thank you, I would love to come and have a cup of tea with you,' Anna replied.

'And here she is!' Fiona concluded.

Robbie's appointment that evening was with the local church, St. Stephen's in Richmond, Surrey. On Friday evenings, he met with the Sunday School group as a volunteer to take a Bible class and then play football with the youngsters afterwards. He picked up his bag containing

16

a sweater and his trainers, inserted his notes into the side pocket and bade Anna and Fiona farewell.

'I'm very pleased to have met you,' he said to Anna. 'Perhaps we shall meet again?'

'Who knows?' Anna replied with a smile, hoping that would be the case. She was attracted to his lazy smile; it was something to do with how his eyes half closed... and his curly but neat brown hair now that it was visible... the way he moved...

Smiling back, he said, 'Bye then, lovely to meet you,' and, 'see you later, Mum,' and left the house, thinking no more of it, other than feeling pleased about his mum meeting someone locally that she could have a friendly chat with. Just what the doctor ordered, he thought as he made his way towards the church meeting room, hoping that Anna would come to tea again soon.

The meeting with the Sunday School group on that particular evening was very poignant. One of the members, Bethany, who was just eighteen, had recently lost her father to a brain tumour. She stood up and explained to the rest of the class why she believed in God and also that she was in no doubt that her father was in heaven. Robbie listened, deeply moved, as she openly expressed her feelings and he thought how very brave she was to stand up in front of everyone at such an emotional time in her life. There was not even a tear in sight; just a calm young lady explaining to the rest of the group what had happened to her father and that he was now free from pain and suffering and how she believed his soul had found eternal peace.

After the reading and prayers, Robbie and the boys played a robust game of football that continued for quite a long time on that warm summer evening. Bethany and the girls meanwhile prepared light refreshments and played music, some of them dancing together, others just chatting socially, until it was time to pack everything away and lock up for another week.

It was after ten when Robbie arrived home and to his surprise and delight, Anna was still there, talking with his mum in the lounge.

Fiona had a smile on her face and Robbie thought she looked happier than he had ever seen her.

'Well,' he said, 'you two must have a lot in common and certainly a lot to talk about.'

Fiona nudged Anna. 'Aye, I think we get along really well,' she replied. 'Doan't you, Anna?'

When Anna laughed the huskiness was more pronounced and made her even more attractive. Robbie was intrigued by her.

'Oh yes, I think so, too, Fiona,' she replied. A mischievous smile played on her lips as she spoke.

Robbie was a little bemused; this young lady appeared to have succeeded in bringing his mother out of her shell after years of hiding herself away, just letting life pass her by. She seemed a different person... and who else, other than family or close friends had ever called her Fiona? It was always Mrs Munro. He looked at Anna, catching her eye, and smiling back at her, drawn to her obvious love of life, her ebullience. She has something, he thought to himself; something really special... she is gorgeous. What am I waiting for?

'Makes you thirsty,' Fiona said, suddenly getting up, 'all this *chenwaggin'*. Time I put the kettle on.'

As Fiona went into the kitchen, Robbie took his opportunity.

'It's Saturday tomorrow, Anna,' he began, 'and I was wondering if you would like to take Lucy for a walk in the park with me?'

There was that radiant smile again.

'I'd be very happy to take Lucy for a walk in the park with you, Robbie,' she replied. 'It would be lovely.'

Lucy, lying at Anna's feet, wagged her tail with enthusiasm. She adored company and had not been far from her all evening.

''Lucy thinks so as well,' she said, stooping to fondle the dog's ears.

Robbie sat down next to Anna and she turned towards him.

'Can I ask you something?'

'Sure, fire away!' he replied, then noticing her puzzled expression, 'oh, sorry, er... yes, of course, what is it?'

'What is this... 'chen waggin'?' She nodded towards the kitchen. 'Fiona, she has it?'

Robbie laughed. 'Oh, that is a bit of cockney – London slang – that Mum has picked up,' he explained. '*Chin* wagging, it means talking a lot. That's what the two of you have been doing all evening, hm?'

'Ah, then it is something like chatterbox, uh?'

19

'Exactly,' he confirmed, 'chatterboxes, both of you! And here comes the other one,' he grinned as Fiona entered the lounge, carefully carrying a tray on which were three mugs of hot chocolate and a plate of digestive biscuits.

Saturday came, and Anna took particular care with her make-up and her hair, which was inclined to take on a life of its own if not securely held in a ribbon or the various coloured velvet scrunchies that she favoured. She had been attracted to Robbie as soon as they met, even though he was covered in soot and grime. He had an open, honest face, warm, welcoming eyes and a wonderful, slightly crooked smile that lifted her spirits. She was looking forward to getting to know him.

Anna turned up at Robbie's house on a bicycle.

'Nice bike,' he said, greeting her at the gate.

'Yes, but it is only borrowed; my employer allows me to use it to get around. I have found it very useful and of course it saves bus and train fares.'

'Okay, well, I'll wheel it round the back; it will be safe there.' He took the bicycle from Anna and ran his hands over the saddle.

'Lucky saddle,' he remarked softly and mostly to himself, finding it amusing and grinning at what he'd said. Anna smiled but said nothing.

She was wearing a trench coat over her favourite dress – the green with black stripes that suited her perfectly. She had style, grace and poise. He was captivated by her beautiful blue eyes, set wide in her open, oval face. She had prominent features and an adorable dimple graced her cheek when she smiled. Her light brown hair was long and wavy, with fair highlights and when not tied back, fell unrestrained about her shoulders.

They headed off towards the park, Lucy on her leash trotting happily alongside them, her tail appearing to be on a spring. They chatted easily, getting to know a little more about each other and Anna mentioned her meeting with Fiona the previous day.

'Your mother, she is a friendly person,' Anna said, 'and I immediately liked her, but there seemed to be a sadness about her… I felt that she was a bit lonely.'

'Yes, well, Dad's away working a lot of the time; he's a civil engineer,' Robbie explained, 'and when he is not away, he spends a lot of time on the golf course or visiting friends. Of course, I am at work full time as well, so she does spend a lot of time on her own.' He hesitated. 'And… she hasn't been too well; Mum's an alcoholic, you see. She is getting help now, but of course it isn't easy for her.'

Anna nodded. 'I know she is an alcoholic.'

'Did she tell you that herself?'

'Yes, she did. It seemed to be a relief for her to talk about it and as you say, it is not at all easy for her.'

Robbie felt slightly piqued that his mother would open her heart to a complete stranger she met by chance in the park and yet had kept her condition so well hidden that not one of the family even guessed she had a problem until it began to affect her health.

'She has never wanted to talk to any of us about it,' Robbie said defensively. 'In fact, she kept it to herself for years; we all knew she liked a drink – she always has, but none of us had any idea that it had become a problem… an addiction. Then once we knew, my sisters and I all wanted to help her and we tried and so did Dad, but she always either changed the subject or clammed up altogether and refused to admit she had a problem—either to herself or anyone else.' He shrugged helplessly. 'We just wanted her to be well and happy.'

'Sometimes it is easier to talk to a stranger,' Anna said gently. 'Families do not always understand. Your mother is a nice woman. She is warm and caring.' She laid her hand gently on Robbie's arm. 'And she will make it… she will get well, because she wants to.'

Robbie placed his hand over Anna's and closed his eyes for a moment, touched that she seemed to care and was not at all judgemental.

As they walked, they were asking lots of questions about each other.

'Did Fiona mention that I am from Switzerland?' Anna asked.

'No; she didn't say a lot last night; she went to bed shortly after you left, but I could tell from your accent that you were either Swiss or Dutch. Actually, I thought you sounded a bit German.'

Anna laughed, disarming Robbie with the amazing husky, throaty sound. 'That is because I am Swiss-German and not Swiss-French. My home is in Basel, in the north. And you, Robbie? Were you born in Scotland?'

'Yes, I am Scottish,' Robbie replied, 'but we left when I was a child, so I lost the accent as I grew up.'

22

'But yours is a northern accent, surely?' she asked. 'Not London?'

'You are right—Yorkshire, to be precise. That's where my sisters and I grew up and went to school. You seem to understand me all right, though?'

Anna smiled. 'Oh yes, and I understand your mum mostly, too… just a few words have me confused, you know?'

Robbie laughed. Yes, I know – like chin-wagging!'

'Ha ha, yes, that is definitely a new one to me!' She changed the subject. 'Have you ever been to Switzerland, Robbie?'

'No, never. In fact, I have never been abroad.'

'Oh, then you will have to come and have a visit with me because I am going back there soon when my course at Richmond College finishes.'

Robbie was interested in her studies; he was about halfway into a degree course in science with the Open University.

'What have you been studying?'

'English.'

'Your English is excellent; you have done very well.'

'Thank you. That is what your mum said, too. Also, I am au pair for a family in Barnes and I speak only English to them and to the children, so I have improved a lot by living in your country and conversing with English people…' she laughed again, 'and now I have also found some Scottish people.'

'So, you have your meals and everything provided, do you?'

23

'I have full bed and board, yes, and a little pocket money for the extras, you know.' She lowered her voice which, already having a husky quality, sounded like the soft, growling purr of a tigress. 'They are extremely rich and very generous… I am very lucky. And they are very understanding if I ask for extra time off,' she added, 'as long as someone is there for the children, of course.'

'How many children have they?'

'There are three—their daughter and two young boys. They are delightful children and very well behaved most of the time, although the youngest son can be very er, mis…chiefous? He plays the jokes a lot, you know?' She pulled a face, remembering the huge, lifelike spider she had discovered on her pillow one night.

'Pranks.'

'Yes, that is it… he *pranks*!'

Robbie stifled a laugh. He could listen to her for hours. Suddenly he felt a wave of anxiety. She had said was returning home when her course ended.

'So, when does your course finish?' he asked.

'Two more weeks to go and then I have four more weeks with the children before I return to my homeland.' She looked downcast and gave him a rueful smile.

'Fancy me being here for a year and then I meet you just before I am due to leave!'

Robbie's anxiety turned to mild panic. The girl he loved – yes, he already knew on this, their second meeting, that he was falling in love with her – was about to leave the country and there was nothing he could do about it.

24

'I will come to Switzerland to see you, Anna,' he assured her.

'Oh please do, Robbie; I would like that very much.'

He was seized by further distress when he remembered that he had arranged to go on a camping holiday with his church group in a week's time. His steps faltered, and he stopped for a moment. Looking at Anna with a frown, he sighed.

'What is wrong?' she asked. 'You are feeling unwell? You have quite a bruise around that cut now.'

'N… no,' he stumbled, 'I am fine. It's just that I have made arrangements to go away next weekend for a week's camping holiday with my church group. I… well, I am going to miss you, Anna… I want to spend as much time as possible with you…'

Again, that gentle touch on his arm as she replied, 'I will miss you too, but it will soon go by.'

His heart skipped a beat. 'You will?'

'Will what?'

'Miss me… I mean, I know we have only just met, but already—'

'Ssh,' she hushed, placing her forefinger against his lips, smiling into his eyes. 'Don't say any more. We will survive. Okay?'

'Okay.'

They exchanged addresses and telephone numbers as well as photographs. Anna showed Robbie a family photograph that she carried in her wallet.

'These are my two sisters, Silke and Evelyn, and my brother, Max.'

25

Robbie noticed that all three girls had the same strong features and their brother resembled the older woman in the picture.

'Is that your mother?' he asked her.

'Oh yes, we all call her Mama... dearest Mama. Marianne—she is French.'

'And your father?'

'Papa is Italian,' she replied, 'but he was not present when this picture was taken. He and Mama are separated, but they still work together. They run a Ferrari dealership in Basel.'

Robbie's ears pricked up. 'Did you say Ferrari? Wow!'

'Yes; it is a prosperous business. Marcel, my sister's boyfriend, works for them as a mechanic. Mama looks after the accounting, Papa, he does the sales and after-sales and they have a couple of general hands as well.'

'Lucky Marcel—working on Ferraris and in a relationship with your sister!'

'Marcel is a very lucky boy,' Anna agreed. He stays at our apartment with Evelyn, and Mama adores him of course because he is French, so they get on very well together and she spoils him. But that is her nature. Papa— he can be difficult and has a temper, but we all get along.' She smiled. 'You will get on well with Marcel. He is – how do you say – 'hip' young man with long hair, but he is very likeable and good for my sister, too.'

'Great. I shall look forward to meeting him – and the rest of your family, of course.'

'They will make you welcome, Robbie; they will adore you; I know they will.'

Fiona had mentioned having two daughters but had not elaborated further.

'Do you have a brother, Robbie? Your mum mentioned your sisters'.

'No, just the girls,' he replied. Sophie and Emily.'

'Lovely names! Do they live nearby?'

'Emily lives near Isleworth, where she works as a vet, and Sophie is married with her own family down in Hampshire.'

'So you are an uncle… is that right?'

'Yes, my love. You are right, I am an uncle.'

'Hampshire is very pretty. I was taken on a day out with my employers and the children to the New Forest. It was breathtaking, and the children loved the ponies!'

'Yes, lovely area.' Robbie, however, was more interested in talking about his future visit to Anna's home in Switzerland.

'We'll write to each other,' Robbie said 'and of course we can phone, and I will try to come and see you in October or it may have to be November. I don't have a passport at the moment, but I can get one between now and then.'

'Wonderful,' she agreed, 'that sounds good and so that's what we'll do. But now we must make the most of this lovely day.'

Holding hands now, they carried on walking along the path through the trees, with Lucy watching and staying close by. The conversation turned to music.

'I like Blondie and Duran Duran,' Robbie said. 'Oh and Depeche Mode, and I like The Shadows—a bit old fashioned, I know, but they have a great sound.'

'My favourite singer is Tracy Chapman,' Anna replied. 'I could listen to her all day long.'

'I know she is very popular,' Robbie replied.

'Do you like musicals, Robbie?' Anna asked.

He replied that he had never actually seen or been to a musical.

'What are they usually about? Are they like operas?'

'No, not at all. They are very different... they are like opera in that they are stories set to music with singing, but there is spoken dialogue in a musical, with intermittent singing and often dancing. In opera, the singing is constant—every word is sung. And musicals are usually much more fun and a lot easier to understand. You must have heard of *The Sound of Music*, surely?'

'Well, I have heard Mum talk about it. In fact, I think she has a recording of it somewhere.'

'So,' she laughed, 'what are you waiting for? Tell her you would like to watch it sometime. You will enjoy it, I know.'

'But I don't have time to sit around watching movies, you know. When I am not working, I am usually busy with my Open University course work, or out with my Bible study group or—'

She cut him off, pushing his chest playfully with the palm of her hand, 'Stop making excuses—you work far too hard and anyway, you will love it; I know you will. It is set in Salzburg in Austria, not that far away from where

I live in Switzerland, and the scenery and songs are magical. Salzburg is a very beautiful, very romantic city.'

'I should imagine so, yes,' he replied, wondering what he had missed. But it was true—what with his job, his studies and the volunteer work, he never seemed to find the time for entertainment.

'What are you studying with Open University?' she asked him.

'I am going for a Bachelor of Science degree,' he replied.

'Really? That is interesting.' She smiled, remembering their first meeting. 'And I think will lead you to something more worthwhile than sooty old chimneys, uh?'

He laughed. 'I would hope so, yes... but at least I know how soot is produced and what it consists of. Chemically there is more to it than just being black and dirty.'

They strolled along, past the lake, towards the wooded area, relaxed in each other's company, Lucy now on her leash, restrained from chasing any wildlife.

'Would you like to go to a live musical?' Anna suddenly asked.

'Erm, I would like to, yes. After all, I do like music.'

'Then why don't we go to one?'

'Well, yes... did you have a particular one in mind? Could we perhaps see *The Sound of Music*?'

She laughed. 'No, silly, that was years ago. You will have to watch your mum's videotape to see that.'

'Oh. Okay. Which one then?'

'Well, I think I would like to go to see Les Misérables. It is on at the Palace Theatre in London right now. It has won awards and is very much acclaimed. I want to see it before I go home.'

'Then we shall go and see it,' he replied, having no clue at all what the show was about and not really that bothered if it meant spending an evening with Anna.

'And you are sure you can tear yourself away from your chimneys and your studies?' she asked, a mischievous twinkle lighting up her eyes.

Robbie grinned. 'I said we shall see it and see it we shall.' He made a mental note to go to the booking office and get two tickets, if possible, for the week after his holiday.

As they continued chatting, she mentioned the headlamp for her father's Daimler.

'I promised I would try to get one for him,' she said, fishing a scrap of paper out of her handbag with the model and series number written down. 'But everywhere I try, they just shake their heads. It seems impossible. Poor Papa, he is going to be disappointed, I fear.'

Robbie held out his hand for the paper. 'Let me have that,' he said, 'and I will have a look around the local scrap yards. There may be one out there somewhere waiting for a good home.'

She laughed and gave him a hug. 'You are a good, kind man. Thank you for offering to help; you may have more luck than I did.'

He hugged her back. Their relationship was underway.

Chapter 2

A week later, on the Monday morning, Robbie set off with his friends, David and Paul, to summer camp in Devizes for a week. Jack and Simon went in another car and David's fiancée, Julie, also travelled separately with her friends, Louise and Mary.

The weather was glorious as they packed the car—perfect for a camping holiday.

At that time, Robbie was driving a Ford Consul. It was his pride and joy and it was roomy enough to take the three of them and their equipment comfortably. As soon as everything was on board they left Richmond for Wiltshire, where they would be living under canvas for the next seven days along with many others, all of whom belonged to or were associated with Bible study groups.

Their destination lay approximately one hundred miles west of London and traffic was steady on the M4, but they encountered a great many caravans either leaving or heading to their destinations. These were fewer in number when they left the motorway and drove along the A roads, taking in some beautiful scenery as they went. It was about two hours later that they turned off the main road, leaving the heavier traffic behind for the quieter, rural route that would take them to their campsite and their home for the week ahead.

As they drove slowly down the country lane, David spotted some tents pitched in a field about a quarter of a mile distant.

'That must be it!' he said, pointing to his right.

Seeing the hand painted CAMP SITE signpost just ahead of them, Robbie confirmed that it was indeed and turned onto the dusty track that led to the twenty-acre field, belonging to a yoghurt manufacturing company. The owners had turned the cows out to the neighbouring pastures in order to rent this one out as a camping ground for the church youth groups.

The dust rose in clouds as they drove down the bumpy track.

'This must be terrible in wet weather,' Robbie commented, barely able to see where he was going.

'Great for a mud race,' David replied.

'Great for the cows as well,' Paul grinned. 'Can you imagine... mud-racing cows... ha-ha, instant milk shakes!'

David groaned, and Robbie ignored Paul's quip; he would make a joke out of anything but at least he was always cheerful; sometimes irritatingly so.

They quickly found the site, where a few other groups were busily pitching their tents and unpacking camping stoves, sleeping bags and sundry items of portable furniture. Robbie parked the car in a fairly clean spot, relatively free of dried cowpats and near to some trees and the freshwater stream. He and his passengers unloaded their tent and began the business of laying groundsheets, pitching and securing the three-berth tent and unloading the rest of their gear. By the time they had finished the operation, they were more than ready for their first brew of tea, made from water from the stream, boiled on a primus stove.

As the kettle boiled, David put up their picnic table between the car and the tent, arranged three mugs, a bowl of sugar and a carton of milk on its surface and unfolded and positioned three canvas garden chairs.

'Home from home,' he said, sipping his tea. 'Doesn't it taste different?'

'Tea made al fresco always tastes different,' Robbie said, 'but yes, I agree that this is a damn good cup of tea.'

Paul nodded toward the field at the other side of the stream where a herd of Friesians grazed peacefully, their tails constantly swishing in an effort to keep free from flies.

'Probably tastes different because of them,' he remarked, shading his eyes and scanning their field. 'Their drinking place appears to be upstream and cows are not briefed in hygiene, are they? I mean, they drink the water, so they are just as likely to pee in— '

'Yes... All right, Paul, if you don't mind!' David exclaimed.

'Just a thought,' Paul replied, winking at Robbie and grinning broadly.

'Well kindly keep that kind of thought to yourself!' David retorted. 'The tea tastes fine.'

'Sure it does—and anyway, the water has been boiled,' Robbie added, trying to keep a straight face.

'Exactly—and no one is forced to drink it if they don't want to!'

Still amused, Paul was about to utter another wisecrack when an elderly man approached.

Robbie got up from his chair, smiling and extending his arm to shake hands with his old friend, Harold, the Group Leader.

'Good to see you, Harold.' He indicated his companions, 'You know David and Paul of course, don't you?'

After greetings were exchanged, Harold said, 'Don't suppose you experienced chaps would mind helping dig out the lats?' He pointed to a secluded spot beyond some distant trees where two young men could just be seen, wielding spades. 'This is their first time and I'd be grateful if you could give them a bit of guidance.'

'No problem, Harold,' David replied, swallowing the rest of his tea. 'Shovels in the usual place?'

'Yes, in the stores. You'll find all you need in there.'

While David and Robbie made their way to the cowshed that for at least one week every summer was upgraded to Stores, Paul made himself useful by clearing away the tea things and washing up. He asked Harold if many campers were expected.

'Should be fifty tents, give or take,' Harold replied. 'We usually have a good turnout and of course this glorious weather will help. You lads have picked yourselves a decent spot here; nice and cool under the trees.' He removed his hand from his pocket, motioning towards their tent.

The sprightly seventy-six-year-old was married to Doe (short for Dorothy) who was as gentle as the animal that her name conjured in the mind.

'Well, I'll leave you to it for now m'boy,' he said before continuing with his tour of duty. 'See you all later.'

As David and Robbie approached the latrine area, they could see that some sort of disturbance was taking place. One boy was slicing the air with his shovel and another was shouting, 'Ouch! Aw, that really hurt...'

'What on earth is going on with these two?' asked David.

'Dunno,' Robbie replied, 'but I think we'd better intervene before someone is seriously hurt, or worse. If you can distract him, I'll try to grab his shovel!'

They hurried to the scene, relieved to discover that they were not witnessing a potential murder... at least not homicidal.

'Flaming wasps,' gasped the one wielding the shovel.

'Spiteful things,' shouted the other, rubbing his neck, 'I haven't done them any harm!'

'Have you been stung?' Robbie asked the vocal one, an eighteen-year-old called Martin.

'Yeah! Twice; they are all over the place!' he ducked and swerved out of the way of another wasp diving at his face.

'There must be a nest nearby,' David replied. 'They can be really angry when disturbed.'

'You got that right,' the youth answered.

'Well,' Robbie began, edging a little distance away from the latrines, 'we have come to give you a hand, but I suggest we vacate the scene for half an hour or so to let them settle and then see how it looks.'

Meanwhile, the other boy, Tommy, had noticed a large number of wasps buzzing around an old bird box nailed to a tree trunk about six feet from the ground.

'Look, he pointed, 'I bet that's where the nest is.'

'Aha,' said David, advancing a few steps to get a closer look at the buzzing, dancing, yellow-and-black mass, 'that's where the blighters are. Right, come on, away from there. We'll have to find another place for the lats... can't be risking getting stung every time nature calls!' He looked around and walked in the opposite direction towards another area secluded by trees.

'Let's try here,' he suggested.

Later that afternoon, with the latrines dug and made as private as possible and a notice pinned up on a tree near the former lats site, warning of the wasps' nest, David and his mates took a walk round the field, meeting up with several friends and acquaintances from previous years. Julie and her friends, Louise and Mary, had also arrived and had pitched their tent a little further down from Robbie and David. Further on still, David's brother, Simon, and Jack, his passenger, were just securing their guy ropes. They stopped for a brief chat and carried on with their tour of the camp.

They located the 'bathroom' which was a zinc bath in a tent pitched on its own a distance away from the others.

If it was not in use, the bath was upended in front of the tent entrance. If the bath was missing, it meant that it was in use and the bathroom was 'engaged'. None of them could recall ever passing the 'bathroom' and finding the bath missing.

By late afternoon, as Harold had predicted, there was a total of about fifty tents, mostly khaki-coloured, on the field and to anyone just passing, it could have been a military platoon on training exercises. During the evening, small communes were formed, and simple but nourishing and tasty meals were cooked, eaten and cleared away. It was still hot well into the night and many took refuge under the trees or in their tents, the latter affording more protection from insects, though feeling rather muggy inside. Even in the heat of summer, there was still hot chocolate on offer before bed every night and most of the campers liked it. It was Robbie's favourite and he never missed out on partaking. The wasps were still there in abundance and turned up, unwelcome and uninvited, whenever meals or drinks were being prepared.

Each evening, the campers assembled for a Bible reading before retiring. Robbie was honoured to be asked to take one of the Bible readings – Samson and Delilah being his subject, no less. He felt very nervous and later admitted that at first, he was petrified at the thought of leading a study in the presence of so many people, but as the reading went on he began to enjoy it and was pleased to have been offered the opportunity. When Robbie phoned Anna the next day, he told her all about it and how anxious he had felt.

'At the time, honestly I wished I had not agreed to do it,' he said, 'but now I am glad I did because it was a wonderful experience.' He also told her that he had managed to book two tickets for Les Misérables for the following Monday evening.

'I hope you are not doing anything on Monday evening?' he asked.

There was a pause.

'Well, yes... I am, as a matter of fact,' she replied.

'Oh, no.' Robbie's heart sank to his boots. 'I know I should have mentioned it first, but I wanted it to be a surprise.'

She laughed. 'Robbie, I am teasing. What I am doing on Monday evening is going with you to see Les Misérables. It is a wonderful surprise and I am looking forward to it very much. Thank you!'

The camping holiday was not without incident. One afternoon, they staged a 'Hunt the Senior' competition, in which the local children participated. The idea was for the seniors, being the group stewards and leaders, to make whatever fancy dress was possible out of their own clothing and anything else they could find that might be of use and go into the town, where the children then had to identify who they were. Robbie decided he would be a brickie, mainly because he didn't really want to be bothered at all but thought he had better show willing. He put on a scruffy pair of jeans and his work boots that he had worn whilst digging out the lats, and a clean but shapeless grey T-shirt that he had put to one side to be used as a cloth. As it turned out, his meagre efforts at dressing up proved to be a waste of time anyway because nobody taking part was allowed to go into a shop or business during the competition but Robbie, spotting a tea shop, was attracted to it like a magnet. He instinctively went in and finding the place empty, selected a table in a corner at the back. He ordered a pot of Earl Grey and a plate of cakes and was therefore seen by no one except the tea shop owner who had no clue about what was going on except that he only had two customers—one of them a rough looking brickie, drinking posh tea and eating fancy cakes!

However, there was an episode that began as a bit of fun but could have proved far more serious when Paul, the joker, went a bit too far with his disguise. He decided it would be fun and cause some excitement to impersonate a bank robber. Unfortunately, this time, his actions turned out to be a prank too far, especially as he was then also foolish enough to walk openly through the shopping centre with a borrowed nylon stocking stretched over his head and face, wielding a toy gun that looked genuine at first glance. So realistic and menacing did he look that a small boy nearby began screaming with fright and people in the immediate area hurried away, finding refuge in gift shops or cafés. The police were alerted and within minutes an armed response unit was at the scene and Paul was disarmed, unmasked and arrested. He was actually locked up for a few hours until Harold had to go and vouch for him and get him released. It was a stupid hoax and Harold made it clear that he was not impressed by what he considered irresponsible conduct by a senior.

No one was harmed, and Paul apologised to Harold and to the police and to anyone he had alarmed with his tomfoolery, but the incident was the subject of lively discussion for the next two or three days.

On the last evening there, Harold agreed that this year they could assemble around a campfire for the final reading, traditionally led by himself. He closed the proceedings with prayers and thanksgiving and told the gathering that anyone who wanted to could sit around the campfire and sing songs for a while. Jack had brought his acoustic guitar and the singing and even some dancing continued until well after dark. It was a joyful conclusion to what had been a very happy week and as Robbie sipped his last mug of hot chocolate, he reflected that although he had missed Anna and thought about her a lot, he was also glad that he had been here to take part. The bonhomie of such occasions was something special and showed humanity in its best light, demonstrating the community spirit at its best.

The following morning, Robbie, Paul and a few volunteers took a last walk around the field making sure that no litter was left and that the lats were properly filled in and the area left completely clean and safe. The remains of the campfire were damped down, and the field was left tidy and in good order. Then it was time to pack up and hit the

40

road; back to Richmond and for Robbie, back to his beautiful new lady, Anna.

Unfortunately, the drive home was neither smooth nor successful. The car suddenly began making strange noises.

'What's up with the engine, mate?' Paul asked. 'Surely you didn't forget to give her a drink of water in this heat?'

Everybody laughed, but it was clear that something was mechanically very wrong. They were approaching a service station and Robbie slowed down and managed to limp into a parking space. There was a cloud of smoke and a nasty smell of hot metal, and people were turning to stare at them as they drove in. The guys scrambled out of the car and suddenly there was an explosion as the engine blew up. From the smell and all the smoke, they thought it was going to catch fire and frantically grabbed all their belongings, stacking them up near the grass bank where they had stopped.

They went to get a cup of tea and when they returned, the engine had stopped smoking, although it was still giving off some heat. Robbie very gingerly lifted the bonnet and found everything blackened underneath.

'Don't touch it,' David advised. 'Ring for a breakdown truck and let them deal with it.' He shook his head. 'Looks knackered to me,' he added.

Eventually the breakdown service arrived, and the mechanic confirmed the worst. David was right; the engine had seized completely and was beyond repair, so the car was towed straight to the scrapyard. David's brother,

Simon, came to the rescue and picked them up and they finally reached home late, hungry and tired.

Such was a camper's lot!

Chapter 3

Robbie wasted no time the next morning phoning Anna.

'Ah, my wanderer returns,' she said. 'And how are you today after your holiday in the tents? Did you all have a good time?'

Robbie told her they had all enjoyed their week at the camp, that the weather was amazing, and they'd had some fun.

'I missed you,' he told her, 'and I thought about you every day, especially last thing at night before I went to sleep.'

'You will be telling me next that you dreamt about me, too,' she said with a laugh.

'Of course I did—who else would I be dreaming about?'

She laughed again. 'I missed you also and it is good to have you back, Robbie.'

'Well you nearly didn't,' he replied and told her briefly about the car seizing up on the way back and having to get a lift home.

'Anna was alarmed. 'And you are all right?' she asked. 'No one was hurt?'

'No, not all—just my pride. We are all fine, don't worry. Listen, Anna, I have to go to work now, so I will see you later this evening—about six-thirty, okay?'

Anna went about her chores with an extra spring in her step on that Monday morning. She had missed Robbie, although he had phoned her regularly from Devizes. Now he was back, and this evening would be escorting her to see Les Misérables in a West End theatre. What should she wear, she wondered? She had just bought a new dress in the summer sales; this would be the perfect occasion to wear it. She would put her hair up as well. And her sandals would be fine. She would have to repaint her toenails, though.

The afternoon seemed to drag on but finally she went to find her employer and told her that the children had eaten their tea and were now watching their favourite TV programme.

'May I leave them in your hands now and go and get ready to go out this evening?' she asked.

'Yes, of course,' was the answer. 'Thank you… and have a lovely evening.'

Anna had already laid out the new dress on her bed. She looked at it and then put it back in the wardrobe. Robbie liked her in the green dress, the one with black stripes; she would wear that one again tonight with a light jacket.

As they waited for the tube, Robbie told Anna that she looked stunning.

'I love you in that dress,' he told her. 'It was made for you. Tell me you wore it especially for me… did you?'

'I might have,' she replied. 'Only I know the answer to that.' She smiled, adding, 'Thank you for the compliment!'

'I'm sorry I didn't wear a suit,' he said, 'but in this weather, a jacket...'

'Would be too uncomfortable,' she finished, smiling up at him. 'You are fine as you are, looking cool and casual!'

The train, when it rumbled in just afterwards, was not too crowded, being a Monday evening, but passenger numbers were markedly increased when they changed to the Piccadilly Line at South Kensington to take the train for Leicester Square. However, they still had time in hand before the show was due to start.

'Have we time for an ice cream?' Anna asked, looking longingly at the treats on offer as they passed one of the pavement cafés.

'If we are quick.' Robbie, never one to miss the opportunity of a sweet treat, picked up a menu from one of the tables. 'What would you like?' he asked.

Anna ordered a knickerbocker glory, served in a large, tall glass and Robbie went for a Peach Melba. Ice cold, on a hot summer evening, they tasted delicious and so refreshing.

Anna dabbed her lips delicately with the paper napkin. 'Wow!' she exclaimed. 'That was the scrumpiest I have ever tasted!'

Robbie laughed, shaking his head slightly. He loved how she could give a sentence a better meaning by using the wrong expression.

'Isn't that what you say… scrumpy?'

'Scrumptious,' Robbie gently corrected her. 'Scrumpy is rough, strong cider. And then we have a word 'scrumping' – that means pinching apples – we used to do that as kids!'

'Pinching?' she asked, confused, squeezing her thumb and forefinger together. 'How does one *pinch* apples? And why?'

'No, no, I meant *stealing* apples—we sometimes say pinching or nicking…' he broke off, smiling at her bemused expression.

'Ach! She said, smiling back at him, 'I think that I will never understand completely the English language.'

'That makes two of us,' he replied, taking her arm. 'Anyway, come on, it's time we were moving!'

Robbie bought a box of Terry's chocolates from a corner kiosk and they then walked the short distance to the theatre, a grand, imposing red-brick Victorian building. When it was built in 1891, it served and was known as The Royal English Opera House and opened with a production of Arthur Sullivan's opera, *Ivanhoe*, which ran for a hundred and fifty-five performances. Unfortunately, the theatre was a failure as an opera house and was hastily converted into a variety theatre the following year and became very successful. Then, as Music Hall began to lose its appeal and die out in the 1960s, it was replaced by the musical. Today, modernised with comfortable seating and tasteful décor, the theatre is well known for hosting popular and long-running musicals.

Friendly and helpful staff assisted them to their seats in the front stalls, right where the action was and although the show had been running for two years at this particular venue, there were not that many unoccupied seats. As the minutes ticked away before curtain up, the buzz of conversation intensified and the atmosphere was charged with anticipation. Then the orchestra assembled in the pit, adding their tuning up sounds to the mix, before playing the overture as the lights began to dim.

Robbie felt for Anna's hand, giving it a squeeze as she turned to look at him.

'Happy?' he whispered.

'I am very happy, darling,' she murmured, 'and so looking forward to this. It is going to be an evening to remember.'

They sat, holding hands, in the front row, with the box of chocolates on Anna's lap, open and ready to dip into and as the curtain rose on the opening scene they sat back, nothing more on their minds than enjoying a wonderful evening out together.

During the interval, they stayed in their seats rather than joining the queues for the bars.

'So,' said Anna, choosing a soft-centre chocolate, 'are you enjoying my choice of musical?'

'It's amazing,' Robbie replied. 'The songs are absolutely wonderful and the costumes, the scenery, the cast with Michael Ball—everything is fantastic!'

'That's a yes, then,' she said, smiling. She leaned towards him. 'I knew you would love it. I think it is pretty amazing too—and even better than I expected!'

It was the start of their relationship and it was magical! Robbie's first real love. She was twenty-two and he was twenty-nine and had worked hard all his life on building sites and also in shops and driving jobs around London, so he'd had little opportunity to form a relationship with a girl. He intended to enjoy the experience as much as he possibly could.

After the show, they caught the tube home, chatting all the way about the show and Robbie saw Anna safely home to her employers' grand residence in Barnes. They kissed goodnight and arranged to see each other later in the week for a walk in the park, or perhaps on Barnes Common.

He told his workmates all about it the next morning and although they pulled his leg about love's young dream and a whirlwind romance, they were genuinely over the moon for him and also understood how difficult it could be to meet someone, as they all worked long hours and had very little time to themselves for socialising.

Robbie had enjoyed his first musical so much that he wanted to see another one and on his way home after a busy day at the building site, he bought an evening paper. He wanted to see what else was on at the moment that both he and Anna might be interested in. As soon as he saw that Brigadoon was on at the Victoria Palace Theatre, he decided to get tickets for it. He kept it as a surprise for Anna and did not tell her until he saw her on Thursday evening that he had planned another night out in town on Saturday.

'Really, and where are we going this time, if I may ask?' she replied, faking a harsh tone.

'Well, I am taking you to see Brigadoon at the Victoria Palace,' he announced. 'It's a revival of the original Werner and Loewe production and is about a mythical Scottish island and I think will be really entertaining, with a lot of Scottish music and highland dancing.'

'A story about your homeland? Scotland, I know, has a lot of history; it should be interesting, and I shall look forward to that!'

As before, Robbie made the short journey to Barnes to meet Anna and then they travelled by underground to Victoria. The theatre was almost opposite the station entrance, so there was not much of a walk this time and they did not stop to have any refreshment before they went in.

The cast gave a robust and rousing performance; the highland dancing was superb, and Anna was impressed by the piper who played during the wedding and funeral scenes.

'Have you not heard bagpipes played before, Anna?' Robbie whispered, noticing her rapt expression.

'No, I am sure I have not. The sound is so...' she paused, searching her mind for the English word she wanted, '... haunting – and a little bit sorrowful, but *so* beautiful.'

Robbie squeezed her hand, pleased that she was enjoying herself and that he had made a good choice for their night out. This time they each had a choc ice in the interval and chatted as they waited for the second half.

When they came out, they waited for the crowds to disperse and Robbie asked Anna if she was hungry.

'Shall we have good old English fish and chips al fresco to round off the evening?' he suggested.

'Why not?' she laughed. 'Yes, actually, I would like some.'

They found a fish bar and had a wait of about ten minutes while some freshly battered cod sizzled to crispy perfection in the golden, boiling fat, and then sat on a nearby wall and ate them. The meal tasted so good as they sat there together with the sights, sounds and aromas of central London drifting around them on the warm, gentle breeze.

As it was such a lovely evening, they walked to St James's Park underground and from there made their journey back home. On the way, Robbie, inspired by the musical, gave Anna a potted history of Scotland, telling her all about the Clan Cameron and Culloden and Robert the Bruce.

'Robert Bruce,' Anna said, 'I have heard something about Bruce and a spider… or is that another Bruce?'

'He was Robert the First,' Robbie replied, 'known as Robert the Bruce and legend has it that while waiting out the winter of 1306, he watched a spider on the cave wall trying time and time again to spin its web. Every time the spider fell, it pulled itself up to begin again, never giving up. Bruce took inspiration from the spider and resolved to continue his campaign against the English, concluding with the Scots' victory at Bannockburn.'

'That is intriguing,' Anna said. 'Is it true or purely legend about the spider?'

Robbie shrugged. 'Who knows? His victory at Bannockburn is certainly true, but of most interest to me of course, coming from Stirling is the Battle of Stirling Bridge where William Wallace defeated the English. There is a monument to him; a tower, overlooking the site.'

What with the kilted dancers and bagpipes in Brigadoon and Robbie's historical knowledge, Anna's spark of interest in Scotland was becoming a burning desire to know more.

The train slowed into Richmond station.

'I would like very much to visit your homeland,' she told him.

'You would love it,' he replied, 'and I would love to take you there, but it is quite a distance to travel – almost four hundred miles – and I can't take time off work yet, but one day I will take you...' he promised.

Chapter 4

Anna's time in the UK was running out and she wanted to meet Robbie as often as possible during these last few days and make the most of their time together. She could not see him as much as she would have liked because they both had work commitments, she with her au pair duties in Barnes and Robbie's long days working on the building site, as well as his travelling time.

When Anna had free time in the evenings she would often cycle to Robbie's home where Fiona would cook them all a meal and they would then relax afterwards, either going out for a walk with Lucy, watching television, or just chatting. Sometimes Robbie's dad, Mike, was at home or, if not working away, could be found nearby enjoying a round of golf on the Richmond Park course.

The more that Anna listened to Fiona, the easier it was to understand her Scottish accent and so conversation became much easier between them. However, if Anna thought she was finally mastering her broad tones, she had not reckoned on the thick Glaswegian burr of Rab C. Nesbitt, a character who appeared in a popular TV programme of the same name. The programme was politically incorrect, contained adult humour and was often very near the knuckle but because it was so funny, clever and perfectly timed, the producers got away with it.

Rab's creator, Ian Pattison, himself referred to Rab as a jovial psychotic.

Gregor Fisher was the actor who skilfully brought the character to life and, strong accent apart, made him instantly recognisable as an unshaven, overweight drunk, wearing his signature string vest, trainers and grubby headband. Fiona was amused by the programme; it was one of her favourites and was being aired one evening while Anna was visiting.

The episode was centred around unemployment and what was then referred to as 'the dole' and what Rab regarded as his wages. In Switzerland there was no real equivalent and Anna had no understanding of the situation, let alone the dialogue.

'Och, Robbie, the puir wee hen, she has'nae a clue, look ye!' she exclaimed, nodding towards Anna and struggling to keep a straight face at Anna's perplexed expression.

Robbie glanced at his mum and then at Anna, whose obvious confusion gave her a look of bewilderment as she sat forward in her chair, hands clasped tightly across her middle, mouth slightly open and a deep frown puckering her brow as she tried to make sense of it all.

'Excuse me?' she said, shooting Fiona a look of confusion, not getting the 'wee hen' bit.

Fiona, unable to answer, pressed her lips together tightly, keeping her gaze on the TV screen and avoiding eye contact with either Robbie or Anna.

'What is he talking about?' she asked Robbie. 'Can you please translate? I am completely lost.'

Robbie tried to explain that it was a humorous send-up of a particular section of the population who did not work, did not want to work and would do anything to stay 'on the dole' and never work.

'It's almost like a cult, you might say,' he managed to add, struggling to stifle his amusement.

Anna, still at a loss, kept quiet for a few minutes and then in her frustration shouted at the television screen.

'They talk so fast! I cannot keep up with… *Mein Gott*, *now* what is he doing?'

Her outburst was too much for Robbie and his mum and they both collapsed into giggles, until eventually the tears rolled down their cheeks.

Anna's perplexity slowly melted away and she too began to laugh, though she was not quite sure what was so funny as to provoke such hilarity.

'S... sorry, Anna,' Robbie stammered, wiping his eyes. 'We are not taking the mickey out of you, honestly, it's just that… your face… oh, it was just so funny…' Seeing that Anna was looking rather uncomfortable now and fearing they had upset her, he composed himself.

'Perhaps a cuppa, Mum?' he asked sliding a glance at Fiona who was also now back in control of herself.

'Aye, laddie, the cup that cheers!'

'Who is this Mickey?' Anna then demanded, looking even more baffled.

The expression on Anna's face and the way she spoke was too much for Fiona. Halfway out of her chair, she crumpled back into it, her whole body shaking with another fit of laughter.

Fortunately for all of them, Anna did not take offence and saw the funny side of it. However, that remained the first and last occasion that she ever watched Rab C. Nesbitt! Fiona never forgot it and smiled with amusement at the memory of that evening each time she watched it on television.

Much more to Anna's taste and liking was *The Sound of Music*. It was her favourite musical and as it happened, Fiona's as well. As Robbie had still not found time to sit down and watch the video, Anna suggested that she come over one evening so that they could watch it together. So she came for a meal, arriving on her borrowed bike and Fiona played the tape. Both ladies had seen it several times and knew what to expect but for Robbie it was a brand new experience and he was completely overawed by the story and the characters and he thought the music and songs were out of this world.

'Imagine seeing it on the big screen,' Robbie,' Anna said.

'Yes,' he replied thoughtfully, 'I bet that's something else! The scenery is magnificent!'

'*My Fair Lady* is another one well worth a wee look,' Fiona, told him.

'Ah, yes,' Anna said, smiling. 'That has some very amusing moments with Eliza Doolittle!'

One evening when Anna was visiting, she mentioned that she had the whole day free on Friday.

'Would you be able to take a day off, Robbie?' she asked. 'I know you are very busy with your work, but as I only have one more week after this, I wondered if we could go to Hampton Court Palace?'

'I'm not sure, Anna,' he replied. 'We are just finishing a job at Isleworth. I might be able to finish at lunchtime.'

'That would be lovely,' Anna replied, treating Robbie to her radiant smile. 'Will you see if you can? I would like to go to Hampton Court—I believe it has so much important history?'

'It has,' Robbie agreed. 'I will do my best,' he promised.

'Aye, a most interesting place,' Mike nodded. 'It's years since I went, but well worth a visit.'

Anna liked Mike and on the few occasions that they had been together, had got on very well with him. Mike was full of admiration for her, in fact thought the world of her and treated her like another daughter, loving her almost as much and hoping that Robbie would eventually marry her and she would become one of the family.

The following day, Robbie asked his foreman if he could finish at lunchtime on Friday, explaining that his girlfriend was soon to leave the country and he would not have the opportunity to see her again for at least two months.

'Take the whole day if you want to, son,' Mr Collins replied. 'We're just about done with this job and it's not as if there's much else to do before the weekend.'

When he told Anna that evening, she was very happy as she had wanted to visit Hampton Court during her time in London, but never had the opportunity.

'Can we go on the underground?' she asked, 'or is it better to go by bus?'

'By bus,' Robbie replied, still without transport following the incident with his car on the way home from the camping holiday. 'The nearest tube station is Wimbledon, not really helpful.'

'Never mind about buses, you two,' Mike said. I'll drive you there and come and pick you up in the afternoon. How's that?'

Anna flung herself at Robbie's dad, wrapping her arms around him and kissing his cheek.

'Oh, you sweet man,' she declared. 'That is so kind of you!'

Robbie grinned at the sight of his dad, rather flushed and straightening his glasses.

'Cheers, Dad; that would be great.'

It was just before eleven the next morning when Mike dropped his passengers off in the main car park at Hampton Court Palace and turned his Ford Orion towards the exit.

I'll pick you up about three-thirty,' he said, 'round about here, if that's at all possible. Have a good day, now!'

They waved Mike goodbye and made their way to the imposing gatehouse—a magnificent structure very much in keeping with the rest of the palace and a perfect statement of the character of the building and its past residents. It was another glorious summer day and Anna, being very interested in history, was excited to be visiting such an important building and learning all about its origins.

Robbie bought a copy of the official guide book which was crammed with information and made fascinating reading, detailing the most popular things to see and do… Henry VIII's palace, the Tudor kitchens, state apartments, the maze and gardens being amongst them. Packed with historical data and lavishly illustrated with colour photographs, it was an essential guide as well as a fantastic memento of a wonderful day out.

Anna soon had her nose buried in the guide.

'Thomas Wolsey,' she read from the guide book, 'English churchman, statesman and a cardinal of the Catholic Church. When Henry VIII became King of England in 1509, Wolsey became the King's almoner and took over the site of Hampton Court Palace in 1514.'

Robbie looked over her shoulder as she continued slowly reading.

'Previously it had been a property of the Order of St John of Jerusalem. Over the following seven years, Wolsey spent lavishly to build the finest palace in England at Hampton Court.'

Unfortunately,' Robbie said, 'although at the time Wolsey was Henry's favourite, it was not long before the king was plotting his downfall with his courtiers. Wolsey gifted the palace to King Henry. He…Wolsey… died a couple of years later, I think.'

'Yes,' Anna found the words with her finger, 'it says that he passed the palace to the king as a gift in 1528 and died in 1530.' She looked up from the book. 'Henry the eighth was notorious for his brutality, was he not? And how you call it... wo-man-ising?' she enunciated

'Well he was certainly notorious,' Robbie replied, 'after all... six wives? And yes, history books tell us he could be brutal.'

Anna continued reading as they walked behind a group of people, 'Henry added the Great Hall (the last medieval great hall built for the English monarchy) and the royal tennis court. The Great Hall has a carved hammer-beam roof. During Tudor times, this was the most important room of the palace. Here, the King would dine in state seated at a table upon a raised dais. The hall took five years to complete and so impatient was the King for completion that the masons were compelled to work throughout the night by candlelight.' She turned to Robbie. 'Such inhumanity,' she said, horrified at the thought, 'imagine that – expecting those poor men to work by candlelight!'

'It was their only form of lighting in those days,' Robbie pointed out – candles and flaming torches—'

'I know that! But all night? And such heavy work. How barbaric!' She quickly looked down as the couple just ahead of them turned round, hearing her outburst.

Robbie, faintly embarrassed, smiled back at them and taking Anna gently by the arm, guided her to an alcove where solid oak tables were laid out with various artefacts, mainly from the Tudor era.

Apart from another protest, this time about the unjust treatment of Anne Boleyn, the rest of their visit was uneventful and they both enjoyed exploring the house and gardens and soaking up the atmosphere of palatial grandeur that surrounded them.

After a light lunch they walked in the grounds and sat near a wooded area, enjoying the view in the sunshine.

'I shall really miss you, Anna,' Robbie said, sliding his arm around her shoulders and hugging her close to him. 'I have enjoyed being with you these past few weeks.' He looked into her eyes. 'Meeting you has changed my life... I never thought I would meet anyone like you.'

'I will miss you too, Robbie,' she replied, taking his hand in hers. 'But we shall soon be together again and I cannot wait for you to come and visit Switzerland and meet my family. The time, it will soon pass, you will see.' She smiled and kissed his cheek, snuggling into his shoulder, her eyes half closed, feeling the sun's warmth on her face.

They relaxed, chatting and dozing, oblivious to other visitors, until it was time to make their way back to the main entrance to look out for Robbie's dad. As they waited, Anna spotted a classic Daimler parked nearby.

'Look!' she exclaimed, tugging at Robbie's arm. 'That is just like the car that my father asked me to get a headlamp for!'

'Wow,' Robbie replied, admiring the sleek lines and gleaming chrome, 'I wouldn't mind taking that for a spin! I bet it fairly guzzles petrol, though.' He grinned at Anna. 'Do you think the owner would notice if we took a headlamp?'

Anna giggled. 'Robbie! Ha yes, I think a gaping hole might be quite noticeable, don't you?'

'Haha, I reckon so, yes. But after all, it's got two and we only want just the one!'

They were still laughing when Mike drew up in his less stately and more modest Orion.

'Well, it looks as if you have been enjoying yourselves?' he asked as they clambered in and he quickly drove to the exit before the car park attendant noticed them.

'Ah,' breathed Anna, 'we have had a most interesting and enjoyable day and I would not have missed any of it for the world. Thank you, both of you, so much'

In the next few days they saw each other as often as possible although Robbie had started a new job a few miles away and was getting home later in the evenings and Anna was busy packing, checking her travel documents and buying gifts to take home for her family. Robbie could not see Anna on the Friday evening because he had his church youth group meeting so they arranged to have a meal at Robbie's house with his parents on the Thursday evening.

Anna arrived earlier than the arranged time of seven pm.

Mike answered her ring at the door.

'Come on in, luv, I'll take your coat,' he greeted her, hanging up the trench coat that Robbie loved to see her wearing. 'Lad's not home yet; must have got held up somewhere, but I shouldn't think he'll be much longer.'

Anna smiled. 'He is working near Hammersmith, I think.'

'That's right. Rush hour can be terrible!'

Anna did not understand rush hour, when to her mind the traffic was almost at a standstill and therefore just the opposite. Another one of those weird English expressions.

Fiona was agitated. 'Och, I didnae want tae keep the wee haggis warm. It's best eaten piping hot!' She had prepared haggis for their last meal together, partly because it was Robbie's favourite and partly so that Anna could sample the Scottish national dish. She kept going to the window and looking down the street. Finally, she declared that they would wait no longer.

'Come on and sit ye doon,' she said to Anna, motioning to the table. 'I'll serve it while it's hot and m'laddie'll just hae to put up wi' it!'

'I'm sure it's not his fault, luv,' Mike said. 'He'll be held up in traffic.'

Ten minutes later, Robbie's key was heard in the door and, hearing voices in the dining room, he poked his head round the door.

'Sorry, everyone,' he said, 'the traffic was a nightmare.'

'Aye, didn't I tell thee?' Mike said, waving his fork at Fiona.

'Smells good,' Robbie grinned, instantly recognising the distinct, slightly spicy aroma as he went upstairs to wash his hands, leaving Fiona to retrieve his supper from the still warm oven.

Anna privately thought she had never smelt anything less appetising and had been hoping it tasted a lot better than its aroma suggested. Taking her first mouthful she had not been over-impressed with the taste either but made the best of it by smothering it with salt and black pepper. Failing to finish all of it, she blamed a late tea with the children in Barnes for her lack of appetite. She was, however, very careful not to offend her friend Fiona and was very gracious in her appraisal of her first (and last) taste of haggis, which for her, ranked equally with Rab C Nesbitt.

After a spell of television and a chat their evening came to an end and it was time for Anna to say goodbye to Fiona and Mike.

'Thank you so much for your friendship and your hospitality, Fiona,' she said, hugging Robbie's mum and kissing her on both cheeks.

'Ye'll always find a welcome here, lassie,' Fiona replied, 'and I hope we'll be seeing ye again afore too long?'

Anna promised to visit when she came to the UK again.

'And I will write to you, Fiona, to see how you are.'

'Take care of yourself, lass,' Mike said, also the recipient of a hug and double kiss, 'and safe journey home.'

In the hall, Robbie took his door key off the hook behind the door and picked up a sweater, tying the sleeves loosely around his waist. He also picked up a box, inside of which was a bulky item badly wrapped in torn newspaper. He removed the paper and showed Anna a Daimler headlight to fit the make and model that was scrawled on the scrap of paper.

'This is why I was so late home,' he told her, grinning with pleasure at the expression of amazement on her face. 'I went to the scrapyard from work and then had to catch a bus—'

'Robbie!' she squealed, flinging her arms around his neck and kissing him. 'That is wonderful; Papa will be so happy!' She paused, looking thoughtful. 'It will be all right to take it through customs? I will not have to declare it?'

'No,' he replied. 'It will be fine. I will wrap it safely and give it to you on Saturday with the receipt just in case there are any questions.'

'Thank you so much, you are my hero!'

'My pleasure, darling,' he replied. 'I am glad I was able to get one. Now, we must go or you will be in trouble for being late back.'

Saturday turned out to be an overcast, rather humid day and reflected the mood of Anna and Robbie as they spent their last few hours together before Anna was due to fly home to Switzerland. Robbie had borrowed his dad's Orion and he picked Anna up in Barnes and took her for a drive. They stopped off at a teashop and had delicious home-made cakes before returning to Barnes where they sat in the car for quite a while, discussing their future plans.

'I will come and visit you as soon as I can, Anna,' Robbie said, taking her hand. 'I expect it will be in October or November. I will get my passport sorted out soon.'

'I cannot wait for you to visit my country,' she replied. 'I know you will love it and there is so much that I want to show you. Can you not make it before then?'

He knew he could postpone it no longer... he had to tell her now. He took a deep breath.

'Anna, I haven't mentioned this before, but... well, I do Formula Ford racing,' he gabbled, 'and there is an important race coming up soon—the penultimate of the season and quite a few points at stake.'

She stared into his eyes until he was forced to look away.

'Formula what did you say?'

'Ford. Formula Ford. It... well, they are racing cars, I—'

'You go motor racing?' she cut in. 'Not to watch them; you actually take part in the motor races?'

As he had feared, his revelation worried her; the reason he had not told her about it until now.

'Yes,' he replied, 'It's very exciting and great fun— something I really love doing. For the thrill of it,' he added.

'And what if you are badly injured or even kill yourself?' she asked. 'Then what? Do you think that would be *thrilling* for me?' She leaned closer. *'Do you?'*

'Well, no,' Robbie was beginning to wish he had not told her. 'But listen, Anna, there are strict safety regulations and the cars are also perfectly maintained,' he insisted, 'they have to be. There really is nothing for you to worry about...'

65

Her blue eyes flashed angrily. 'No, of course not. Why should I worry? After all, it cannot be of any importance at all if you could not even mention it to me until just before I am going to leave and now I shall be powerless to try to stop you!'

'Trust me, Anna, it is perfectly safe. There is no need for you to worry, honestly. And anyway, I am not going to be stopped, not even by you; it's part of my life; I enjoy it.'

He felt her stiffen and she turned away as he tried to take her in his arms. For a few moments she sat, rigid, staring out through the car window but seeing nothing. Robbie could think of nothing to say while she was so dismissive and sat awkwardly beside her, waiting for her to speak. It seemed an age before she turned towards him, relaxing and appearing to relent.

'Okay, I will not worry,' she said quietly. 'It is your life, your choice after all, but I just want to have you fit and well and all in one piece to come and visit me afterwards, okay? Is that too much to ask?'

'No,' he replied, 'and when I come to see you, I promise I will be fit and well and all in one piece.' Smiling at each other, they drew close together in a final, prolonged and passionate embrace.

Monday morning and the day of Anna's departure. She was excited at the prospect of going home and seeing her family again after a year's absence and at the same time sad to be leaving Robbie behind. He was good company and she would miss having him around. She paused as she

66

packed her last bits and pieces, looking at the photograph he had given her—a typical likeness of him in crisp, white, open-neck shirt and faded blue jeans. He smiled back at her from the frame. Always smiling, she thought, extending her finger and gently stroking his image behind the glass before carefully wrapping the photo in a scarf and adding it to her suitcase.

Robbie was awake early after a restless night, his mind filled with thoughts of Anna's departure and how much he was going to miss her in the coming weeks. Slipping on his jacket and taking the dog's lead from the hook in the hall, he called Lucy and opened the front door. The street was cool and quiet at that hour and they walked undisturbed.

He had not been prepared for Anna's vehement response when he told her about the Formula Ford racing; in fact, although he expected her to be concerned for his safety, he had thought she might have been more enthusiastic about it, knowing her love of adventure and her positive, optimistic attitude to life. He supposed it was a natural reaction, really. After all, it rated high on the list of dangerous activities, even though fatalities were few compared to mountaineering, horse racing, base jumping and the like...

Robbie reflected on how quickly he had become attached to her—and she to him, apparently. A whirlwind romance of the kind that he had read about in books and seen in films but never thought would or could ever happen to him. As he walked with Lucy trotting happily beside him, Anna's smiling face came into his consciousness; he heard that sexy, throaty laugh and felt her lips on his… the sweetness of his first real love. He really did not want to do anything to jeopardise their relationship at this early stage. Anna was special; very special. He would play down the motor racing; not mention it unless she did.

He looked at his watch and turned for home. Home— the place where he would shortly have breakfast, get ready for work and return to at the end of another busy day. Home, where he slept and ate and had pretty much taken his humdrum existence for granted, living for the moment and not really having a life plan other than achieving his science degree and finding a decent career for himself. He'd supposed the rest would follow all in good time—a home of his own and a wife and family. Or not. Then, when he met Anna for the first time – at his home – it was as if he had found a piece of jigsaw that he had not even known was missing—a vital piece that completed the picture, made his life whole.

Tea break time on the building site and instead of sitting down with the lads to consume whatever they had saved in their lunch boxes for the afternoon break, Robbie stayed where he was, working on the foundations of a new building. There, surrounded by the general chaos of buckets, barrows and cement mixers, he stood, hands in his pockets, eyes watching an aircraft as it gained height, having recently risen from a runway at Heathrow. He doubted it was Anna's flight as it was headed due north,

68

but she would be up there somewhere right now, homeward bound, returning to her family after a year's absence.

'Farewell, my lovely,' he whispered. 'See you soon.'

Chapter 5

Surprisingly, although Robbie obviously missed Anna, her absence did not affect him too badly and his lovesick feeling was not as overpowering as he had anticipated. For one thing, he had a lot of work booked and he enjoyed his job on the building sites in the fresh air with his mates. They also helped keep his spirits up with their banter and the obligatory disparaging but always good humoured disagreements about football. He continued to take the church youth group on Fridays and also obtained a new set of wheels after the unfortunate demise of his Consul.

By way of a change and with his mind and energies focused on the upcoming Formula Ford race meeting, he had settled on a Ford Transit minibus. White, with a red stripe, it looked the biz – smart, spacious enough to carry passengers as well as all his gear, and robust enough to tow his racing car. He was spending a lot of time in practice and preparation and this latest mode of transport was ideal.

He and Anna exchanged letters about every ten days and spoke on the phone once a week until a postal strike meant that for a while no letters were being delivered or received, so they relied more on the telephone. Inevitably she would ask him about the motor racing and try to persuade him to give it up.

'Hey, I came seventh in my last race,' he told her. 'My personal best and I know I can improve even more and maybe—'

'It is far too dangerous, Robbie, and I worry about you so much. I want you to promise to give it up?' she begged.

'I promise… to be very careful, Anna,' he replied, laughing. 'It is not that dangerous and I will be fine, trust me!'

'If you go motor racing and get killed and do not come back,' she said, 'I will have your nest egg, remember that.'

He grinned to himself. Some nest egg, he thought. 'Fair enough,' he answered, 'that's the deal then… have my nest egg.' He paused for a moment. 'But you should know something,' he continued, 'dead or alive, my nest egg is not worth an awful lot.'

He loved to tease Anna but she was not remotely amused and sensing the anxiety, hearing the tension in her voice, he changed the subject, telling her that he missed her and loved her very much and would be seeing her very soon now.

'And don't worry, my darling, as I promised, I will arrive fit and well and all in one piece!'

Three weeks later, Robbie's British Airways flight touched down at Basel Mulhouse airport, smoothly and on time. He waited for his luggage and made his way to customs where, to his consternation, although he had nothing to declare, he was stopped by a customs officer.

Requesting Robbie's passport, the official opened it, studied the details and with an expression devoid of emotion looked into Robbie's eyes.

He pointed to Robbie's military style holdall. 'The bag—on the desk, please, sir.'

Robbie placed his bag on the desk and was then told to stand still with his arms raised. At this point a second official walked up to the desk and frisked him.

'Okay,' he nodded to his colleague.

'You will please open the bag, sir,' the first officer requested and the second officer began to take out his tightly packed shirts, jeans, underwear, socks, shaving and other toiletry items, laying them all out on the desk while the first official unfolded or unrolled them, laying each item to one side after thorough examination.

Then the various compartments were unzipped and emptied and Robbie watched, embarrassment growing as all his belongings, including family photographs and even his grandfather's war medals and some old coinage, were exposed and laid out on the desk like items in a car boot sale. Having completed his search, the officer turned the bag upside down, examined it minutely and then shook it vigorously, the action producing one last remaining item from a small side pocket. Opening the packet, checking that the contents matched the description on the label and now satisfied that Robbie was neither a terrorist nor a drugs smuggler, the customs officer took a step back, indicating with a slight nod and an arm gesture that he was free to repack his bag and leave the terminal.

'Enjoy your stay, sir,' he said, handing the standard pack of condoms back to him.

Anna was in a flap. After a bad night, she had overslept—today of all days, when she wanted to tidy up and get a few supplies in before Robbie arrived. She was sitting in front of her mirror while her sister finished styling her hair.

'That will do now, Evie,' she said, raising her voice over the buzz of the hairdryer. 'I am going to be late.'

'You are already late,' Evelyn shouted back, 'and if you do not let me dry it properly it will just go frizzy and then *that* won't be right... just hold still, will you, I am nearly done now!'

Anna was officially on holiday from the florists where she worked and Evelyn had taken the afternoon off, wanting to be there when Robbie arrived. As sisters they were very different but also very close and supportive of each other.

'Enough now,' Anna said, dismissing the dryer with a shake of her hand. She peered closely into the mirror. 'Oh, my God, there are still bags under my eyes – he will think I am a wreck. I hardly slept at all last night, you know—'

'Anna, you do not have bags under your eyes! It is the light in this room; these wall lights are fine for creating atmosphere but not much else. You look great and Robbie will think so too.'

'I look pale and tired,' Anna protested, applying blusher to her cheeks and then refreshing her lipstick.

Evelyn fetched her handbag and took out a large pair of Prada sunglasses.

'Here. Wear these if you are so worried about your looks. Now come on, move it. The poor guy will be thinking you have left him high and dry at the airport!'

Robbie stood near the exit of the arrivals hall where the telephones were and where Anna had told him she would be waiting for him. He looked around. There was no sign of her. He had been held up for at least half an hour in customs... had she tired of waiting for him and gone? Or perhaps assumed he was not on that flight? After his less than welcoming experience he now felt nervous and unsettled. He walked up and down, looking at the faces milling around—many, many faces but not one of them was Anna's. He decided to stand still where he could be seen, nearer the exit doors—it would be easier for her to spot him than if he were pacing up and down.

He checked his watch. He had been standing here for fifteen minutes. She must have either left, or she could have been held up. Relax, he told himself, she'll be here, waving and smiling as only Anna can. He shivered a little, feeling the October chill in spite of the early afternoon sunshine. He paced up and down, taking care not to move too far from the doors.

After another twenty minutes he began to wonder if she was coming. She had sounded so positive on the phone the day before. Had she mistaken the time? Or the day, even? No, he decided that was not possible. He hoped she was all right and had not been involved in an accident. Or had she been and gone?

After waiting for half an hour, he decided that she was not coming. She was, after all, an hour late now. She must have dumped him. Now what was he to do? The logical course of action was to ring Anna's home to see if anything was wrong.

Knowing nothing about the operation of the Swiss public telephone network, he had just made up his mind to try and get through to her number when the automatic doors slid open and, tripping herself up on the slightly raised metal frame, possibly a side-effect of wearing the dark glasses, Anna fell headlong into the hall.

'Robbie!' Unhurt and unperturbed, she scrambled to her feet and ran towards him, the non-tameable hair, silk scarf and familiar trench coat, unbuttoned and billowing out behind her, revealing her green mini skirt and an expanse of shapely leg, turning a few male heads in her direction.

Relieved and filled with longing for her, he let his bag fall to the ground and held out his arms. Hurling herself straight into them she clung to him as they embraced.

Releasing her, he held Anna at arm's length. 'You are late!' he said, feigning annoyance. 'I have been waiting here for almost an hour; I thought you weren't coming!'

Knowing that he was teasing her, she hung her head, studying her black patent, buckled shoes.

'Sorry, Robbie… I was delayed.'

'Never mind, you are here now and—'

'Delayed, doing myself up for you,' she interrupted. 'I wanted to make myself look beautiful for you.' She pushed the shades on to the top of her head, losing them in the tangle of hair that Evelyn had taken such pains with.

'Well, as I was about to say… you are here now and looking more beautiful than ever!'

They hugged again and Anna took his free hand in hers as he picked up his bag in the other.

'How was your flight? You landed on time?'

'Oh yes, bang on time—there was no delay until I got to customs!'

She laughed. 'But Robbie, it is always slow going through customs. There is all this extra security everywhere these days.'

'Tell me about it! They obviously thought I was a threat to national security – I have only had my luggage searched and all my stuff tipped out on the desk and scrutinised. In public!'

Anna clasped her hands together, controlling her urge to giggle at his dismayed expression. 'Oh, poor Robbie, that must have been so stressful for you.'

'It was. Embarrassing as well, I might tell you.'

'Never mind, it is all over now. Come! Let's go,' she said, quickly leading him out to her bronze Mazda in the car park. 'I can't wait to introduce you to my sister!'

The drive from the airport to Anna's apartment in Basel took about fifteen minutes. Robbie was impressed by the clearly signposted roads and well-ordered traffic and thought about his days as a delivery driver around the Home Counties and the long queues at roundabouts. Here, everything seemed to move smoothly. All vehicles were required by law to be driven with dipped headlamps in daylight and this seemed to add a certain sparkle to the general fresh, clean appearance of the city.

Anna, a confident and competent driver, pulled up outside the modern high-rise apartment block where she lived on the second floor, with her sister, Evelyn. Robbie brought his bag from the car and as Anna skipped on ahead to unlock the door, he took in the immediate surroundings. Again, he thought how clean and orderly everything seemed to be compared to London which, at that time was being extensively developed and building sites and traffic chaos were the norm in most districts. Those building sites, however, provided him with a decent living, enabling him to indulge his passion of Formula Ford racing which was already becoming an issue with Anna and one which he knew he had to handle with kid gloves. She had not mentioned the subject so far but he supposed it would only be a question of time and he was ready for it. He had no intention of giving up his passion but at the same time he could not bear the thought of losing Anna.

'Come on, slow coach!' she called, hair and coat being swept along by the current of air created as she ran up the steps towards the main entrance.

There was a lift waiting on the ground floor but Anna was already halfway up the first flight of stairs. Robbie followed, struggling a little, not so much with the weight of his bag but the bulk of it now that it had been unpacked and searched and his possessions roughly stuffed back inside in any fashion. The incident had unnerved him and if he was honest, he still felt quite shaken.

77

Inside the apartment was a small hallway and cloakroom and leading off to the left was the lounge where Evelyn sat drinking coffee on a very comfortable looking sofa. She smiled and clattered her cup down on the low table, jumping up from her seat to be introduced to Robbie.

He saw another Anna before him—not quite a twin, but a more dynamic, larger-than-life version of Anna. Evelyn sported a similar, if anything thicker, shock of untamed hair, auburn in colour and escaping the restraints of the white silk ribbon much like a river bursting its banks. Her orange dress seemed to swirl and flutter as she advanced towards him, flashing him a dazzling smile, enhanced by her very white teeth and very red lipstick. Her blue eyes shone with genuine delight and long, chunky earrings dangled and swung in all directions and Robbie marvelled that they did not get tangled up in all that hair. She was as stunning as Anna, he thought; they were both stunners.

'I thought you must have changed your mind,' she said in very good English, 'was your flight delayed?'

'No,' put in Anna before Robbie could reply. '*He* was delayed.' She rolled her eyes and jerked her thumb towards his bag, just inside the door.

Evelyn looked at him, still smiling and raising an eyebrow questioningly.

'I... well, I know it was not the brightest idea to use a military style bag,' he agreed, 'but it's just the right size. And anyway, you were also an hour late,' he reminded Anna in a mock rebuke, receiving a shrug and a broad grin for a reply.

Evelyn kissed him on both cheeks. 'Well, you are here now and welcome,' she said. 'Would you like some coffee, Robbie?'

'I... yes, I would love some coffee, thank you,' he stumbled, flushing slightly and resisting the urge to touch his face.

As Evelyn busied herself in the tiny kitchen, Anna showed Robbie where the bathroom was and then opened the door to her bedroom.

'Put your stuff in here for now, Robbie,' she called to him. 'You can unpack and shake out the creases later when you have recovered.'

Robbie looked around the compact bedroom that contained a double bed, wardrobe and a small chest of drawers that also served as a bedside table, accommodating a reading lamp and some literature. The room was cell-like and calm, with seemingly not an item out of place but Robbie supposed that the space being small, tidiness was essential.

They had not yet discussed sleeping arrangements but he assumed he would be spending the nights on the sofa and that was fine with him. He had no expectations of any intimacy with Anna; indeed, so far they had gone no further than kissing, but he liked to think that she might be encouraged to relax a little more in her own domain... and after all, he had come prepared for such an eventuality.

Chapter 6

Evelyn set down the tray bearing freshly made coffee, toast, butter, two boiled eggs and a pot of honey. Muesli was already on the table along with dishes, cups and cutlery. She tossed her auburn mane, holding it away from her eyes as she poured coffee for Robbie. In Switzerland, breakfast typically included bread, butter or margarine, marmalade or honey, maybe some cheese or cereals, plus milk, hot or cold chocolate, tea or coffee. Lunch could be as simple as a sandwich or a birchermüesli, or it could be a complete meal.

'Help yourself, Robbie,' she said, waving a hand at the food on the table. 'I hope you will like our Swiss breakfast.'

'Thank you. It all looks good,' he replied, transferring some muesli to a bowl and reaching for the jug of milk.

'Did you sleep well?' she asked, smiling and twitching an eyebrow.

'Yes. Yes, I did, thank you,' he replied. His thoughts went back to the previous night. It was fortunate that he was very tired after travelling, he thought, and that he had pretty much drifted straight off to sleep after kissing Anna goodnight.

It had come as something of a surprise and a delight when Anna had told him he could sleep in her bed.

'Really?' he had asked, hardly daring to believe his ears. 'Are you sure about that?'

'Of course I am sure, darling. I would not invite you to otherwise.'

'Wow! I thought you would prefer me to sleep on the couch...'

Anna shrugged. 'If you prefer to sleep on the couch, then do so,' she replied, 'but I tell you now that it is not so comfortable as my bed with its warm, soft duvet.'

'No, no.' He shook his head. 'I will be more than happy to share your bed.' He feasted his eyes on her pleasing body, a glint of expectation in his eyes. 'Thank you, Anna,' he said, holding out his hand to her, 'that will make me very happy.'

He had misunderstood of course and Anna, realising he had the wrong end of the stick, quickly made her intentions clear.

'Robbie,' she said quietly, 'you must understand that I am not inviting you into my bed to make love to me. It is just that I think it will be more restful for you to sleep in my bed rather than that lumpy couch. There must be no... what do you English call it... the hanky panky! No, you must understand I am not ready for that. Okay?'

'Of course, Anna,' he replied, struggling to hide his disappointment, 'and you know that I would not want to do anything that might offend or upset you.' Silently, he wondered how it was going to be 'more restful' for him to have to lie beside this beautiful creature he was in love with and not be able to touch her. Perhaps the lumpy couch would be better after all? Or she might change her mind...

So, she continued, he was to go to the bathroom while she undressed and got into bed at night and there would be a similar routine in the mornings. Robbie was a guest; a guest in a country whose customs he knew very little about. His hostesses were charming and kind and he did not intend to abuse their generosity.

Anna came to the table as Robbie was drinking his second cup of coffee, apologising for keeping him waiting. She looked fresh and fragrant in a pale blue dress, with a long cream cardigan. A darker blue ribbon secured her hair.

'I see that my sister has been looking after you,' she smiled, pouring coffee into her cup.

'Yes, she has. She warned me not to wait for you—that you always take a long time in the bathroom. That is why I started breakfast without you,' he explained.

'That is okay, I am only having coffee anyway.'

'You don't eat breakfast?' This was something he did not understand at all; how could anyone go without breakfast?

Anna's throaty laugh filled the space between them. 'Do not look so alarmed. When I am working, yes, I have something. But this week I am on holiday and anyway, we shall be having a special treat later on at the Markt Platz coffee shop—they have the best drinks and cakes in town.'

Finishing his coffee, Robbie leaned back in his chair.

'Sounds good to me,' he said. 'I can manage coffee and cakes anytime.'

'Yes, I remember,' she replied, leaning across the table towards him. 'If it is hot, sweet or spicy, Robbie will like it.'

He smiled, touched that she remembered his tastes and reached across the table, squeezing her hand. Smiling, he looked into her eyes. 'It sounds perfect to me.'

Their conversation was interrupted by the slamming of a door and Evelyn's footsteps hurrying up the hallway.

'Have a lovely day, you two,' she called, looking into the lounge briefly before grabbing her coat from the hall stand to go out to the salon near the market, where she worked as a hairdresser. *'Tschüss!'*

'Tschüss!' Anna responded.

Robbie, turning in his chair, caught only a brief glimpse of a yellow, figure-hugging, woollen dress; the auburn abundance being tied back this morning with yellow ribbon, and the ever present smile enhanced with orange lipstick.

'Evie is always running late,' Anna told him, shaking her head.

Robbie smiled in reply. Just a guess, but he suspected it ran in the family; in any event, he would not mention again that Anna herself had been an hour late at the airport yesterday.

They sat together at the breakfast table for some time, mostly discussing the more interesting places to visit in Switzerland during this, his first trip abroad.

'So,' Anna concluded, 'it would be a good idea to look around Basel today. We will go to the Markt Platz and you can have your cakes and then I thought you might like to see Basel Cathedral?'

'I have only seen photographs of the cathedral,' he replied, 'so yes, that would be a real treat for me.'

'You are quite interested in the architecture and history of famous buildings, aren't you, Robbie?'

'Very much so; I find it fascinating to learn why and how these places were built and also how they have evolved over the years.'

'Great, and also during your stay, I think you would appreciate a visit to the Natural History Museum.'

'Now that would be a real treat, Anna. I am very interested in natural history and science... you remember I am studying for a bachelor's degree in science with the Open University?'

'Ah, yes, of course, your studies. How are you getting on?'

'Very well. I am hoping at the end of it all that I can find science-related work—you know, to be permanently employed in a profession rather than relying on labouring or seasonal work.'

'That would be a big step up for you, 'Anna replied, adding, 'but one which you are capable of taking if you set your mind to it. '

'Well, it's what I want to do, really.'

'Then, if it is truly what is in your heart, you will find a way. I have similar ambitions, you know. I love my job in the flower shop but I feel...' she searched for the word, '... restricted. I loved my time in Barnes and living near to London and I have an urge to visit other European cities, for I think they all have a beauty and character of their own...'

As her words trailed off her expression became wistful.

'With your command of the English language,' Robbie said, 'and the winning way you have with people – you know, putting them at ease, being helpful, you should also be making the most of your talents – perhaps in the nursing profession, or—'

'I am not... cut out? Is that right, yeah? I am not cut out to be a nurse. All that blood...' she shuddered. 'But I would love to travel.' A worried frown then creased her brow. 'Are you are still involved with that motor racing? Please tell me you have given it up?'

Robbie sighed inwardly. Here we go...

'I wondered when you were going to get round to mentioning that. No, I haven't given it up; in fact there is a special end of season event next month at Silverstone. I would like you to come and watch the race if you could get a few days off to come over?'

Anna sat up straight and folded her arms, staring at him across the empty cups and dishes.

For some moments, neither spoke.

'What?' Robbie asked, breaking the silence.

'Robbie, I think you already know the answer to that one, uh? Are you serious? Come and visit you, of course. But watch you get killed?' She shook her head, her dangly earrings clattering, seeming to support her sentiments. 'Now, if you would be very sweet and take the dishes into the kitchen, I will clear the table before we go out.'

They travelled by tram to the Markt Platz and after consuming an enormous wedge of walnut and chocolate cake washed down with a glass of steaming hot chocolate, Robbie was keen to see Basel Cathedral, known locally as The Basel Minster (*Münster, German*) at close quarters. Being one of the main landmarks and tourist attractions of Basel, Robbie thought it added definition to the cityscape with its red sandstone architecture and coloured roof tiles, its two slim towers and the cross-shaped intersection of the main roof.

'Wow!' he exclaimed, gazing up at it. 'That is magnificent!'

'It is listed as a heritage site of national significance in Switzerland,' Anna told him. 'Originally it was a Catholic cathedral but today is part of the Reformed Protestant church.'

'When was it built?' Robbie asked her.

'Well, it goes way back. In the eleventh century it was built in Romanesque style – the Romans had a fortress on this hill. But by the early sixteenth century it had taken on a Gothic look when the southern tower was completed.'

'Hm. It has seen a few changes then.'

'Oh yes. The original tower was destroyed in 1356 by the Basel earthquake and when rebuilding began, the two towers were built.'

'Ah, twin towers!'

'No. Not quite. You will notice one is not so tall as the other.'

As they walked through the cloisters, added in the thirteenth century and home to the tombs of several and varied eminences, Robbie was strongly reminded of the windows of Westminster Abbey.

Inside the cathedral, the grandeur was breathtaking and Robbie was blown away by its immense arches and columns; the expansive windows that had been witness to events both bloody and saintly, from medieval to more modern times. There were ancient paintings on silk, and wooden inlaid treasure boxes containing relics of gold. Also on show were paintings and sculptures and rustic statuary that had all been added at various times during its one thousand year history.

On the way out, two hours later, Robbie turned in the doorway to look back at the massive stained glass windows, their vivid colours so vibrant that the bright sunshine outside seemed dull in comparison.

'Can we walk along the river bank?' Robbie suggested.

Anna had other plans.

'Could we perhaps do that next time?' she suggested. She pointed vaguely in the direction of the Town Hall. 'You will want to visit the Natural History Museum... we could make a day of it, have lunch and then walk by the river afterwards. How does that sound?'

'It sounds perfect,' Robbie agreed. 'So what are your plans for the rest of today?'

She beamed at him. 'There is a Tom Hanks movie showing at our local cinema, *Turner and Hooch*. Would you like to see it?'

'Turner and Hooch... oh, the detective and a dog?'

'Oh, you have seen it already?'

'No. I've seen a couple of reviews. It's an American comedy.'

'Yes!' Anna squealed, delighted that he knew something about it. 'Shall we go?'

Robbie was happy to go along with whatever Anna had planned; just being in her presence again was a joy in itself. They walked hand in hand, occasionally stopping to look in a shop window. Robbie thought everything about this city was amazing; the memory of his very first trip abroad would stay with him always.

They hopped on a tram, hopping off again after a few minutes.

'The cinema is just around the corner,' Anna said. 'Wait here for me just a moment, will you?'

She went into a small confectioner's shop, emerging a few moments later with a huge smile on her face.

'Bought something nice?' Robbie queried. 'You look very pleased with yourself.'

'Try this,' she said, still smiling as she peeled away the red wrapper from a bar of chocolate and broke a piece off for him, popping it into his mouth.

When he could speak, he read out the name on the wrapper.

'Frigor?'

'Do you like it?'

'Wow! It tastes like food from the gods,' Robbie answered. 'More, please!'

Giggling, she fed him another piece of the chocolate. 'That is all for now, okay… we will have the rest while we watch the film.'

Robbie had never tasted chocolate like that in his life; even Belgian chocolate was not as good as that.

Linking her arm in his, they made their way to the cinema, which was about half full and the timing could not have been better as the film was just starting. They found seats a little way in from the aisle and three or four rows up in the stalls and settled down.

A few minutes later, a man on his own came and sat two seats away from Anna. She noticed from the corner of her eye that he kept glancing at her and she looked across at him. He smiled at her and briefly held up his hand as if he knew her. She did not know him; in fact had never seen him before but smiled back to be friendly and then turned her attention back to the screen.

Robbie, at this point unaware of the man, whispered something to Anna about the film. Leaning towards him to hear what he was saying, the next thing she knew was that the man had moved into the empty seat right next to her. She took a closer look at him, wondering who he was. Feeling uncomfortable, she snuggled closer to Robbie.

After that, it seemed that the man had got the message and remained sitting there quietly, watching the film. But then he began fidgeting and shifting about in his seat, searching in his pockets. Finally locating what he wanted, he opened a packet of Ricola herbal sweets and nudging her arm, indicated that she take one.

Anna shook her head. 'No, thank you,' she said, offering a weak smile.

The man was insistent. 'Please... you are welcome...'

'What's going on?' asked Robbie, bending forward to see who Anna was whispering to. 'Do you know that guy? Is he being a nuisance?'

'No, I don't know him. He has just offered me a sweet, that's all. It is fine, really.'

Robbie was suspicious and leaned in front of Anna to speak to the man.

'The lady is with me, okay? And she does not want your sweets,' he told him.

The man stared at him blankly.

Robbie stared back. Perhaps he did not understand. He flicked his hand as if swatting an insect away. *'Tschüss!'* he said, using the first Swiss word that came to mind.

The man sat back in his seat and peace was restored except that Robbie did not trust him and kept an eye on him but he seemed to have settled down now. It had obviously been a misunderstanding and the guy had not realised that Anna was with him. All the same, Robbie could not help a feeling of resentment, even a touch of jealousy that someone should try to take liberties with Anna when he himself did not dare to.

They had reached the bit in the film where Scott crashes the Cadillac into a concrete barrier, when Anna felt the man touching her just above the knee. She cried out and slapped his hand away. Robbie was out of his seat like a rocket, ready to tackle the nuisance but Anna didn't want any trouble. Grabbing Robbie's hand, she dragged him into the aisle and found alternative seats a little further back where several other people sat. A few people in the nearby seats turned and glared at them, telling them to be quiet and a rather robust lady wearing a green-and-gold uniform appeared very quickly and asked if there was a problem.

'No,' they both answered in unison.

'No problem,' Robbie said quietly. 'Just a misunderstanding.'

The uniformed person stayed around for a few minutes and then left, leaving them to watch the film to the end without further incident.

'You didn't know that guy, did you?' Robbie asked Anna when they came out of the cinema.

'No, I did not and nor do I want to,' she flashed. 'What makes you think I know a creep like that?'

'You are too nice, that's the trouble,' he fumed, 'and it can be mistaken for encouragement.'

'How dare you suggest that I encouraged him? I did not want to make a scene, that's all.'

'Anna, I did not say—'

'Robbie, we have to be able to trust each other,' she said, her blue eyes staring intently at him. 'If you cannot trust me when we are together, I am surprised you trust me to be faithful when we are six hundred miles apart!'

'But I do trust you… I didn't mean… you have got it all wrong, Anna, I was concerned about you,' Robbie replied. 'I love you… and of course I trust you.'

She softened and leaned into his chest, looking up at him. 'I am sorry; I know it is all strange for you, and not easy to deal with. Can we forget it? Put it behind us?'

'We should not be bickering but making the most of our time together,' Robbie replied and held her close, kissing her forehead. Anna was a very attractive young woman and this kind of attention, he thought to himself, was something he was going to have to get used to.

They arrived home later than intended and Anna pointed to a souped-up pale blue Renault with black stripes parked near the apartment.

'Ah, Marcel is back. I have told you about Marcel? He works for our father and he also lives here with us.'

'I remember... Evelyn's boyfriend,' Robbie nodded. 'And you also told me he was French?'

'Oh,' she laughed, 'Marcel is very French! That is why he gets on so well with our mother. She adores him! Tomorrow, we are all going to have dinner with Mama. She is so looking forward to meeting you.'

'Marcel works with Ferraris, right?'

'Yes, he is Papa's mechanic and has been spending the weekend with his family in Lausanne,' Anna explained. 'It is very beautiful there—you would like it, Robbie.'

Evelyn and Marcel were laughing at the popular Benny Hill Show, which was being aired on television in over a hundred countries at that time, when Anna and Robbie entered.

'Ah, the wanderers return,' said Evelyn, muting the sound with the remote control. 'Robbie, I want you to meet Marcel. Marcel, this is Robbie...'

Marcel rose from the sofa, offering his hand and Robbie shook it. He saw a lean but strong young Frenchman, a little taller than himself, not so muscular but very masculine regardless of the neat moustache, long curly hair and a gold hoop adorning his left earlobe.

Marcel's dark eyes held a permanent look of amusement and it was sometimes difficult to tell whether he was mocking or being serious.

'Hi! So you made it finally, uh?'

Robbie smiled. 'Yes, and what a great country.'

'Uh-huh,' Marcel nodded, 'good place to live and work, yeah. I am just going out to have a beer. Want to join me after your long day exploring the city?'

Robbie could think of nothing nicer and nodded to Marcel. 'Oh yes, I would. Thank you.'

'Are we having dinner in this evening? Or shall we eat out?' Anna asked her sister.

'Well if Marcel is taking Robbie for a drink, perhaps we can get a meal ready while they are out?' Evelyn suggested. 'Unless we all go and have something to eat at the bar?'

'We will eat here,' Anna decided, 'as we are all invited to dinner with Mama tomorrow.'

Evelyn nodded and turned to Robbie. 'I am relying on you to make sure that Marcel does not stay too long at the bar and the pair of you come home before the dinner burns.'

'Oh, no pressure, then,' Robbie answered, smiling. 'Do you think he will take notice of me?'

'I am sure he will behave himself with you, Robbie,' Evelyn added. 'He does not listen to me, of course, but...' she winked, '... French, you see!'

Marcel ordered a lager for Robbie and a beer for himself and carried them to a small table in the busy bar that Marcel frequented, regarding it as his 'local.'

'Proscht!' he said, raising his glass.

'Proscht!' Robbie replied, taking a long pull of the cold, pale liquid. 'I am really interested in your job servicing Ferraris. Do you get to drive them very often?' he asked.

'Oh yes, when they have been worked on,' Marcel replied, the amusement in his eyes very apparent, 'we have to test drive them, but also we work with other makes, not just Ferrari.' He grinned. 'I have heard that you are a racing driver, yes?'

Robbie told Marcel that he took part in Formula Ford racing, describing his Merlyn MK 24A in some detail, while Marcel was interested in engine size and performance.

'There is a prestigious race coming up next month,' Robbie told him 'the last of the season. I am hoping to do well there and beat my own personal best of coming seventh.'

'That is impressive,' Marcel said. 'Those races require a lot of skill—and courage, too!'

'Anna wants me to give it up,' he replied. 'She says I will kill myself!'

Again the merriment in Marcel's eyes. 'The ladies... ah, they make the big drama, yes... but they do not understand the excitement, the exhilaration, the thrill of it all, uh?' He laughed. 'Tell her you will give her the world

94

and everything in it as well as the moon and the stars, but you still keep the motor racing for you, uh?'

'I have pretty much told her that already; she knows I would do anything for her.'

'Make her feel special, pamper her—the ladies love the attention, but do not give in! Once you do that...' he treated Robbie to a classic Gallic shrug, complete with pouting lower lip.

They chatted amicably, at ease in each other's company, about cars, football and women.

'I suppose you met Evelyn through your work with her father?' Robbie asked.

'Yes, that is true, but it was not he who introduced us; it was Marianne, the girls' mother. You know, I think she had a soft spot for me. She was always saying she would like me to meet her daughters and then one day Evie called at the dealership with something for her mother, *et voilà*! We have been together ever since.'

'Love at first sight?' Robbie asked, remembering his first impressions of Anna.

Marcel laughed, shaking his head. 'Er, the instant attraction, certainly. Love...' Again the shrug.

'That is exactly how it was with me and Anna,' Robbie replied. 'Well, at our first meeting I was attracted to her and then when I saw her again later that same evening, I realised she was special; I was kind of hooked.'

'Anna is the more serious one,' Marcel told him. 'She can be a little bit reserved and she can also be a little bit sharp if—'

'Tell me about it,' Robbie interrupted.

'The car racing, uh?' Marcel grinned. 'I can very well imagine Anna's objections. Evie—she is a fireball; hot temper; hot headed.' He grinned. 'Hot. But fascinating when you know how to control the burner.' He grinned again; his eyes half closed. 'Two magnificent ladies, uh?'

Robbie could not argue with that. He wondered what their father was like to work for.

'Giuseppe is fair with the hours of work and the pay is okay,' Marcel replied. 'But he also has a temper and then he can be abusive... a bully, you could call him, but I am okay with it; I can handle it.'

'Is he going to be at the family dinner tomorrow evening?'

Marcel shook his head. 'No, no; he is away in Maranello this week, at the Ferrari factory. There is a new model being launched in Europe and he is there to secure a deal.'

'Oh, okay.' Robbie felt relieved in a way, although he had hoped to be able to go round the showroom and also have a look at some of the classic cars that Anna had told him about.

As if reading his thoughts, Marcel added, 'Marianne is holding the fort – she is the real boss, the brains behind the business anyway – I am sure she will show you around the place if you are interested.'

Robbie smiled. 'Am I interested?' He then remembered Evelyn's instructions and checked the time. It was getting late.

'Should we make a move, Marcel? The girls will have the dinner ready, no doubt?'

'One more drink... hey, don't look so worried, my friend. The dinner, it will be burnt anyway – it always is – and if they are hungry they won't wait, they will eat it and then make a fuss and have us believe they were fainting from hunger. Man, they just love the drama!'

'Burnt?' Robbie queried. 'But Anna can cook,' he protested. 'She worked as an au pair and cooking was part of her duties.'

'Her cooking is superior to Evie's,' Marcel agreed. 'Anyone's cooking is better than Evie's, but listen,' he leaned across the table, his index finger raised for effect, 'you have not sampled Marianne's cuisine...' he broke off, bunching his fingers to his lips and kissing them. 'To die for,' he added. 'You will see.'

Chapter 7

Marianne had occupied her modest apartment in the medieval and cultural old town area on the west bank since separating from her husband, Giuseppe Sarri. She was a woman of means but her needs were few and simple and she saw no virtue in taking a more fashionable penthouse with a built-in pool and roof garden in the more modern Klein-Basel, north of the river, just for the sake of it. Here, in Gross-Basel she was near her friends; she had enough room for entertaining, a guest bedroom and a quiet balcony where she could relax by looking out onto the Rhine, something she never tired of.

Today was special; her family was coming to visit and Anna was going to introduce her to the new man in her life. *Un Anglais*, she thought, looking out of her window across the river... well, she reflected, my husband is Italian with Greek ancestors, my children are Swiss-German, Evelyn has her Frenchman and now Anna has found herself a Brit. She smiled with anticipation... this evening's celebration would certainly have an international flavour. She had already planned the meal and included in it would be something to make Robbie feel at home.

In Anna's home, they were getting ready for the visit and because the occasion was going to be more than their normal family get-together, the girls saw it as the perfect excuse to wear their glad rags. In fact, Evelyn had bought an outfit especially: a green-and-white striped dress with a tiered skirt and V-neck, matched with a plain white jacket and white stiletto heels. Anna, a little more conservative, chose a pale grey, mid-length skirt and a pink top with a black swan motif. A black knitted shrug and her black patent shoes completed the look. She left her hair to fall loosely around her shoulders while Evelyn had attempted to contain hers with wide green ribbon tied in a huge bow.

Marcel had brewed some coffee and he and Robbie chatted while they waited; neither of them were ambassadors of formal dressing, preferring jeans and T-shirt or even working gear, but by wearing jackets, both had achieved an acceptable smart casual look and their sweaters meant they could also get away with not wearing ties.

'Always they take so long to get ready!' Marcel said. 'The nails; the make-up; the earrings, uh? The hair...' his dark eyes brimmed with merriment as he mimicked someone brushing their hair.

Robbie laughed. 'Anna is nearly always late,' he remarked, pulling a face. 'I thought she had dumped me when she didn't show up to meet me at the airport.'

'But she did come, uh?'

'Yes, an hour late and her excuse was that she had been doing herself up for me!'

Marcel laughed, the light dancing in his eyes. 'Hah! That is Anna... always honest.'

Marcel drove them the short distance to Marianne's apartment knowing that one of the girls, more likely Anna, would come to his rescue if he drank more than the legal limit for driving home. He was not a heavy drinker and was not often the worse for wear, but Swiss laws were very strict and he did not want to risk losing his licence which would also mean losing his job.

As the foursome climbed the steps to the main door of the building, Robbie could see that it had once been one of a row of grand residences, most of which had been sold off over the years and converted into apartments. He saw a similarity with some of the larger, terraced town houses in London, the Swiss versions being far more picturesque with their brightly painted doors and window shutters and nearly all had garrets, many of which were rented out to students.

Before they reached the door it was flung open and a plump blonde woman of medium height stood at the threshold, flanked by a tall young man on her right, and to her left, a smartly dressed young lady with cropped red hair and wearing large glasses. Anna did the honours, introducing her mother, Marianne, and then her brother and sister, Max and Silke respectively. Max and Silke both spoke very good English like their siblings but their mother spoke only French, with a little bit of Suisse-Deutsche thrown in and only a few words of English. Robbie knew no other language apart from what Anna had taught him so when he was conversing with Marianne, one of them would act as interpreter.

Marianne was a woman of the world, a hard working one. Very family orientated, she was a strong mother figure, sweet-natured and charming, oozing serenity from every pore, and she and Robbie liked each other instantly. Robbie had seen a photograph of Marianne but was still unprepared for the rosy-cheeked, homely figure who stepped forward to welcome him. She was what his mother would term a 'bonnie lassie'.

Marianne took in Robbie's muscular frame, finding it pleasing to the eye, her blue eyes smiling at him as he inclined his head towards her to be kissed on both cheeks. He took the action in his stride, now becoming used to the Swiss mode of greeting a family friend.

Silke was the smaller of the three girls and the quietest, carrying herself with dignity and confidence. Max was tall, still a student and very slim, blessed with his mother's high cheekbones. Robbie realised that he was the only child who resembled Marianne and supposed that all the girls took their strong features from their father; all three having large eyes and noses and full lips. The other thing he noticed was that mother and daughters all wore large dangly earrings and all had immaculately painted, unnervingly long nails.

Greetings and introductions over, they trooped into Marianne's lounge where a small table was laid out with red and white wine and glasses for an apéro, or apéritif before dinner. Marianne stayed to drink a toast with them and then headed back to the kitchen where she was well underway with the cooking.

Robbie wondered what they would be having and thought the aromas wafting around suggested *'le rosbif'*. As he chatted with Silke, she told him about her work in a bank in Lugano and mentioned that she was married to a bricklayer.

'Really? What a pity he didn't come with you,' Robbie said. 'We would have a lot in common; I have been working on building sites for some time now.'

'He is working some distance away,' she replied, but I am sure you will meet him sometime soon, and then you can both talk the shop to your hearts content!'

'I think they will talk more about cars,' Marcel said. 'This guy races Ford cars in England... more interesting than the brickwork, uh Robbie?'

Robbie cringed inwardly, shooting Anna a glance and catching her deadeye glare.

'Work, cars, football...' Robbie replied swiftly, 'I am sure we will have a lot in common.'

'Liverpool FC!' Marcel said, picking up on the football thread and giving Robbie a chance to change the subject.

'Wimbledon won the FA cup,' Robbie informed him. He saw the merriment in Marcel's eyes. Had he mentioned the racing purely for devilment? He wouldn't put it past him.

'Wimber who? Marcel continued. 'I have not heard of any Wimberdon.' He grinned, showing perfect white teeth.

'And what about Manchester United… they were once the champions, uh?'

'Middlesbrough can run rings round them!' Robbie said.

'Meedles?'

Max joined in the conversation and the girls, having no interest, left them to it, Evelyn and Silke pouring themselves fresh drinks while Anna fled to the kitchen to give Marianne a hand.

Marianne, as always, spoke in French to her daughter.

'And what has rattled my little girl's cage?' she wanted to know, sensing Anna's mood change. 'Your *Anglais*… I like him, Anna. He seems to be a very agreeable young man.' She gave Anna a moment to reply and when she said nothing, continued.

'He has taken the trouble to come here to visit you so I presume that his intentions are serious? What I mean is that he is not just toying with your affections, surely?'

Anna shook her head. 'No, Mama, he is not playing games. He is serious all right.'

'Hm, good, I thought so too.' She looked directly at Anna. 'And you? You are also serious about him?'

'We are in love, Mama, but there is this one thing that keeps coming between us and he won't listen to me… he has just been joking about it with the boys and to me it is not a joke, I have a very bad feeling about it!'

Marianne enveloped her favourite daughter in a comforting, maternal hug.

'And what is it that troubles you so much, my little one?' she asked, gently soothing Anna's hair away from her face.

Anna told her about Robbie's passion for motor racing and her constant worry that it would one day claim his life.

'It is a dangerous sport, Mama, and I have begged him to give it up but I know he won't. Surely he would, if he really loved me?' Close to tears, she clung to her mother for emotional support, feeling a kind of relief that she had at last been able to express her fears.

'Evelyn and Marcel are no help to me,' she continued, 'they just encourage him and—'

'Ssh, ma cherie,' Marianne murmured. 'From what you have told me, Robbie is a young man with a sense of adventure – he enjoys life and is fun to be with, yes?'

Anna's muffled agreement rose from the confines of her mother's ample bosom.

'And you… you are also fond of excitement.' She gently raised Anna's head so that they were face to face. 'You remember the day when you went air ballooning over the Alps?'

Anna said nothing but waited for Marianne to continue.

'You will never know how I hoped and prayed that the flight would be cancelled that day. I was so afraid that something awful would happen – that the balloon would crash down on the mountains and I would never see you again—' Marianne's hand flew to her mouth at the thought of some gruesome and grisly outcome that never was.

104

'Mama,' Anna took a step back. Holding her mother's shoulders now, she searched her eyes. 'Oh, I know now exactly how you felt, though I had no idea at the time. But you did not try to stop me?'

'Would it have made any difference, child? You were so intent on doing it, I doubt if I or anyone could have persuaded you against it! So I had to take a back seat and pray and have faith that you would return safe and well. And of course you did.' She kissed her daughter's forehead. 'Life is short, Anna. We must all make the most of it and take our chances when we can and if sometimes that causes conflict...' she shrugged. 'My advice, *cherie*, is show him that you love him, support him and be there when he needs you...'

'Who needs who?' Evelyn asked as she came into the kitchen and caught Marianne's words. She looked from Anna to her mother. 'Is everything all right in here?'

'Everything is fine,' Anna replied.

Evelyn's eyebrow flickered. 'Good. Because we are all hungry and ready to eat.'

'Then start to take these dishes into the dining room and...' Marianne checked the roast through the glass oven door, '... it will be served in about five minutes, so get on with it!'

Robbie felt honoured that Marianne had cooked a traditional English roast and was particularly delighted when she also produced traditional Yorkshire pudding to complete it. After saying grace with the family he rubbed

105

his hands together in joyful anticipation of what he was about to receive.

'It makes me feel very special,' he told them, 'that your mum has not only gone to the trouble to cook a traditional roast beef but I see has also made Yorkshire pudding!'

'It is not the 'rosbif,' Marcel pointed out. 'I don't know what about the Yorkshire-whatever,' he shrugged. 'But is all cordon bleu. Enjoy!'

Robbie, about to take his first bite, saw his childhood favourite, Bambi, in his mind, thinking he was about to eat venison.

He glanced at Anna.

'It is horse meat,' she said.

Marianne, seated at the head of the table, gave him the most disarming smile and he was lost for words for a moment as the image of a very much alive Red Rum winning the Grand National entered his consciousness. He was aware of everyone watching him and quickly put the forkful into his mouth and began to chew. He was pleasantly surprised by the taste – a lot like beef but with a gamey kind of flavour – and it was so tender it melted in the mouth. He just wished that he could get rid of Red Rum who unfortunately stayed with him, not only for the rest of the course, but also popped in and out for most of the afternoon.

The chocolate gateau that followed the main course was sheer decadence on a plate and Robbie savoured every mouthful of the velvety chocolate mousse, layered with the finest of luxury chocolate and finished with gold dust.

'What do you think?' Anna asked, knowing his weakness for chocolate.

He sighed with deep content as he laid down his fork. 'I think... that is the closest to food heaven I have ever been. Absolutely out of this world!'

Anna relayed his comments to her mother, who smiled with pleasure, nodding her thanks to him.

Coffee in the lounge completed the repast and they spent the rest of the evening chatting and looking through family photographs and videos. When shown a photograph of Giuseppe Sarri, Robbie was immediately reminded of a bull and was amazed that his daughters could be so attractive. Max, in comparison, looked nothing like him, either in features or build, so his initial thoughts about their looks had been spot on.

When Anna ran the promotional video for the Ferrari dealership, his eyes feasted on these extravagant machines designed for speed and glamour and which were accessible only through the pockets of the ultra-rich.

'Man, you will have to come to the showroom,' Marcel said, watching Robbie's reactions. 'We do not have all of those models of course, but I guarantee you will like what you see.' He looked at Marianne.

'Of course,' she replied, smiling. 'No problem.'

Marcel nodded, giving Robbie a thumbs-up sign. 'You happy with that, uh?'

Robbie grinned at him, returning the thumbs-up. 'Very happy. Thank you.'

107

As the evening came to a close and everyone prepared to leave, Robbie went with Anna to thank her mother for making him so welcome and for the wonderful meal.

Replying through Anna, she said what a pleasure it was to have met him and he was welcome at any time, then insisting that if he could visit for Christmas, Swiss hospitality would be on offer at its bountiful best.

Chapter 8

The following day Anna asked Robbie if he would like to visit the Natural History Museum in Basel.

'We can make a day of it if you like,' she suggested.

'Will it take all day to go round, then?' Robbie asked.

'It could easily take *you* all week,' she laughed, 'knowing how you get carried away with the natural sciences. You will find everything there, Robbie, from the largest dinosaur to the smallest ant!'

'Wow… really? And rock formations, minerals… that kind of thing?'

'Yes. And more,' Anna replied. 'Much more. And you said you wanted to walk along the banks of the Rhine?'

'Oh, well yes, I would.'

'Good. It is a perfect day for it,' Anna said, looking through the window and seeing blue sky. 'And I want to see a film afterwards. Then we can round it all off with dinner.'

Robbie was happy. 'Sounds like a plan! What's the film?'

'Big.'

'Big what?'

She laughed. 'What do you mean, big what? Tom Hanks is what! It is a fantasy about a boy who makes a wish to be big and then ages to adulthood overnight.'

'You really like Tom Hanks movies, don't you?'

'Yes, I do. He is a fabulous actor.'

Robbie was like a dog with two tails in the Natural History Museum. With a heritage dating back over 300 years, it was home to extensive collections focused on the fields of zoology, entomology, mineralogy, anthropology, osteology and palaeontology. Robbie had covered some of these studies with the Open University and having read the theorem, could now see the practical and physical formulation that brought it all to life.

'You were right,' he whispered to Anna as they stood gazing up at the giant skeleton of a dinosaur, 'I could easily spend a whole week in here. That's Brachiosaurus: they grew to about fifteen metres tall.'

'It is amazing,' Anna agreed, 'but I am grateful that they are extinct. Just look at those huge jaws and teeth!'

'They have been extinct for sixty-five million years, Anna,' Robbie informed her, 'so no humans were ever at risk and anyway, most were herbivores, apart from T-Rex.'

The rock and mineral section was of special interest to Robbie as that was his field and they spent some time there. Apart from admiring an impressive display of crystals and fossils, Anna did not have much interest but stayed with him and listened to his comments.

'I think you should be an archaeologist,' she told him. 'I can see you on a dig with a little tool, carefully scraping the dirt away from old relics.'

He smiled. 'No, Anna, I am more interested in the geological structure of the earth rather than its social history, though the ancient human settlements do give an insight to life as it was during the stone, bronze and iron ages.'

They continued to explore the exhibits until Robbie felt he could not absorb any more. The museum was also filling up with visitors and the comparative quiet atmosphere was now giving way to a general and continual buzz of conversation.

'Are you feeling hungry?' Robbie asked.

Anna laughed. 'A little, yes and you... well you are always hungry.'

Robbie was tempted to make a comment about his hunger for her, which was becoming increasingly more difficult to contain and not helped by the fact that he shared her bed but not her body.

Anna took his hand. 'Come, we will find some lunch and then have our walk by the river.'

The opportunity lost, he said nothing of what was on his mind as they headed for the exit.

The River Rhine looked particularly beautiful, sparkling in the autumn sunshine as Robbie and Anna ambled along its banks after a light lunch. They were discussing their jobs again.

'Robbie, will you help me to apply to British Airways as a stewardess?' Anna asked.

'I will do what I can,' he replied, 'but I don't know anyone at BA, or much about them, I'm afraid. I imagine you would have to get an application form. You might even have to be a UK resident.'

'Oh. I see.' Anna could not keep the disappointment out of her voice. It may not be as simple as she had hoped. And she felt he was not being very encouraging.

'Robbie, be truthful; do you not want me to get a good job and better myself?'

Astonished, he stopped in his tracks and turned to her.

'Anna, what a thing to suggest! Of course I want you to do well and find happiness and I know you have set your heart on being an air stewardess, but I don't want you to raise your hopes and then be disappointed if it doesn't work out.'

'But you could perhaps help me to get an application form?'

'When I get home I will ring their recruitment centre and see what I can find out. You know I will help you as much as I can.'

'Okay, if you would, darling.'

Robbie thought what a typical Aquarian she was – a paradox, if ever. Tough, yet gentle; fierce yet affectionate; faithful yet detached; stubborn yet willing to compromise.

'Have you thought of applying to your own airline?' he quizzed.

'You mean Swissair?' She pouted, giving him a dubious look. 'No. That would mean me still working here in Switzerland while you are back in England. What is the point of that?'

He agreed there was no point at all. 'But,' he continued, 'supposing I could find work here?'

'You would leave London and come to live here?'

'If it were a possibility, yes. I love your country.'

'You would do that for me?'

'I would be doing it for both of us, Anna.'

Anna was excited. 'When you come again for Christmas, we will see how far we have got. Meanwhile, I will ask around everyone I know who might be able to find work for you. I am sure you will soon find something suitable for a person of your knowledge and ability.'

They walked back, arm in arm to the cinema and again were lucky to get in just as the main film was about to begin. Fortunately, this time there were no attempts by strange men to molest her and they both sat back and enjoyed the movie which was funny and very entertaining.

Afterwards, they found a restaurant and had dinner to round off their day. On this occasion, Robbie tried *wienerschnitzel*, a traditional Austrian dish but one which was also very popular with the Swiss. After a dessert dripping with delectable Swiss chocolate and then a coffee, they made for home, both feeling easy in each other's company after an enjoyable day together.

Later that night, Robbie completed his bathroom routine and went into the bedroom where Anna was already in bed, sitting up against her pillows, reading. Robbie climbed into bed next to her.

'Did you enjoy today, darling?' she asked, putting her book down on the bedside table.

'It was magical, Anna,' he replied. 'I have enjoyed every moment. Thank you for making it so special.'

She kissed him with more passion than usual; something he had not experienced before. He felt that she was ready to consummate their relationship; she was different, relaxed, receptive… and ready.

He moved closer to her and kissed her again and her response encouraged him to take a step further. He fondled her breast through her nightie and her reaction came as a shock to him as she cried out and slapped him.

'No, Robbie! I have made it clear that I am not ready for this!' she responded.

Robbie put a hand to his stinging cheek. 'Anna, I am so sorry, I thought you… Sorry, I misread the signs…'

Marcel was up early the following morning and was surprised to see Robbie sleeping on the couch. He walked past him to the kitchen to make coffee and then went back into the lounge, carrying two mugs of fresh coffee. He gave Robbie a gentle shake.

'Hey man, why are you sleeping on the couch, uh?'

Robbie stirred beneath the spare duvet that Anna had thrown at him and heaved himself into a sitting position, rubbing his eyes, disorientated for a few moments. Then he remembered.

Marcel jerked his head towards Anna's bedroom. 'You and Anna… you have a falling out, uh?'

Robbie nodded, gratefully accepting the coffee that Marcel offered.

'Yes. I erm… I misread the signs.' He thought back to the passionate embrace. 'She seemed… I really thought she was ready to… well, to be honest, she seemed to be asking for it and then… well next thing I'm banished to the couch.'

114

'Too amorous for her, uh?' Marcel's eyes danced with mirth.

'No! Well, it had not been my intention – I thought it was hers—'

'Women,' Marcel put in, 'how to understand them, uh? Do not worry, *mon ami*, Anna will come round. She is...' he paused, searching for the word he wanted in English, '... unpredictable, perhaps sometimes volatile, but then in the next moment all is forgiven and life carries on as before.' He nodded. 'It will be fine, you will see. Now drink your coffee, man, while it is hot.'

Robbie sipped the steaming black liquid. 'And Evelyn?' he enquired. 'Is she like that too?'

'Ah, my Evie,' Marcel smiled wistfully. 'She is different to Anna but I would say they can both be awkward. Evie has a hot fiery temperament like her father but I can handle her fine.' He grinned. 'I tell her I will bring a television in the bedroom because what does she do? Always, when the football or rugby is on, she wants my attentions—and sometimes if I am thinking of going for a beer.' He shrugged. 'Like I said, the women, they can be awkward.'

As Marcel had predicted, hardly any tension remained between Anna and Robbie. Anna met him coming out of the bathroom and asked him if he had managed to get any sleep on the couch.

'Some,' he replied. 'I was restless, worrying that I had offended you. Anna, please forgive me, I didn't mean to—'

'You are forgiven,' she told him, 'and you can sleep in my bed again tonight if you want to… as long as you can behave yourself. If you cannot, then it will be the couch.'

Robbie was about to ask her if she thought he was made of stone and then thought better of it, remembering that he was a guest.

She looked at him, wrapped in a towel, looking forlorn. 'You had better get some clothes on!'

No more was said and Robbie decided he would not mention the incident again unless she did. What he did not know was that she had just been confiding in her sister and there had been a few tears.

'But Anna,' Evelyn had said, 'if you really wanted to, why did you stop him?'

'I don't know… I think I was a bit shocked that he was so sudden and then I found I had these… feelings for him. It wasn't until after he had gone that I realised how strong these feelings were and how much I wanted him, but it still felt wrong…' She broke off as her emotions overcame her and Evelyn held her as she cried softly on her shoulder for a few minutes.

'Then it was not the right time,' she told Anna. 'You will know when it is and trust me, it will have been worth waiting for. It is not so good to rush into these things before you are ready. You have plenty of time. Let it take its natural course and you will be so glad you did.'

Unusually, all four of them sat down to breakfast on that Friday morning and, much to Robbie's relief, the atmosphere was very congenial.

'What are you two planning to do today?' Evelyn asked, looking from Robbie to Anna.

'We haven't actually made any plans,' Anna replied. 'I thought a quiet day, maybe showing Robbie around the locality – cakes and coffee included, of course – and relaxing.'

'Evie and I are going to see a movie this evening,' Marcel added. 'Would you like to make it a foursome and have dinner afterwards?'

Anna turned to Robbie. 'What do you think?'

'Of course,' he replied. 'I would like to do that. What is the film?'

'*Green Card*,' Evelyn said. 'It is a romance and apparently very funny with that Frenchman, erm, Gerard…'

'Depardieu!' Marcel obliged.

'Yes, him, and Andie MacDowell.'

That being agreed, Marcel then slurped a last mouthful of coffee, grabbed his jacket and left for work with a cheerful 'Ciao, guys!'

Evelyn went off to battle with her hair, eventually giving up on it – when she sorted out one tangle, another seemed to take its place – and also left to go to her work at the salon, leaving Anna and Robbie with the day stretching ahead of them.

To Robbie's great relief, there was no more mention of his faux pas and he and Anna spent a relaxing day enjoying each other's company, bringing to Robbie's mind those happy days spent in Richmond Park when they first met.

The evening was a much more lively affair, only to be expected in the company of Evelyn and Marcel, with whom there was never a dull moment and hardly ever a quiet one.

Robbie's time in Basel was now running out. He was due to fly back to London on Monday and Anna had planned a full weekend. On Saturday they would visit Zurich and then she wanted Robbie to see Lucerne which she knew he would really enjoy, both for its architecture and scenic beauty.

Being the largest city in Switzerland, Zürich was located at the north western tip of Lake Zürich. It was a hub for railways, roads, and air traffic and the airport and railway station were the largest and busiest in the country. Zürich was founded by the Romans. Their official language was German, but the main spoken language was the local variant of the Swiss German dialect.

Of the many museums and art galleries, they visited the Swiss National Museum and the Kunsthaus, which was packed with fine art and sculptures.

Robbie was aware that most of Switzerland's research and development centres were concentrated in Zürich and the low tax rates attracted overseas companies to set up their headquarters there. He could perfectly understand why.

Next stop on the agenda was Lucerne and as they waited for a train, Anna asked Robbie what he thought of Zurich.

'To be honest,' he said, 'I am a bit disappointed.'

Anna was surprised by his response. She knew how much he had enjoyed the visit and studied his face, knowing how good he was at hiding his emotions behind an impassive mask. She could read nothing.

'In what way disappointed?' she asked.

'Well, we have been here... how long,' he consulted his watch, 'at least four hours and in that time I have not spotted one gnome. Not one, or anything looking remotely like one!'

'Get outta here!' she exclaimed with a giggle. 'Gnomes of Zurich... you know perfectly well what that refers to – and where it originated, in your own country—'

Robbie burst out laughing. 'Of course I do, Anna. Sorry, I couldn't help winding you up. Good old Harold Wilson... responsible for many a misunderstanding, I might add!' He ducked as she took aim with her handbag, grinning when she missed by a mile but protesting when the follow-up caught him squarely on the back of his head.

Fortuitously, the Lucerne train then came into sight, slowing and then coming to a halt at the platform and they boarded. Robbie helped his lady and her handbag into the carriage, realising that the gap between train and platform was apparently not just confined to the London Underground or indeed the UK.

As they approached their destination, the snow-capped mountains were visible, the famous Mount Rigi towering above Lake Lucerne. Although not the highest of Lucerne's three local mountains, Rigi was renowned for spectacular views.

The colourful old town with its preserved medieval architecture, sat sedately between Lakes Lucerne, Zug and Lauerz, under the protection of the three mountains, Rigi, Pilatus and Titlist, the highest. All peaks were accessible by cable cars, gondolas or cog railway, though they had to forego that pleasure to enjoy exploring the old town where they found a delightful restaurant and had a traditional rösti for lunch.

Afterwards they walked to the Chapel Bridge (*Kapellbrücke*), a wooden pedestrian bridge that spanned the River Reuss. Named after the nearby St. Peter's Chapel, it was built in 1333 and was one of the oldest covered wooden bridges in Europe. It was about 170 meters and originally was constructed as part of Lucerne's fortifications… connecting the old part of town on the right bank with the new part on the left, it served as protection from any attack that came from the south of the lake.

Anna pointed towards the roof. 'Just look at those, Robbie!'

'Wow!' Robbie exclaimed, raising his eyes to see triangular paintings hanging in rows from the interior apex of the roof, depicting historical events and legends of the area. 'What an amazing place!'

There were more than 150 paintings by a local seventeenth century Catholic painter, Hans Heinrich Wägmann, but time as ever was ticking away and they had to leave to get their train back to Zurich and then home to Basel.

Too tired that evening to even accompany Marcel to the bar, there were no repetitions of the previous night… Robbie fell asleep as soon as his head touched the pillow.

'So Anna is taking you to our capital city on your last day with us,' Evelyn said. Marcel was still in bed and Evelyn was sitting at the table in her dressing gown, drinking coffee with Robbie. Anna was in her bedroom in front of the mirror, making herself beautiful.

'Yes,' Robbie replied. 'I am especially looking forward to the medieval architecture of the Old Town and, of course, the Einstein Museum as well as his former residence.'

'You will find many things there to interest you; and it is not all ancient, you know. There are boutiques, bars and cabaret venues—some of them in vaulted cellars, there is also modern art and the cafés attract locals as well as tourists.'

'It sounds fascinating.'

Evelyn poured a coffee for Marcel and got up from the table.

'I hope Anna does not keep you waiting too long,' she said. 'Have a lovely day!'

Anna put in an appearance shortly afterwards, looking gorgeous in a royal blue mid-length skirt, with an orange-and-blue top weighted with a long, double string of large black beads, a black woollen jacket, black tights and knee-length black boots. Her hair was flowing free, already tangling with her jet earrings that had been a birthday gift from her mother.

They walked the short journey to the station and took the train which arrived in the capital about an hour later. Set in the heart of Switzerland, Bern was the gateway to the Alps. The capital could also easily be reached by car or by the bus links. Although Bern had a very good public transport network it was best to explore the city centre on foot and this was what Anna and Robbie elected to do.

The old town of Bern was a UNESCO World Heritage Site and thanks to its six kilometres of arcades, which the locals referred to as 'Lauben', it boasted one of the longest weather-sheltered shopping promenades in Europe. Anna was naturally keen to explore the fashion and shoe shops and Robbie bought her a brightly coloured scarf that caught her eye.

The medieval air of the city with its many fountains, sandstone facades, narrow streets and historic towers, was unique and an experience that Robbie enjoyed immensely. He was becoming more and more enchanted with this fascinating country and less and less inclined to fly home to London and leave it all behind.

He was interested in the Albert Einstein House where the physics genius had lived in a second-floor apartment with his wife and son in the early twentieth century. It was out of the question to leave the city without visiting the Einstein Museum. A tour of the Fine Arts Museum brought their sightseeing trip to a close and they went off in search of food and a much needed sit down. It was getting close to dusk as they waited for their train back to Basel and darkness had fallen when they reached the apartment. This time tomorrow, Robbie thought, he would be drinking hot chocolate with his parents in their semi-detached in Richmond and all this would seem a world away.

Robbie's flight to Heathrow was scheduled for two p.m. and Anna pulled into the parking area at ten-thirty, giving them time for their goodbyes and ensuring that Robbie met the check-in deadline of eleven o'clock.

'Anna, I don't want to leave you now. I want to stay here with you...'

Anna heard the emotion in his voice. It did not make it any easier for her but she put on a brave face; she needed to be firm with him.

'Robbie, you know you have to go home. All good things come to an end, remember, and look, we will be together again in two weeks' time.' She frowned. 'Not that I want to watch you kill yourself in that horrible racing car that you insist on telling me is not at all dangerous, but—'

'Anna, you don't understand. I want to stay here and make a life with you in your beautiful country – for always – not just for visits and special occasions.'

But Robbie, there are procedures, conditions...'

'I don't mean now, this minute – though if that were only possible... a dream come true. No, I am thinking a few weeks ahead – when I come for Christmas, I could maybe look for work then.'

'What kind of work? On the building sites?'

'Not necessarily; I would like to do something interesting like working in one of the museums or art galleries, but I would take anything going if it meant we could be together.'

Anna agreed that it was what she wanted as well, but that it would take time. 'And I have always set my heart on working for British Airways,' she added.

Robbie reached out and held her hand. 'If that's what you really want, then let's go for that and we will live in London?'

As the PA continued with its intrusive announcements of arrivals, departures, delays and final boarding calls, Robbie heard his flight to Heathrow mentioned.

'I suppose I should go and check in,' he said. 'Can we both give some thought to this and try and reach a conclusion when you come to London next month?'

The announcements garbled on and people swarmed in every direction, some hauling and some pushing their baggage, some having no clue where they were meant to be. For Robbie and Anna the moment they had both dreaded was here, it was time to say goodbye. Oblivious to the surrounding chaos, they came together in one last embrace and for them the world stopped until, breaking apart from him, Anna whispered, 'God speed, my love,' and was gone.

Robbie turned at the automatic doors before going to find the BA desk. The bronze Mazda was in a queue waiting to turn right into the traffic, heading for home.

Chapter 9

For Anna life was a little flat after Robbie's departure and she somehow felt incomplete without him. She went back to her work at the florists but hoped that she would soon hear from Robbie that he had managed to get her an application form to join the flight crew of British Airways. How wonderful it would be if she could arrange to go for an interview during her forthcoming flying visit to London. She and Robbie talked on the telephone and she was anxious to know whether he had been successful.

'Anna, it is not that easy,' he explained. 'Every time I ring up, the lines are always engaged and even if anyone should happen to answer my call, I am put on hold and eventually have to hang up.'

'Perhaps I should ring them myself?' she suggested.

'You can try, but honestly I think you will be lucky if you get any response. I will try writing them a letter and see if that gets any results.'

'How will that help? If they cannot answer the phone, they will hardly reply to a letter?' In two weeks' time, Anna was visiting London and she thought perhaps she and Robbie could go to their offices personally and find out about recruitment.

'We have nothing to lose,' Robbie replied. 'Let's do that.'

Meanwhile, Robbie was preoccupied with getting his racing car in tip-top condition for the forthcoming race at Silverstone. He had done well in his last race and this one was going to be extra special because Anna was coming to watch him and he not only wanted to impress her with his driving skills, he also wanted her to see for herself that it was not the death trap she imagined it to be. They had not talked about the event much because Anna still had serious doubts and also thought that Robbie spent far too much money on something that she considered to be a life-threatening activity.

Anna was arriving at Heathrow on Friday afternoon. Robbie had arranged to drive his Ford Transit to pick her up. As usual, she was late but this time it was because the flight had been delayed and out of her control. She waved to him as she approached the waiting area and once she had spotted him, he stood back a little, away from the press of passengers coming through.

She ran up to him and putting her bag down at his feet, fell into his warm embrace, both delighted to be reunited. He took her bag and led the way to the short stay car park. It was dry and not too cold for November.

'How was your flight?' he asked.

'It was fine,' she replied, 'once we were cleared for take-off. There was a hold up at Basel for some reason.'

He studied her for a moment. She was wearing a woollen grey belted coat over a black skirt and red roll-neck sweater, red tights and her favourite black knee-length boots. Her hair was secured in a black velvet scrunchie and a grey-and-white chiffon scarf floated about her shoulders.

'What?' she said.

'You are more beautiful than ever,' he told her.

Anna laughed. 'And you are still charming the birds, I notice!'

Oh! How he had missed that sexy voice, the throaty laugh that was Anna's trademark.

'Only one bird,' he replied, helping her up into the passenger seat of the Transit.

'Oh, this is your new transport?' she said, looking around the cab and the seats in the back. 'It is different to what I imagined... is like, er, minibus?'

'Is exactly a minibus,' he said, smiling. 'You can always go and sit in the back if you don't feel safe in the front with me!'

She poked her tongue out at him. 'I am okay here in the front; it is high up and I can see a lot! The seats are not so comfortable though...'

'No. I am sorry about that but I didn't buy it for comfort, I needed it to—'

'To tow that damn racing car; that is why you bought it!'

'Not solely for that. I sometimes use it to take football fans to Brighton.'

'Hm.' Anna gave him a half smile and changed the subject. 'How are your parents?'

'They are fine. Dad's working but he's at home at the moment. He is looking forward to seeing you... well and

Mum, of course. She can't wait to have a chinwag as you might imagine!'

Again, the husky laugh. 'And how has she been? Is she still off the drink?'

'Yes, she is doing very well. She had to have a spell in hospital... she needed a lot of support to get through the withdrawal symptoms, you know. They were pretty bad, but she is home again now, attending AA and looking good.'

'I am so pleased to hear that.'

'She told me only the other day that meeting you was a kind of blessing sent to her – she has not touched a drop since that day she met you in the park.'

'Oh!' said Anna. 'That's amazing!'

'It's you that's amazing,' Robbie replied, indicating to turn left into his road.

They talked about Evelyn and Marcel and Robbie said it would have been good if Marcel could have come to watch the race.

'Yes; he said he would like to. I told him he was welcome to take my place as far as the racing was concerned, except that I really wanted to see you again. I have missed you so much.'

'I have missed you too,' Robbie replied. 'It seems longer than three weeks. By the way, I finally made contact with British Airways.'

'You did? And did you manage to get me an application form?' Anna asked, excited that there had at last been some response.

Robbie shook his head. 'I'm afraid not, my love,' he said gently. The guy I spoke to was really friendly and very helpful, but he told me there was already a long list of applicants who have all completed the checks etc and ticked all the boxes and are just waiting for the call. There are other vacancies, but mostly for ground staff – you know, check-in, baggage handling, cleaning – all that kind of thing.

Anna sighed, disappointed. 'So I can forget my dream of living in London and working for BA?'

'Don't be too despondent,' he told her as he pulled up outside his home. 'I have a dream, too.'

She looked at him, eyebrows raised, requesting more explanation.

However, their discussion had to wait as Fiona, who had been looking out for them, was already at the door to greet them.

'Och and here she is, ma bonnie wee lassie!' she cried, running out through the door and into the street, helping Anna down from the cab and hugging her.

'How are ye, hen? My, ye're looking just fine,' she enthused, 'just fine!' She ushered Anna indoors and Robbie followed, putting her bag down in the hall. Within minutes the kettle was boiling and tea and Dundee cake were served as a stopgap until dinner.

'Your Dad'll be here aboot six,' Fiona said. She smiled at Anna. He's aye looking forward tae seeing his wee lassie again.'

Anna smiled, her whole face lighting up. 'It will be good to see him, too. I expect he is still very busy?'

'He's away overseeing some bridge work down Kingston way.'

'Oh, not too far away, then,' Anna observed.

'Makes a change! He was aye up in Liverpool last week so I didnae hae him under ma feet!' She sighed. 'It was quiet wi'oot him, all the same.'

The British Formula Ford Championship was an entry level single-seater motor sport category, originally designed to give racing drivers their first step into car racing after karting. Drivers from across the world were attracted to the UK to compete in the series, and successful Formula One drivers such as Ayrton Senna and Jenson Button won their first single-seater titles in the FF Championship. The championship was run to various Ford regulations over the years, based on the engines provided for the championship by Ford Motor Company. Formula Ford was unique in the world of motor racing. Unlike most other kinds of competition, it was open to the amateur and to those less well-off but it was also sufficiently dynamic for the championship to count in the world of motor sport.

A large element of potential cost depended on whether you were able to maintain and run the car yourself. Self-preparation reduced costs dramatically and if you happened to have a mate who was a mechanic, you could save even more.

The car that Robbie raced was a maroon pre-74 category Ford Merlyn MK 24A 1600 and bore the number 58. Robbie did a lot of work on his Merlyn himself. His father took an interest and also went with him to the circuits whenever he could. Other, more technical, maintenance was carried out by the local garage at reasonable cost. His mechanic at Silverstone, Nick Bell, was second to none and had a reputation for putting the safety of his drivers above all else.

The racing car was designed to work at its best when it was set up as intended by its designer. This applied to any car, be it a new Formula Ford or an old F3 car. For the enthusiast, working on these speed machines was DIY at its most enjoyable.

Driving a single-seater open wheel Formula Ford racing car was unlike anything else. Strapped into the confines of the cockpit with the help of your mechanic, steering movements, acceleration and braking were all exaggerated due to the lightness of the car, but the procedure was no different from Formula One – crash helmet on, full harness seat belts tightened to the max and the engine was fired up. Edge out onto the circuit and then it was up to you – you were on your own.

Robbie's crash helmet was navy blue (for Scotland) and around the crown was a grey circle motif, broken into five equal segments – each one representing a family member – Robbie, Fiona, Mike, Emily and Sophie.

On general practice days such as today, all kinds of cars were taking part from E-type Jaguars and minis to modern rally cars, each having varying speeds and degrees of control. There was no competition, so no pressure to perform and Robbie was hoping that this would put Anna's mind at rest so that she would not worry so much about his involvement in the sport.

Robbie himself was very relaxed as he and his father, with the help of the local mechanic, loaded the Merlyn onto the trailer and secured it for the journey. He and Mike had worked on it in their spare time and the mechanic had fine-tuned it. The machine was in its best possible condition and Robbie had high hopes of a good practice session.

'See you later, Mum,' Robbie called to Fiona who stood in the doorway to wave them off. Anna climbed into the van, sitting between Mike and Robbie who was driving. There were a few pockets of mist as they left the capital and headed north towards Towcester but already the sun was beginning to shine through and it promised to be a clear day which was exactly what was hoped for.

Anna sat quietly, looking out at the road ahead, occasionally looking alarmed when the trailer hit a bump in the road or a pothole.

'Are you okay?' Robbie asked her, concerned that she was not her usual exuberant self.

'Of course. But I will be honest, I am not looking forward to this racing business. I am thinking I would have been happier spending the day with your mum while you and your dad are doing this.'

'Hey lass,' Mike said, placing a comforting hand on her arm, 'now there's nowt for you to be worrying about—you'll enjoy it once you get there and pick up the atmosphere of the place. 'Nowt quite like it, is there Robbie?'

Robbie grinned. 'It buzzes,' he replied. 'Literally. When you're out there in the stands and you hear the engines negotiating the bends, and then full throttle on the straight… Dad's right—there's nothing to compare, really.'

The journey took about forty-five minutes and it was action stations immediately once they arrived, parking the van and unloading the car. Once the formalities were completed, Robbie took Anna to the stands where she would have a bird's eye view, not just of him but of all the cars involved in the practice laps that day as well as the surrounding rural landscape, comprised mainly of pasture and woodland.

She shivered in spite of the sunshine; grateful she had worn her woollen coat. Looking around her, she could see quite a few spectators gathering.

'Okay, luv?' Mike said. You'll have a grand view of everything from here. See you a bit later and we'll have us a bite to eat.'

'Aren't you staying to watch?' Anna asked, not comfortable at being left on her own in this strange, busy, noisy place.

'Nay lass, I'll be in t'pits with Nick, doing me bit if he wants a wheel change or owt.'

Robbie kissed her on the cheek. 'It won't take too long; we'll be finished this run in an hour or so. Now don't forget to wave to me… see you later!'

'Robbie!' She ran after him and hugged him tightly. 'Good luck, darling. Please come back safe!'

He kissed her again. 'Don't worry, Anna—just relax and enjoy the experience.'

134

Anna's vantage point was Copse Corner, providing a great view of one of the fastest corners as cars could be seen speeding down the National Straight into this fast paced bend. She stood in the concrete terraced area in front of the General Admission stands. For the devotee, watching from Copse Corner was awesome because you got to see how well the down force works on the modern racing car. They seemed absolutely glued to the track as the aerodynamics pushed the car into the ground. The turn in speed could be incredible and mind blowing to watch! You often saw drivers running amazingly wide through this turn as they found the absolute limit of grip.

Anna, however, neither knew nor cared about the aerodynamics or statistics involved in what she still saw as a pointless but expensive and perilous activity. She stood, shading her eyes against the sun, looking for Robbie's maroon car with the number 58. Finally she focused on what seemed to her to be the only one of that colour, but she could not see its number. He was some way back on the starting grid and there were all kinds of cars taking part, including souped-up Mini Coopers and a rather grand vintage Bentley. The noise rose in a crescendo as the drivers revved their engines in readiness for the off.

Keeping her eyes on the maroon car, she had a good view as it approached the corner and the number 58 was clear, confirming that it was indeed Robbie. He and several others negotiated the corner and zoomed onward towards Maggots and Becketts; the next sharp corner being Stowe. She relaxed a little, still not finding it enjoyable but not feeling quite so worried about Robbie's safety as the drivers were obviously experienced and driving responsibly, Robbie included. Perhaps it wasn't that bad after all. She watched closely as he approached Copse Corner for the second time and in spite of herself, felt a surge of pride at his skill and courage.

It all happened so quickly. Robbie was just ahead of the vintage Bentley going into the corner when a rally car zoomed up and recklessly overtook the Bentley right on the apex of Copse Corner but lost control and didn't make it, clipping the front of the Bentley at speed and spinning into Robbie's wheel with such force that it resembled a rugby ball and then somersaulted through the air, landing on top of Robbie's car—small and light in comparison to the solidly built rally car.

Anna cried out, horrified. The sound of the collision was horrendous—the explosive impact of the vehicles, screaming rubber on tarmac, harsh screeching metal against metal and glass shattering was a sound like no other and something she never wanted to hear again. And then a deathly silence fell before the emergency services came speeding to the scene. Anna's hand covered her mouth as she strained her eyes to see what was happening. Thick smoke veiled most of the shocking scene from her sight. As the fire hoses were utilised, the smoke gradually reduced to steam and then eventually cleared. She could see the Bentley driver walking off the track to the side and then she saw the driver of the rally car, hanging upside down. She could not of course see Robbie. What had happened to him? He must have been crushed to death underneath it all!

136

'Robbie! Robbie?' She hurtled from the stand, her feet barely touching the ground in her panic to reach him. Several stewards stood around the scene obscuring her view and she tried to push past them to get to Robbie.

A steward's muscular arm quickly barred her way.

'Hey, sorry, lady, you're not supposed to be here,' he said, taking her arm and escorting her away.

She shook him off, insisting that he let her stay.

'He is my boyfriend,' she said, 'I saw it happen. Please! What is happening? Is he dead? Please tell me he is not dead.' She began crying hysterically, her fists pummelling the man who had to call on all his strength and determination to keep her at a safe distance.

'He is upside down, love,' a first-aider told her, 'and has a few cuts and bruises. Once we get him on the ground, we can check him over properly but we think he should be okay. He's talking.'

'Not him! Robbie—the driver of the car underneath! What has happened to him?'

She noticed a first-aider crouching near Robbie's car, shaking his head.

'Leave it to the doctor,' she heard him say. 'Best he deals with this one.'

'Noooooooo!' she screamed. 'I knew he would kill himself; I told him it was too dangerous but he would not listen and now he's—'

'I'm the lad's father,' a voice said behind her. 'I'll look after her.'

She fell into Mike's arms, sobbing, unable to speak to him.

137

'Mike,' one of the stewards acknowledged him. 'A bad do—bloody fool overtaking like that,' he said, referring to the rally car driver. 'Best of it is, he's only a mechanic on a test run.'

Mike pointed to Robbie's car. 'What's… is he…?'

'He's trapped. The guys are ready with the cutting gear, but it's tricky; we're waiting for the doctor.' The steward lowered his voice. 'He could have a… neck injury; have to be careful… you know.'

'Broken his neck, you mean?'

The steward shook his head. 'We don't know.'

Anna, in her confusion, heard only 'broken' and 'neck' and to her confused mind that meant he was either dead or dying. No one survived a broken neck, did they? An anguished howl erupted from the very depths of her being.

'I knew it! I had such a bad feeling about coming here today. I have had it all along and now I know why. He is dead, my Robbie, he is dead—'

'Anna,' Mike shook her gently. 'He is not dead. He is trapped and probably has a neck injury and we are waiting for the doctor to come to oversee his removal from the car. One false move and…'

Anna was still inconsolable. 'Then if he is not dead he will be paralysed… my Robbie, so active and then to be cut down…'

Mike held her as the rally car driver was released from his safety harness and removed from his car. He was clearly shaken but able to walk and led away to an

138

ambulance for further examination. As soon as the driver was freed, a hoist moved in and lifted the rally car free.

'Can you hear me?' the doctor asked Robbie.

'Yes.'

'Can you tell me your name?'

'Robbie Munro.'

'Okay, Robbie. Are you in pain?'

'My right shoulder and head and my left leg are hurting.'

'Pain in your leg? That's a good sign—means you have most likely escaped a severe spinal injury. Can you move your right leg... got any feeling in it?'

'It's very cramped in here. Yes. I can feel pressure on it.'

'Good. Any pain in your neck? Top of your spine?'

'Not really... shoulder's the worst.'

The doctor, still concerned about a possible neck injury, fitted a neck brace to provide support as firemen with cutting gear then set to work to release Robbie, demolishing most of his beloved Merlyn in the process. Eventually, he was carefully transferred to a stretcher and taken to a waiting ambulance.

Anna, relieved that her beloved was not dead, but still distressed about his condition, sat down on a nearby bench with Mike and waited for further news.

Inside the ambulance, the doctor gave Robbie a thorough examination. Surprisingly, given the speed of the rally car and the impact of the collision, he had suffered nothing worse than a few cuts to the head and face, a badly bruised

139

left leg and dislocated shoulder, yelping in agony as the doctor manipulated it back into place. He then immobilised the arm and gave him a shot of morphine to settle the pain.

'You're a very lucky fellow,' the doctor told him. 'Nothing broken, no evidence of concussion. Your safety harness saved your life – that and the protective shell of the snug cockpit – and from what the recovery team told me and what I saw with my own eyes, you were merely inches away from having your head severed from your body.' He shook his head in disbelief. 'Damn lucky! Your car's completely knackered, of course…'

Robbie emerged from the ambulance limping slightly with a bandaged head and his right arm in a sling. Anna ran to him, tears of relief streaming down her cheeks. He put his good arm around her shoulder.

'Hiya!' he chirped.

'Oh, Robbie, thank god you are all right – I thought you were dead; I still do not know how you survived. I saw it all happen; it was worse than a nightmare.'

'Take more than that to finish me off,' he grinned. 'Pretty spectacular though, ay? I wouldn't mind a cup of tea? Or some hot chocolate, preferably.'

Mike went to organise some refreshments and Robbie had to report to the stewards. This was a mere formality as the incident had clearly been a result of the rally car driver ignoring the strict rules that governed on-track behaviour. He was subsequently penalised for causing an avoidable accident by driving recklessly.

When Robbie arrived back, Anna was still tearful.

'That is it!' she told him, wiping her eyes. She blew her nose and took a deep breath. 'Robbie, either you give up the racing or I am giving you up… don't speak,' she said, raising her palm as he opened his mouth to respond, 'I told you it was dangerous and I knew it would be only a matter of time before something serious happened. You must make the choice – me or the racing because I cannot go through all that stress every time you enter a race – and that, you tell me, was only a practice! You have even frightened the life out of your father—and thank God Fiona was not here to see it!'

'I see.' Robbie folded his arms, feigning attitude. 'So you are giving me an ultimatum?'

'Yes, I am.'

'So, you or the racing?'

'Me or the racing. I mean it.'

Robbie sighed and looked down. 'I see… well, in that case, Anna, you leave me with no choice. I cannot give up the love of my life just like that—'

Anna gasped. She had not for one moment thought that he would choose his precious motor racing over her. He had told her that *she* was the love of his life.

'Well then, that is that. I will go back to my homeland on the first available flight. If you prefer to end your life on a motor racing circuit that is your choice, your business!' She stood facing him defiantly, hands on hips, eyes brimming with tears.

'Anna, Anna, please let me finish… I just said I cannot give up the love of my life and I meant it. You are the love of my life; *you*, Anna – and this whole episode has made me realise just how much you mean to me.' He held his arms out to her. 'Come here... I am sorry for the anxiety and stress I have caused you and will do my utmost to make it up to you. I promise.'

As it turned out, Robbie had no choice but to stop racing after that because it was going to be too expensive for him to rebuild his car and a replacement racing car was out of the question. The best he could hope for was to fix the main damage, sell the car and cut his losses. The car would be sold as safe to race but needing all the usual refinements to make it successful. He would miss the thrills and excitement and the camaraderie but he could not afford to be sentimental. He also felt the time was right to quit. He had gone as far as he could and with new ambitious drivers coming into the sport, he was unlikely to improve on his personal best of coming seventh— no mean achievement considering the opposition and the very nature of the races. And today he had been lucky to survive a horrific crash; next time... who knew?

Two days later, Anna and Robbie were back at Heathrow for Anna to begin her return journey to Basel. She thought she should have taken a taxi and let him rest but his leg was much better and he had no problem driving the van. He insisted on carrying her bag with his good arm as they approached the terminal.

'Well, you will have plenty to tell Evelyn about,' he said. 'And Marcel will find it amusing.'

'Marcel is amused by everything,' she retorted, 'but Evie will understand what I have been through.'

'I am sorry I put you through all that,' Robbie replied. 'But I have drawn a line under it now. My Formula Ford racing days are in the past.'

'You do really mean that?' Anna asked, still needing reassurance. 'I know it was important to you.'

He kissed her hair. 'Not as important as you, Anna. You mean everything to me.' He paused, looking her straight in the eye. 'I want us to start a new life together. Look, the job with British Airways is a non-starter, we know that. Why don't you contact Swissair when you get home? You will stand a much better chance in your own country. And when I come to visit you for Christmas I thought perhaps I could spend some time looking for work – there must be something I could do – and then we can be together all the time. What do you think?'

Anna suggested that she could probably find interesting work for Robbie with the pharmaceutical and chemicals giant Ciba-Geigy.

'Your kind of thing. They manufacture and test chemicals. I have a friend who is a police officer and she knows a security guard there. I could ask her to find out a bit more. You would have to apply for a work permit, of course.'

'But that is no problem if it means we can be together. I think that is a great idea.'

'Okay, I will talk to Martina. Once you have a job, then it is no problem getting a work permit. But don't raise your hopes too much, I am not sure if she can help. And yes, I will approach Swissair.'

They kissed goodbye and Anna picked up her bag and walked through the barrier to the platforms. She turned as she went through and waved, blowing him a kiss.

'Love you,' he mouthed, feeling happier now that he and Anna had talked things through and reached a new understanding. He felt very optimistic about the future and was looking forward to making a fresh start.

Chapter 10

Anna bought a coffee and sat down to relax in comfort in the arrivals lounge at Basel Airport. With four days to go before Christmas, she had just completed her interview with Crossair and had half an hour to kill before Robbie's flight was due in at 1.30 p.m.

She thought the interview had gone very well and was satisfied that she had given her best. Having tried British Airways and Swissair, she was put off by their long waiting lists, and one of the Swissair staff she spoke to had advised her that she was much more likely to be successful with the smaller, lesser known but rapidly growing Crossair, a subsidiary of Swissair at that time. She had contacted Crossair almost immediately and they had invited her for an interview, coincidentally on the day that Robbie was flying in to spend Christmas with her.

She looked around her, taking in the atmosphere and watching various aircraft as they taxied, took off and landed on the runway beneath her vantage point high up in the lounge. There had been several snow flurries and more serious snowfall was forecast so ground staff were busy organising snow-clearing vehicles ready for deployment when needed. She was optimistic that she had a future in this industry and at this particular airport and could not wait to tell Robbie her exciting news.

She drank her coffee and wandered through the lounge until she heard the PA system announcing the arrival of Robbie's flight number from London Heathrow, and then made her way to the point near the doors where she had arranged to meet him.

Robbie was looking forward to sharing the Christmas festivities with Anna and her family, having already met them all in October of course, with the exception of Anna's father, Giuseppe Sarri. The name Sarri was of uncertain origin, but Giuseppe himself was Italian. Robbie was anxious about how he would get on with Anna's father. He knew that Anna was not over fond of Giuseppe because of his womanising that had led to her parents' separation. Marcel, who worked for him, had described him as being a bad-tempered bully, so he had very mixed feelings.

After their affectionate reunion, Anna and Robbie walked out into the cold December air to where her Mazda was parked.

'Smooth flight, darling?' she enquired.

He nodded. 'Yes, the flight was fine. Bit of a bumpy landing though – puts you on edge a bit!'

Anna rolled her eyes. 'You, on edge. After almost losing your head in a racing car!'

'Well, isn't the landing the most dangerous thing about flying?'

'Of course not,' she replied, shaking her head. 'Where did you hear such a thing... from one of your science programmes, no doubt?'

He grinned. 'Probably.'

146

'Anyway,' she began, unable to contain herself any longer. 'I am hoping that I will soon be able to put your mind at rest regarding all flying procedures.' She gave him a sideways glance.

'Go on then,' he urged, 'tell me how your interview went?'

'My God! I thought you would never ask!'

'I am waiting for you to tell me, for heaven's sake. Did you get the job?'

'Oh, Robbie, I really hope so. It all seemed to go very well and I have such a good feeling about it all. They are going to let me know in a day or two.'

'So will you know before Christmas?'

'Well, I doubt it, actually. The airport of course is open over Christmas but their general offices will be closed after tomorrow.' She smiled. 'But straight after Christmas, I would think!'

As Anna and Robbie entered the apartment, Marcel was trying to secure a medium-sized spruce tree to a stand in a corner of the room.

'Hi, man,' said Marcel, bear-hugging Robbie. 'Just in time to help me with this, uh? It keeps falling over!'

Evelyn appeared from the kitchen. 'Robbie, hallooooo!' she greeted him with her usual enthusiasm, embracing him and kissing both cheeks as usual. 'Are you well? How was your flight? Would you like some coffee?'

'Evie, just make the coffee!' Anna laughed, accustomed to her sister's excitability.

Marcel grinned. 'I think he would rather drink a beer, uh man?'

'Yes and both of you ending up like that Christmas tree, leaning over!' Anna retorted. 'Honestly, Marcel, you have no idea! And anyway, why are you not at work?'

'This is work,' he told her. 'I was sent out to buy three Christmas trees – one for your Mama, one for Papa and one for us. And now you expect me to put the thing up and decorate it. Huh!'

'But you do not have to do it now,' Anna said. 'Well, maybe you could put it up – straight, if possible – and Evie and I will decorate it ready for Christmas Eve.'

Christmas trees are popular in Switzerland and Anna explained that they are often bought and decorated as late as Christmas Eve.

'Some people like to use real candles on the tree, which are traditionally lit on Christmas Eve when the presents are being opened, and also on New Year's Eve for good luck,' she added.

Evelyn came into the lounge with the coffee and amidst much laughter and merriment the four sat down and chatted about Anna's interview, Robbie's flight and Christmas in general, including London's Regent Street lights. Marcel wanted to know more about Robbie's crash at Silverstone but Anna immediately intervened.

'That subject is strictly forbidden,' she insisted. 'If you two must talk about that, then do so in private because I do not want to be reminded of it!' She shuddered at the memory of it all. 'My God, no…'

Marcel shrugged and pouted his lower lip. 'Okay, okay!' He winked at Robbie. 'Over a few beers later in the pub, uh?'

As it turned out, they spent the evening at home. When they had finished chatting, Robbie unpacked and had a shower and the girls disappeared into the kitchen to prepare a meal, leaving Marcel to wrestle with the tree.

Swiss people usually indulged in a Christmas dinner both on Christmas Eve and Christmas Day, and sometimes again on Boxing Day, depending on how many relatives there were to visit. It came in handy that there was more than just one traditional Christmas meal. Anna and Evelyn had planned a lovely meal for just the four of them on Christmas Eve. They had a Christmas ham and scalloped potatoes with melted cheese and milk baked into it, followed by walnut cake and Christmas cookies. The tree was beautifully decorated and there were also a few real candles included to keep up their tradition. They did not follow the tradition of opening their presents on Christmas Eve, however. That was to take place the following day when the whole family was to gather at Giuseppe's apartment for their Christmas Day dinner.

Robbie was made very welcome with the rest of the family to Giuseppe's apartment above the garage for Christmas dinner. Giuseppe, as host, had decided on beef and Marianne and Evelyn did the cooking. Anna helped with preparation and then the clearing away afterwards and Robbie and Marcel washed up with some, but not much help, from Max, who could be quite aloof, preferring his own company.

They had lit the candles on the tree and exchanged presents and then began their celebrations with a few drinks and raised their glasses wishing each other *'Schöni Wiehnachte'* while dinner was getting underway in Giuseppe's kitchen. Anna gave Robbie a Tissot Alpine Granite watch with a yellow hour hand and a red minute hand, representing the colours of Swiss hiking trail markers. It was a very rugged, masculine watch and he was delighted with it. Anna, on the other hand, was disappointed with the carpet bag that Robbie had bought for her, but graciously thanked him and later put it away at the back of a drawer.

Robbie had worried needlessly about Giuseppe. He was a big man with strong, bullish features and a large nose. He also had a loud voice with an Italian accent and he did have a domineering manner, but in truth, his bark was far worse than his bite.

Anna's father asked Robbie if he was interested in cars and of course when the answer was an enthusiastic yes, they got on like a house on fire. Leaving the festivities, he took Robbie all round his showroom which was actually more of a museum-cum-showroom, as he not only had his Ferrari dealership cars, but also an impressive collection of vintage Ferraris, including a Dino and other classic vehicles, examples being a Standard 10 from the 1930s, a 1950s Jaguar FS, a Riley RMA and a 2½ litre Bentley. There was also the Daimler that had needed a headlamp and he thanked Robbie for getting hold of one for him. He had recently taken delivery of the very latest top of the range Ferrari and took him out for a ride in it there and then. That was a special treat for Robbie and he never forgot the sound of the engine as the car roared down the street: that deep, throaty, reverberating growl that was unique to the Ferrari.

He told Giuseppe about his Formula Ford racing and that he'd had to give it up after the accident in practice.

'Ah, *si*, Anna—she told me all about the racing. She said it was very dangerous... what she think if you go racing in one of my Ferraris, uh?' They both laughed at his joke and Robbie remarked that it would be a dream come true.

'As a young man I also raced,' he told Robbie. 'Only at junior level, you understand, but I know all about the thrills and spills and thrust of the sport.' He held his clenched fist to his chest. 'It gets into the blood, you know that!'

Robbie had only had a brief look round on his last visit and Marcel had taken him out in one of the showroom cars, but he had not realised the true extent or quality of Giuseppe's operations. He was a man who definitely knew the business inside out and managed it very efficiently with Marianne's input as co-director. They were a good team and it was obviously the reason for continuing with their working partnership after their marriage broke down. He must be a very rich man, Robbie thought, and yet could very easily be mistaken for a deadbeat when he was seen out walking with his equally scruffy but much loved Old English Sheepdog called Enzo, in honour of Enzo

151

Anselmo Ferrari, the Italian motor racing driver and entrepreneur, founder of the Scuderia Ferrari Grand Prix motor racing team, and subsequently of the Ferrari marque.

Before they left the party later that evening, Giuseppe beckoned Robbie over. 'Come with me for a moment?'

Marcel watched with amusement as Robbie got up from his seat next to Anna on the couch and followed.

'Old Pa is rather hogging young Robbie, don't you think?' he remarked in almost perfect cut-glass English.

'Yes. I am surprised but pleased, you know, that they are getting on.'

'But who could not get along with Robbie?' said Evelyn.

Silke, inclined to be acerbic, agreed. 'Yes, I have to admit he is very likeable, for *Engländer*, anyway.'

A few moments later, both men returned. Robbie was wearing a navy blue Ferrari blazer that the older man had long outgrown, bearing the famous Ferrari logo on the breast pocket.

Robbie had been lost for words. 'But… wow! Are you sure you want to part with it?'

'Yes, I am sure.' He indicated his expansive chest and abdomen. 'It no longer fits me. You will wear it well and with pride, *amico mio*.'

Marcel's eyebrows shot up and his dark eyes widened with surprise. '*Mon Dieu*,' he whispered to Evelyn.

The Boxing Day dinner at Marianne's apartment was a smaller affair. Silke and her husband were going to see his family, Max had been invited to spend the day with some college friends and Giuseppe said he had made other arrangements too. Marcel had suggested that this 'other arrangement' was most likely blonde, thirtyish and curvy but none of them really cared one way or the other. They had all enjoyed Christmas Day with him and there were no arguments or disagreements, which was all that really mattered.

So there were just five of them to tuck into Marianne's choice for Boxing Day, a meat fondue – Fondue Chinoise, or Chinese hotpot made with veal, which was delicious and filling. For dessert there was Viennetta, a shop-bought, multi-layered ice cream cake, only available at Christmas, and a special treat.

It was a cold day with light snowfall, but after they had eaten their meal and cleared away, they wrapped themselves up and took a stroll through the beautiful old part of the city. The shop windows had all been beautifully decorated to encourage customers to buy and Robbie was impressed not only with the quality of the goods on display, but also the tasteful way they were presented. He mentioned it to Anna.

'Even Bond Street does not come close to this standard,' he said.

Anna smiled. 'We Swiss have a flair for bringing out the finer elements. It is quite an art, you know!'

Back in the warmth of Marianne's apartment, she made hot chocolate which they drank with Christmas Cookies that she had made to her own recipe. And so Christmas itself was over for another year and this particular one had been special in many ways for Anna and Robbie. For Robbie certainly, it held a kind of magic—he kept expecting to wake up and find it had all been a dream… and what a dream!

On 28th December, Anna received a phone call telling her she had been accepted as an air stewardess with Crossair and asking her to make arrangements to go and see them to sort out her start date, staff medical and be measured for her uniform. She was very excited and could hardly wait to get to the appointment that had been made for the 2nd January.

'Oh, I have to wait almost another week!' she grumbled.

'Well and you will have to tell the florist that you are finishing your work there,' Evelyn reminded her, 'and you will have to be trained before they will let you loose as a stewardess, remember!'

'I am sure that won't take very long,' Anna replied. 'And I have already told the flower shop of my intention and that I was waiting for a reply, so it will not come as a complete surprise.'

Robbie was overjoyed for her and now wanted to go ahead with his own plans to live and work here. He had the idea of asking Giuseppe if he could be found a position in his business but he did not want to mention it in front of Marcel and Evelyn. He would wait until he and Anna were on their own.

The four of them went out to celebrate Anna's good news, having lunch first and then going to see a movie –

Hairspray – a dance/comedy film. Robbie particularly enjoyed watching it as it starred Debbie Harry, the lead singer in Blondie, one of his favourite bands at the time.

They looked around the shops, went home and finished off the Christmas leftovers for supper.

Later, lying in bed in the darkness, Robbie mentioned that perhaps he could ask Anna's father if there would be a job for him in the garage.

Anna sat up in bed abruptly and with such force that the mattress bounced.

'What?' She snapped the bedside lamp on, temporarily blinding Robbie who closed his eyes and took refuge in the softness of his pillow.

'I said I was—'

'I heard what you said.' She turned, punching her pillows into shape to support her as she leaned back. 'Are you mad?'

This was not the response Robbie had expected and he was unsure how to respond.

'I… well, I suppose I just thought it would be good to have a job nearby with people I know, and doing something I am interested in, you know, working with cars. And Marcel would show me the ropes.

'Marcel! He would be allowed to show you nothing. He has worked for Papa since college and by now should have a position as Works Manager but he still sweeps the floor and runs errands…' she poked him, '… are you listening to me?'

'All ears!' Robbie sighed and hoisted himself up, resting on his elbows as Anna's tirade continued.

'Because Marcel is considered family, he is cursed and bullied like the rest of us, while the assistant mechanic gets the cream of the work—you saw for yourself that Marcel was even sent out to buy Christmas trees and decorations!'

'Marcel tells me he is happy enough,' Robbie pointed out. 'He has learnt to deal with all that.'

'No, Robbie. He has not. Don't misunderstand me, Marcel is a very charming and amiable young man and I am very fond of him, but he is either too weak, too lazy or both, to stand up to my father and while that situation continues he will remain a dogsbody.' She paused for a moment and when she spoke again her tone softened slightly.

'I do not want the same thing to happen to you. I want better for you... and this work I have in mind at Ciba-Geigy is really right up your street. I think you have a good chance.'

'It's just that your dad and I get on so well—he even gave me his beloved Ferrari blazer and—'

'Robbie, shush,' she said quietly, arms folded defensively now, 'if you want to continue to get on well with him, then do not even think about working for him. Trust me, that would be the kiss of death for your friendship. He will just exploit you... he does that. I would only agree if you cannot find anything else and even then, it would only be temporary, you understand.'

Robbie said nothing, knowing it was useless trying to argue with Anna in this mood. A true Aquarian, Evelyn had said, and he had yet to understand her many moods and how they could change in the blink of an eye. And typical of her nature, having forthrightly said her piece, she calmly replaced her pillows, kissed him goodnight and switched off the lamp.

He lay down in bed again, resigned to the fact that he was not going to be working with Ferraris or with Marcel.

'But what if there are no vacancies at Ciba-Geigy?' he suddenly asked.

'You are just planting obstacles now. I do not know for sure if they are taking people on at the moment,' she admitted. 'But they will be at some stage for sure and anyway, I have a Plan B.'

'Oh, I see, and am I allowed to know what this Plan B is?' he enquired.

'Not yet, because everything is uncertain until I have had a chance to speak to Martina. So go to sleep now and do not worry about it any more.'

'Goodnight then.'

'Goodnight. Sleep well, darling.'

The room finally fell silent, disturbed only briefly by Robbie, trying to have the last word for once.

'I am not worried.'

Then he turned over and went to sleep.

Chapter 11

Nothing was mentioned by either Robbie or Anna next morning and they had breakfast together companionably. Marcel and Evelyn had gone back to work and Christmas, enjoyable as it had been, was already beginning to fade and people were now looking forward to the New Year.

'Robbie, can you ice skate?' Anna asked, pouring a second cup of coffee.

'No. Well, I don't know... I've never tried,' he replied.

She smiled, eyeing him up and down. 'I bet you can, fit guy like you. How's your balance?'

'I did a bit of roller skating as a kid, but that was a whole lot different to skating on ice.'

'Not that different,' she replied. 'I think you will be gliding across the ice like a pro in no time!'

He grinned back at her. 'Right.'

'So you want to try it?'

'Why not? It sounds like fun.'

'Oh, it will be fun all right. That is settled then, we shall go this afternoon. Are you happy to just relax here for this morning? I would like to try to get hold of Martina today if possible.'

'Fine with me.' Robbie got up from the table and began to stack the breakfast things on a tray. 'I will do the washing up.'

Anna thanked him with a peck on the cheek and went to fetch her handbag to find the telephone number of the Basel Police Station where her friend Martina worked. It appeared she was on leave until the next day, so Anna tried her home number. Again without success, so she left a message to call her back as soon as possible.

Robbie was looking through some photographs of Anna and her family when they were younger when the phone rang. Halfway through preparing lunch, Anna came out of the kitchen, drying her hands, before taking the call.

Robbie heard her say Martina's name but as the two conducted their conversation in Suisse-Deutsche, he was unable to keep up with what was being said. All he knew was that it concerned him and the work that Anna was trying to secure for him. There was then some girl talk, judging by the giggles and exclamations before she hung up.

'Great news!' Anna said, clapping her hands with excitement. 'Martina has a colleague in the police force whose boyfriend is a security officer for Ciba-Geigy and she is going to ask him if he can find out from Kurt whether there are any vacancies.'

Robbie was confused. 'So Martina's boyfriend is a security guard?'

'No. You are not listening. A policeman she works with... Kurt is his boyfriend.'

'Oh, I see… I get it.' Robbie thought for a moment. 'This Kurt…?'

'Yes, what about him?'

'He is a security guard, you said.'

'Yes, he works at the main gates. Why do you ask?'

'Well, I was just wondering how much he would know about any job vacancies?'

'He won't,' Anna replied with a smile, 'but Martina says he is acquainted with the receptionist, Kristina, who apparently knows everybody's business and everything that is going on and what she does not know, she will make it her business to find out.'

After lunch they set off for the skating rink which was a few tram stops away.

Anna wore her tight black ski pants and red roll-neck sweater with a green woollen hat and matching scarf and very much looked the part. Robbie thought she looked amazing.

'We will hire skates for one hour,' Anna suggested as they entered the rink. 'That should be enough for your first time.'

Robbie agreed, thinking to himself that one hour would be more than enough and hoping he was not about to make a complete fool of himself.

'Size 42, I think?' she asked, consulting a chart on the wall that converted UK and American sizes into the continental equivalent.

'Fort… oh, yes,' Robbie nodded, realising that the skates were sized in continental numbering. He made a

mental note to never reveal that information to his mates…
the Sooty and Sweep jokes had been bad enough without
adding Bigfoot to their repertoire.

They went to the edge of the rink and sat down to put
on their skates. Robbie thought they felt a bit stiff,
especially the right one.

'You will soon get used to them,' Anna assured him.
'Now… careful how you stand up!'

Holding onto everything within reach, Robbie stood
up.

'Okay, I am standing up, now what?'

'You hold on to my hand, forget about your feet and
don't look down—keep your eyes focused on a point
ahead of you, okay?'

The pair set out onto the ice rink, where skaters with
varying degrees of competence were gliding, slipping and
falling across the surface. With some trepidation, Robbie
took his first tentative steps, sliding and skidding; lurching
from side to side trying to keep his balance. He held on to
Anna, almost pulling her down a couple of times and then
succeeding.

As they fell in a heap on the ice, he still clung to Anna,
holding her in a tight hug.

'Hm,' Robbie murmured, 'you were right, it is fun.
Can we do that bit again?'

Giggling, Anna scrambled to her feet, hauling Robbie
up and helping him to regain his balance; his dignity was
beyond saving.

'Now… let's try again and if you are going to fall
down, try to do it on your own!'

'Aw, spoilsport!'

Robbie eventually found his balance and in a surprisingly short time was skating around the rink unaided, albeit rather shakily, especially when turning. He and Anna then skated together as a pair, synchronising their steps and movements.

'Torvill and Dean eat your hearts out!' Robbie laughed. 'There's nothing to it!' As he spoke the words, he stumbled and bent over. 'Oh, I need to rest my foot a minute,' he gasped as he hobbled to the side.

'Now what is wrong? You were doing so well.'

'Anna, this right skate is killing me.'

'But you should have said... perhaps you need a bigger size?'

'No, they were fine; it's only just come on.' He grimaced in pain.

He sat down in the spectator area and struggled to get the skate off. The reason for his discomfort was immediately apparent. A huge blister had erupted on the ball of his foot. It was red and inflamed, extending from his big toe almost as far as his heel. Once the skate was off, the swelling seemed to increase in size and as soon as he attempted to put any weight on it, throbbed mercilessly.

'Is your other foot okay?' Anna asked. 'Let me have a look.'

'Yes, that feels all right. It's only the right foot.'

Nevertheless, Anna insisted on examining not only Robbie's left foot, which was fine, but also the skates themselves. She checked first that they were a pair.

'Yes, both are the same size and there is a left and a right,' she confirmed.

'Surely they would not give someone two left skates?' In spite of his pain, he struggled to hide a grin at her disapproving expression as she examined both skates.

'Huh! You would be surprised,' she uttered, poking about inside the right one with exploring fingers. 'Ah... I think this is the culprit. Look!' She held the leather insole aloft. It was loose inside the skate and had become screwed up beneath Robbie's foot, causing pressure with each movement until this huge blister had formed.

She looked around and spotted an attendant, calling out to him.

She showed him the skates and Robbie's foot and asked for first aid. In less than a minute one of the medical staff arrived and bathed Robbie's foot, drying it and then spraying it with antiseptic before covering it with protective gauze.

With some difficulty Robbie managed to get his shoe back on, but it was painful and he could not do the laces up.

'Shouldn't you have lanced it?' he asked.

The first-aider explained to Anna that lancing the blister would make it much more painful as well as open to infection and he should let it take its natural course.

Anna collected their coats and they left the rink, Robbie leaning heavily on her for support.

'We had better take a taxi home,' Anna suggested, very concerned at Robbie's plight, 'and you will have to rest your foot and keep the weight off it, okay?'

Robbie was in too much pain to argue and by the time they reached the apartment, he could do no more than collapse onto the couch. Unfortunately, their social activities had to be curtailed for the remainder of his stay. The blister subsided in a couple of days but walking was still painful and difficult. However, he did manage to make it to the Ciba-Geigy works on 2nd January, the same day that Anna was going to finalise her job details with Crossair.

At the main gates, Robbie was asked to produce some ID and state his business. He took out his passport and handed it to the security guard who scrutinised it and then consulted his visitor list.

'Ah yes,' he said, smiling. 'You are Martina's friend from England looking for work?'

'Anna's friend,' Robbie replied. 'She is Martina's friend.'

'Ah yes,' he repeated. 'Martina, she works with my partner, Fritz. He is in police department also. I am Kurt… welcome!' He opened the gate to admit Robbie and then pointed towards the reception area. 'See Kristina at the desk.'

A heavily made-up blonde girl sat behind the reception desk. She smiled.

'Grüezi.'

'Grüezi,' he replied, wondering if she spoke English. He cleared his throat. 'I er… I have an appointment with…' he showed her the name that Anna had written down when she had taken the details over the phone.

164

The girl's face lit up immediately, as if someone had flicked a switch.

'Ah, yes! You are from England,' she said, in good English, clapping her hands twice, 'to work in our world famous laboratories. Kurt has told me all about you. I am Kristina.' She held out her hand and he shook it briefly, thinking to himself that 'Ah yes' must be the standard way of greeting in this establishment. It seemed to be a very friendly, relaxed place considering the size and status of the company and the nature of their work but he was aware that certain standards also had to be met. His overall impression of the Swiss people was that they were courteous, perhaps a little reserved until they got to know you—but friendly and helpful.

She phoned through to someone to tell them that Robbie was here for his appointment.

'Have a seat, please,' she said.

Robbie was not kept waiting long but noticed during the few minutes that he sat in the waiting area opposite the reception desk that Kristina was looking at him, smiling demurely each time she caught his eye. He smiled back at her, wondering if everyone who came here for a job was treated in the same way. He supposed so.

Then the phone rang on Kristina's desk and she asked him to follow her to the interview room. It was only when she stood up that he noticed how very tall she was, and it was evident as he followed her up a short flight of stairs that her feet were proportionate to her height—he guessed size 10 or 11 English size and she must have been more

165

than six feet tall. The thought 'drag queen' came briefly into his mind and then she was showing him into the room.

'How did it go?' Anna asked when she and Robbie met up later for a meal after their respective interviews.

He kissed her cheek. He had planned to pretend disappointment and despondency and tell her that he had been refused, but he couldn't hide his delight at being accepted as a student worker, subject to a full medical examination which was normal procedure for all employees.

'I am now officially a practicant with Ciba-Geigy,' he told her. 'Or I will be once I have their confirmation and I can then apply for a work permit.'

Anna gave a squeal of delight at the news. 'That is fantastic!' she replied.

He caught her by the waist with both hands and swung her round right there in the street amongst busy shoppers and passers-by.

'And you?' he asked

'I have been measured for my Crossair uniform,' she said. 'It is very smart, a grey-and-white striped shirt with a ruffle neckline and a jacket and skirt of grey-and-white check. I have to tie my hair back and wear a black Swiss style hat. Oh and this is for my lapel.' She took a small box from her handbag and gave it to Robbie.

He opened the box to find a gold-plated aeroplane brooch.

'Wow! That's classy!'

166

She smiled. 'Yes, isn't it? Oh and I passed my medical and I am all set to start on 11th January. I will have to attend a two-week training course to get my certificate and then I go up, up and away!'

'I have to go back for a medical on the fourth,' Robbie said, 'the day before I fly back to London. At least my foot should be healing nicely by then.'

'Yes,' Anna glanced down at his right foot encased in a loosely laced shoe. 'Is it still painful?'

'A little bit sore,' he admitted, 'but nothing like it was. It will be fine, thank you, nurse.'

Anna linked her arm in his and they headed for the restaurant to have lunch.

After all the festivities of Christmas and New Year, it seemed quiet and flat the next day. Most people had gone back to work and life carried on pretty much as before. But for Anna and Robbie, new and exciting times lay ahead; for them, life was never going to be the same again. They spent most of the day taking down the decorations and restoring the apartment to some order, chatting as they did so.

'It's amazing how much bigger the room looks with all the cards down, and the tree,' Robbie observed.

'Yes, I know what you mean.' Anna had a wistful look. 'It looks a bit sad now, doesn't it?'

Robbie laughed. 'Marcel's tree looked sad right from the start, leaning over in the corner like a drunk!'

Anna agreed. 'Poor Marcel—he can identify every part of a car's engine and tell you where it is and its

167

purpose, but he cannot get a Christmas tree to stand up straight.'

'I like him; he and I are going to be good friends.'

'Oh yes. As you know, I am very fond of him; he is very laid back and easy-going, but that is part of his trouble. He will never get anywhere or be anything in life because he just drifts along in his own world.'

'But he is happy there.'

Anna gave him a quizzical look.

'In his own world,' Robbie explained. 'He is always happy and relaxed... nothing bothers him.'

'You are right,' Anna agreed. 'We cannot all be ambitious and some are just not motivated. It's just that I think he could do so much better for himself if he could be bothered!'

'He and Evelyn seem well suited,' Robbie remarked.

'Yes. She is also happy-go-lucky and they do complement each other,' Anna agreed. 'How is your foot?'

'It hardly hurt at all in the shower this morning, so I think it is healing. It's still a little bit sore, but not bothering me.'

'I have never seen a blister like it!' Anna exclaimed.

Robbie grinned. 'But then I bet you never met a guy covered from head to toe in soot before, either!'

'Oh my God! Your poor mother—she was mortified to think you had to come home in that state just at the time that she had invited me to tea.'

'I know. Poor Mum.'

'She will miss you.'

'Yes, she will. It's going to be hard for her at first.'

'Do you think she will manage okay without you there? I would not like to think of her going back to her old ways.'

'She only saw me in the evenings, Anna, and then I was either in my room studying, or out with the church youth group. And anyway Dad is at home more often now. She will soon get used to it. And she is doing well with the AA programme. The group is very supportive.'

Anna nodded. 'And they will miss you at the church group also.'

'Oh, that won't be a problem, someone else will take my place easily enough. None of us is indispensable.'

Anna, standing behind Robbie, gently squeezed his shoulder. 'And you have no regrets—about leaving your family and your homeland?'

He turned to face her, stroking back stray curls that fell across her face, taking her into his arms. The kiss they shared was filled more with promise than passion, but there was no doubting the love they felt for each other.

'Does that answer your question?' he asked.

She smiled and nodded. 'Almost... but just in case I didn't quite get it the first time, perhaps we could make sure...'

The next day was Robbie's last full day in Basel before leaving for home. It was also the day he was to have his medical at Ciba-Geigy and he was up early, showered and ready to go soon after breakfast. Having made the journey once, he had the confidence to find his own way there.

169

'Well, call me if you have any problems,' Anna told him, 'but I am sure you will be fine. You found it all right without me when I had to go the airport.'

He was there in good time and Kurt wished him *viel glück* (good luck) as he admitted him through the entrance gates.

As he entered the reception area this time, Kristina was standing behind her desk and Robbie thought she looked even taller than before. Good grief, she must be wearing high heels today, he thought.

'Ah, hallo,' she said, 'you are here for your medical, yes?'

'Yes.'

She wrote something on a clipboard and indicated the seating opposite her desk. 'You like to have a seat, please,' she said in her best English. 'They will not be long.'

He sat in the same place as before and picked up a company brochure which, although written in the Swiss language, gave him somewhere to look other than at Kristina. He could feel her eyes all over him and was relieved when a nurse appeared and asked him to follow her.

This time Robbie was taken to the medical suite where he was measured and weighed, had his blood pressure and pulse checked as well as his vision and provided samples of urine and blood. His embarrassment at being stark naked in the presence of the nurse was heightened when finally asked by the doctor to, 'Cough for me, if you please.' Then he was told he could get dressed and go back to reception to wait. Fortunately, Kristina was engaged with someone else and he went and sat further down from her desk, where he felt less exposed to her constant scrutiny.

He waited for half an hour and was thankful that during that time Kristina was kept very busy and had no chance to ogle or chat him up. The same nurse returned and told him that everything was fine and all his papers would now be sent to the appropriate Swiss Authorities to obtain a visa on his behalf. Back in London, he was to apply to the Swiss Consulate for an entry visa and then his residence and work permit would be available when he returned to Switzerland to work.

Outside in the grounds, he almost had to pinch himself. He inhaled the clean, cool air with a deep sense of satisfaction. He was going to work in a laboratory at one of the world's leading pharmaceutical companies—in a month's time, he would be entering the gates as an employee! He could not wait to get back to tell Anna.

He shook hands with Kurt on the way out and thanked him for his help.

'No problem, my friend, and I look forward to seeing you again very soon.'

That evening, Anna and Robbie invited Evelyn and Marcel to join them in a celebratory meal at a restaurant in town. It had been an enjoyable Christmas for all of them and Robbie was appreciative of the welcome he had received from the family – even Giuseppe and his dog – they had made him feel that he belonged.

'I am looking forward to being back with you all,' he said. 'My proposed start date with Ciba-Geigy is 1st February if everything can be arranged in that time, but I was told that it should all go through without any problems.'

A smile played around Marcel's lips, devilment showing in his eyes.

'You better hope it will, man,' he said. 'You know, at this very moment, the Federal Intelligence Service is probably looking into your background.' He glanced shiftily from left to right, then leaned across the table to Robbie. 'You do not have criminal record I hope, because if so, you know...' he drew his index finger across his throat and then effected a classic but exaggerated Marcel shrug, '... not good, uh?'

Evelyn gave him a playful whack that sounded painful but Marcel, always the joker, merely winked at her and said, '*Merci*, Evie.'

They left the restaurant in good spirits and briskly walked the short distance home, their breath streaming out as vapour in the cold night air. It had been a good night out and perfectly rounded off what had been a memorable experience for Robbie.

Anna was over the moon with her new career and also the fact that she had been able to help Robbie find work that would interest him and hopefully advance his scientific studies. Love at long distance was better than nothing but hardly ideal for building a close relationship or for developing the love they had for each other.

They would soon be together; both with an exciting future to look forward to.

Chapter 12

The flight to Basel, though familiar now, seemed very different to Robbie's previous journeys. They had been necessary to the furtherance of his romance with Anna... the need to be with her and to meet her family and understand more about her country. His love for Switzerland had been as instant as that for Anna and once he had set foot upon Swiss soil, he knew that he wanted to live and work there.

Looking through the window he could see nothing but a mass of fluffy white cloud below the aircraft. It had the appearance of cotton wool—he felt that he could just freefall into it and be enveloped in its softness and warmth and feel safe. He thought about his departure, more than two hours ago now. Mike had wanted to drive him to the airport but Robbie, disliking prolonged goodbyes, thanked him and declined his offer, saying he didn't want a fuss and this way, he felt would also be the least upsetting for his mother.

His mum had been so brave. As he hugged her for the last time he had felt her desperate sadness at being parted from her only son and yet mingled with her sense of loss was her feeling of pride that her boy was going to make something of his life. She had always known he could and hoped he would but the opportunities never seemed to come his way. Now he had the chance to experience the future he had always dreamed of.

He'd kissed her cheek and, as gently as possible, extracted himself from her maternal, possessive embrace.

'We'll be back to see you before long, Mum… and I'll phone to see how you are.' He hugged his dad and then picked up his rucksack, ready to go.

'Look after yourselves now; I'll be in touch.'

'God speed, laddie,' Fiona said, taking her hanky from her cardigan pocket, 'and mind you look after that bonnie wee lassie.'

'No tears, now,' Robbie said, struggling to keep the emotion out of his voice and willing her not to start him off.

'Och and dinnae be such a wee goonie,' she replied, fluttering the cotton square at him. 'It's no for the greetin'… it's for waving ye off!' One thing Fiona was good at – though probably not always aware of – was that she had a knack of lightening the mood.

Settling back and relaxing in his seat for the remaining thirty-five minutes or so before landing, Robbie reflected on his new status. Instead of being exposed to the elements of the seasons on the building sites and studying to be a boffin in his spare time, he was going to fulfil one of his dreams and train to be a boffin with some of the top boffins in the field. He was going to be with the girl he loved and had no doubt that one day they would marry. He loved Switzerland and the Swiss people. Of course, he would be able to continue his Open University studies and a B.Sc.

degree would open many more doors. Who knew where it would all lead?

Anna was waiting for him in the usual place, looking more delectable than ever in a blue-and-yellow striped sweater, navy blue leggings and black knee boots, all topped off with a black faux fur jacket and a yellow scarf hanging loosely. After they had embraced, she looked around, seeing his rucksack at his feet.

'Where is your luggage?'

He indicated the bag on the ground.

'What? That is all you have brought?' she asked with surprise.

'Yes. I have all I need,' he replied. He grinned. 'We men don't need to carry the kitchen sink around with us!'

'Very funny. At least you have not alerted the bomb squad this time,' she said, remembering the previous fiasco as she led the way out into the chill of the late January air.

Anna asked about Robbie's parents and they chatted about their new jobs for most of the way home.

'I have been asked to go in tomorrow,' she said. 'There is a meeting for new recruits, just to clear up any queries we have and to make sure we know where to report to.'

'You must be excited,' Robbie said.

'Yes, I am, but also a little bit nervous, you know?'

'Of course, that's natural, but you will be fine, you'll see.'

'Well, I won't be doing much to start with, just watching what the others do—oh and fetching and carrying and helping to put the passengers at ease.'

'When do you actually start?'

'On Monday, 30th.'

'Oh, my first day is Wednesday, 1st February.'

'Yes, you told me. Did your papers come through all right?'

'They were brilliant in London and they said the other part of it would be dealt with here, so I have nothing else to do, really.'

Anna concentrated as she negotiated lane changes and traffic lights to bring them on to the side of town where their apartment was. From there it was straightforward.

'How was your mum?' she asked. 'Any problems?'

'Much calmer than I expected,' Robbie replied. 'Putting on a brave face for my benefit, of course, but she is genuinely very happy for both of us… said I was to be sure to look after you.'

'What a darling she is!'

'And Dad sends his love.'

In two more minutes, Anna was parking the car outside the apartment and Marcel was at the door to help carry Robbie's luggage.

'Be my guest,' Robbie said, putting his rucksack down on the ground.

Marcel looked around. 'There is more in the car?'

'That's it,' Anna said flatly. 'Travels light, this one.'

Marcel disputed 'light'. 'Weighs a ton,' he puffed as he lifted it. 'Man, you hauled this all the way from England, uh?'

'Well the aircraft was a big help…'

Both men grinned. Marcel dropped the rucksack and aimed a friendly punch at Robbie's upper arm before they went into a bear hug.

Evelyn came out to welcome Robbie, kissing both cheeks and then folding her arms across her chest and hunching her shoulders against the cold.

Once inside, they had coffee and some of Robbie's favourite chocolate cake and then he unpacked.

'I have cleared a space for your stuff,' Anna said, opening the wardrobe door.

'Oh, thanks,' Robbie replied, noting that she had also emptied a couple of shelves. As he wore jeans and sweaters most of the time, they would be useful.

'And you can use those drawers,' she pointed to a chest of drawers alongside the wardrobe, 'for underwear, socks, personal things, whatever.'

He smiled at her. 'Okay. Do you know how good it feels to be here… moving in and living with you?'

She took his hand. 'Yes, I do know how good it feels—I have been counting the days, and now it has finally happened.'

He drew her close and for a few moments nothing else mattered as they embraced and sealed their future together with a passion that had long been needing an outlet.

Pulling away, Anna cleared her throat. 'I will leave you to it, darling, and get on with dinner.'

After a special welcome dinner, they all relaxed with a few drinks and in the manner of friends who have been apart for a while and have a lot of catching up to do, they talked well into the night.

On Monday, 30th January, Anna was up early for her first day working as cabin crew for Crossair. She looked very smart and professional in her uniform and Robbie complimented her.

'You look like you were born for the part,' he said.

'Thank you, darling... do I look all right?'

'You look like a million dollars,' he replied, 'and I really think I ought to come with you to protect you from all the male passengers.'

She giggled. 'I can look after myself!'

He kissed her goodbye. 'Make sure you do. Good luck and see you later.'

Following basic training, the first three to six months were usually treated as a probationary period and during this time, performance was monitored by trainers or senior crew. On passing the probationary period, new recruits became full members of the cabin crew team. Anna knew that if she wanted to live the jet-set lifestyle working as cabin crew she would need to demonstrate hard work, dedication and professionalism around the clock and around the globe and she was ready to give it her all.

Wednesday came and with it, a new month and more wintry weather. Robbie had been asked to report for his first day's duties at Ciba-Geigy at 8.30 a.m. He would be working a forty-hour week and was also serving a probationary period. How long he remained a practicant depended on how quickly he learned and how efficiently he was able to apply his knowledge. If he showed potential and was interested in becoming a member of an elite team, there were excellent prospects awaiting him.

Kurt greeted him at the gates a little before 8.30.

'Hallo, my friend, and welcome,' he said, stretching out his hand.

Robbie shook hands with the security guard. 'Thank you… it feels a bit like coming home,' he replied.

'Well, you know the way by now,' Kurt added, pointing to the reception area. 'Kristina will sort you out, I am sure.'

Robbie had no doubt that she would. He smiled but said nothing, other than, 'See you later.'

As he walked into reception, Kristina was looking at a diary open on the desk. She smiled as he approached, her green eyes looking him up and down.

'Hallo, Robbie,' she purred. 'I was just checking the worksheets. You are going to be working upstairs in the plastics lab for the time being. I will take you up there—follow me.'

She tossed her head, swirling her blonde curls, and led the way with an exaggerated wiggle of her hips. Once again he marvelled at the size of her feet.

He was shown into a laboratory and introduced to the Lab Chief, Professor Martie, and his Lab Technician, Monsieur Jaffra and two other workers, Maryse and Manfred.

M. Jaffra handed him a white coat. 'Try this for size.'

The professor explained that he was to be engaged with finding the melting point of plastic and how long it took before giving off toxic gases. These experiments were all devised and carried out with the good of the environment in mind and Robbie, being an environmentalist, was glad that he was working in this sector rather than the drugs testing centre. Because of his Open University tutorials and his general interest in science, he very quickly picked up the principles of these experiments and made a good impression on the professor, who soon began to entrust him with more important and interesting work.

Meanwhile, Kristina was making her presence felt. Everywhere Robbie went, she seemed to be not far away, and always looking at him and smiling. She was a very pretty girl, pleasant and polite and very good at her job of greeting visitors and putting them at their ease. However, she had the very opposite effect on Robbie. He found her to be nosy and intrusive and she made him feel distinctively uneasy. It was obvious from the outset that she fancied him and was doing her utmost to draw him into her web. And what was unnerving to him was that she made it so obvious—was so blatant about it. She kept flirting with him and following him about, even in the street after work. He was wary of her, suspecting she could cause trouble, and also formed the opinion that she was mentally unbalanced.

Other than that, Robbie loved his work and looked forward to each new day. Sometimes, while he was waiting for results from some of the experiments, he had time on his hands—often four or five hours at a time. He asked the professor if he could be helping with something else during these periods of waiting and was told that as long as he had his work under control and up to date, he could use this time for his own studies and so he took full advantage of that. There were also occasions when they would meet up with other workers who were employed in different fields, so that the student workers would begin to learn how one operation could affect other experiments.

Anna was also enjoying every moment of her new career. Every flight was unique; every passenger had different needs and some were just nervous, while others were hysterical. Those who may have had too much to drink to calm their nerves could be difficult; children were tetchy... there were many challenges for her and she relished each one, dealing with them calmly and professionally, and winning the admiration of senior crew members.

Weekday evenings in the apartment were spent with the four of them chatting about their day. Marcel of course always had some amusing story to tell—maybe something that in itself was not remotely funny but he would manage to bring some humour to it and have them all laughing. The girls had plenty to laugh about and dinner was usually a happy, light-hearted occasion.

On one particular evening, Robbie was subdued, not joining in with the others and seemingly preoccupied. Anna was concerned.

'Are you all right, Robbie?' she asked. 'Robbie?'

He looked at her. 'What? What is it? What are you all staring at me for?' he asked, looking round.

'I just asked if you were all right. You seem a bit far away this evening?'

'Oh yes. Yes, I am fine,' he replied. I've had a rather tiring day, that's all—a lot of concentration, you know.'

'Leave the boffin in the laboratory,' Marcel said, 'and concentrate on the dinner, man.' He turned to Evelyn who had prepared a Swiss chicken ragout. 'This is very tasty. I think we shall let you cook again… what you think, Anna?'

'She can do the cooking every night as far as I am concerned,' Anna replied. 'I have been preparing and serving meals and washing up all day!'

Dinner over, they watched TV for the rest of the evening and finished off the wine.

Later, in the privacy of their bedroom, Anna said, 'Well, are you going to tell me what is bothering you? I know there is something on your mind; you have hardly uttered a word all evening.'

Robbie was hesitant. He did not want Anna to get the wrong end of the stick. In fact, he would rather not tell her at all but if anything should get back to her and he had not mentioned it, she was bound to suspect that something was going on.

'It's Kristina,' he finally managed.

'Ah,' Anna replied, apparently understanding the problem. 'I do not know Kristina—only what Martina has told me that Kurt has told Fritz. I hear that she is a something of a man-eater—and an obsessive one at that!'

182

'You can say that again,' Robbie replied. 'Today she has been an absolute pain—everywhere I went; everything I did, she was there, cosying up to me, fluttering her eyelashes and licking her lips, giving me the come on.'

'Are you sure you are not encouraging her?'

'Anna! How could you suggest such a thing, and why would I? I don't even like her, let alone fancy her... you know you are the only one I have eyes for.'

Anna giggled. 'I am sorry, Robbie, I am only teasing. But honestly, is it that bad? Can you not just ignore her? She will soon get the message, I am sure.'

'But I do ignore her – well, I try to, but she won't be ignored; she makes sure that I notice her – and there's no mistaking her intentions either!' He got into bed beside her. 'And do you know what happened today?'

'Go on.'

'I had a meeting with some of the other practicants in a different lab—there was no need to wear my jacket; I had my white coat on anyway. But when I came back at lunchtime to get my jacket to go to the canteen, my key was missing from my pocket.'

'Your key?'

'Yes—the key to the apartment.'

'But don't you keep your jacket in your locker?'

'Not always. In fact, I usually hang it on the back of the door in reception.'

'Well that is not very clever! What about your wallet?'

'No, that was there; nothing else was missing.'

'So what are you saying? That Kristina had taken your key?'

'No. I'm not saying that at all. When I mentioned that it was missing, she was concerned—you know, asking me if I was sure that's where I had left it and could it have dropped out of my pocket somewhere? Then she remembered the maintenance guy had been round checking the light bulbs, missed his footing on the ladder and ending up grabbing the coats and pulling them down on the floor with him. She hung the coats back up and the maintenance guy, who was thankfully okay after his fall, carried on with what he was doing.

'Well he didn't have your key, did he?'

'No, but Kristina guessed it was probably on the floor somewhere and went down on all fours, eventually finding it over in the corner.'

'Well, good for her – what is your problem with that?'

'My problem with that, Anna, my sweet, is that she now thinks she deserves a special treat for finding it – thank you is not enough, she is hinting at a night out… or more like a night in, knowing her!'

Anna laughed, unconcerned. 'Just play it cool, darling. When she comes in pursuit of you, just turn around and go in the opposite direction. Be rude if you have to. Keep out of her way… stay with the boys. And keep your possessions safe in your locker in future!' She kissed him goodnight. 'Now go to sleep and forget all about her; you are in bed with me, not her.'

Robbie said nothing. He was only too aware that he was in bed with Anna. He had hoped that now he was a resident rather than a guest in the apartment, was paying his way and had made a commitment to Anna by finding work here, she might have relaxed the bedroom rules but nothing had changed. He turned over; it was some time before sleep came.

Chapter 13

Robbie liked Kurt, seeing him on a daily basis when he went to and from work and they quickly became good friends. One lunchtime they happened to meet in the canteen and shared a table. Some of the workers who knew of Kurt's relationship with Fritz were surprised to see him with Robbie and inevitably, a rumour started going round. At that time, homosexuality was not fully accepted. Most people had no problem with it at all, whereas others were tolerant but guarded in their attitude towards it. Humans are naturally curious about each other and the main question being asked was whether or not Kurt had fallen out with Fritz, his long term partner, and replaced him with the young Englishman. The person who was likely to know the answer was of course Kristina and one of the workers asked her if she knew what was going on.

Kristina's curls bounced with the shaking motion of her head.

'There is nothing in it,' she replied. 'They are friends, that is all, having their lunch together. And anyway,' she added in a seductive tone, and hands on hips pose, 'Robbie is mine!'

'Really? I understood that he had a steady girlfriend.'

'Huh! She is too busy flying about in aeroplanes—I see much more of him than she does,' she said smugly. 'Trust me... Robbie is mine.'

Kurt was aware of the idle gossip and when Robbie left for home that evening, he asked if he could have a word.

'Of course,' Robbie replied. 'Problem?'

'No, no – but I thought I should mention lunchtime – I hope you did not feel too awkward about it?'

Robbie shook his head. 'Kurt, it was good to have your company, and no, I did not feel at all awkward. Why should I?'

'Oh, you know, I think a few people were suggesting that we might be involved or something; I did not wish to embarrass you.'

Robbie assured him that he was in no way embarrassed or uncomfortable to be seen in Kurt's company.

'I would like it if we could go out for a nice meal together, somewhere private and quiet where we can have a proper discussion without people making comments,' Kurt said. 'How would you feel about that?'

'I think that is a great idea, Kurt,' Robbie replied. I would be honoured to go and have a meal with you.'

'Does it matter when? I mean, are you normally free in the evenings?'

'Any time is fine with me,' Robbie replied, bidding Kurt goodnight and heading for the tram stop.

A few mornings later, Kurt asked if Robbie could make the following night for dinner.

'Fritz is on duty and I have nothing planned, so it seems a good time,' he said, 'if you are free.'

Robbie said he was free and would be delighted to meet him later. Kurt gave him details of the restaurant and they arranged to meet at eight that evening, exchanging phone numbers in case either of them could not make it.

The place that Kurt had chosen was small but exclusive and tucked away from the busy main restaurant quarter. Their reserved table was in the middle of the busy room but space between the tables was generous so that diners' conversations were kept private. As friends, instead of sitting facing each other, they sat in a diagonal, non-intimate position.

Kurt asked what Robbie fancied to eat from the menu.

'I think the steak,' Robbie replied.

'Then you will want a full-bodied red wine to go with it.' Kurt called the wine waiter and ordered a bottle of cabernet sauvignon for Robbie and a Riesling for himself to accompany his *wienerschnitzel*. Robbie's preference would have been a beer but this occasion was special for Kurt, who wanted to demonstrate Swiss hospitality to his new British friend.

He realised that Kurt was something of a gourmand. He was a big guy—obviously an asset in his line of work, but here was a man who enjoyed fine food, properly prepared and cooked and who did not fuel his body with junk food.

'According to Martina, you are Scottish,' Kurt said, thoughtfully stroking his droopy moustache.

188

'Yes, that's right.'

'A country steeped in history, with much conflict.'

'Absolutely.'

'And a country that produces the finest whisky in the world!'

Robbie smiled. 'Oh yes, we know how to do that.'

The waiter came to the table and took their order, followed by the wine waiter who showed Kurt and Robbie the bottles of their choice and poured a little of each for them to sample.

'So what is your favourite whisky?' Kurt asked when the waiter had gone.

'I have expensive tastes, I'm afraid,' Robbie replied. My favourite of all is an exclusive twelve-year-old organic single malt, Laphroaig. This particular one is selected and bottled for Highgrove—the country seat of the Prince of Wales. The barley is grown in Inverness and matured in a single, numbered, first-use bourbon cask.'

Kurt laughed. 'Well if it is good enough for the future King of England, it should be good enough for you, my friend.'

'Yes—but the difference is that I cannot afford to drink it very often.'

'My taste is not so grand as yours, 'Kurt explained. 'I am happy with The Famous Grouse brand. Blended, of course, but I find it rich, sweet and well rounded.'

'An excellent choice,' Robbie told him. 'The Famous Grouse was first produced by Matthew Gloag & Son in 1896.' He smiled at the look of surprise on Kurt's face. 'I am not an expert on whisky, by the way,' he added. 'My dad drinks Famous Grouse and the details are all on the label—have a look next time you get some.'

Robbie realised that Kurt at close quarters and away from his official post as Head of Security, was really not what he had expected, knowing that he was the gay partner of a policeman. He was fifty-four years old and twice the age of his lover. Tall and well-built, he could easily be taken for a nightclub bouncer. With his short black hair, blue eyes and moustache he was still good looking but not strikingly attractive.

Their meal, when it came, was perfectly cooked and Robbie said that he had never tasted food as good as the Swiss food.

'We do pride ourselves on our cuisine,' Kurt told him. 'It is the one thing that people remark on—our cooking skills.'

'And also for me, your hospitality,' Robbie said, dabbing his mouth with his napkin and reaching for his wine glass. 'I have been made to feel so welcome wherever I have been.'

'I am glad you like my country,' Kurt said.

'I love Switzerland and everything about it,' Robbie assured him.

Kurt smiled. 'Especially the lovely Anna.'

'Yes, especially the lovely Anna—she is, after all, the reason I am here.'

'You met in London; I believe?'

'Yes – well, Richmond – a suburb of the capital.'

'I like London,' Kurt replied. 'Very cosmopolitan, an exciting city of culture and grandeur.' Laying his knife and fork down for a moment, he took a sip of his wine. 'Your steak,' he indicated Robbie's plate, 'it is cooked to your liking?'

'It is perfect, Kurt. Thank you.'

'And when you met Anna in Rich…?'

'Richmond.'

'Ja, thank you… in Richmond; it was love at first sight?'

Robbie laughed out loud, recalling the exact moment of his meeting with Anna.

'Forgive me,' Robbie quickly added, noticing Kurt's bemused look. 'For me, it was instant attraction, yes but I am not sure it was the same for Anna.' He explained that he was covered in soot and looked like some monster that lived in a coal mine.

Kurt found this very amusing and his deep burst of laughter set Robbie off again.

'I had to go out later that evening, to a church function,' he continued, 'but of course I cleaned myself up. And the amazing thing was that when I got home, well after ten o'clock, Anna was still there, chatting with my mum. Heaven knows what they found to talk about, but you know, I was smitten – she was beautiful – and I asked her out the next day. The rest is history.'

Kurt then talked a little about Fritz with whom he shared an apartment in the city.

'I met him when he was barely twenty years old,' Kurt said, 'and with a lot of problems. He had been experimenting with drugs—not the hard stuff, but it could so easily have led to that and he was heading for trouble, for sure. Coming from a broken home, he had no one to confide in or help him to find the right path. The night I met him; he had drunk too much beer. The barman threw him out and he was making a nuisance of himself. A patrolling policeman was about to arrest him but I managed to persuade the officer that I would look after him and gave him my personal assurance that he would not cause any further trouble that night.'

'You did that, for a drunk that you knew nothing about?' Robbie realised there was much, much more to Kurt than he had ever imagined.

'There was something about him… I felt I wanted to try to help him. I took him to my apartment and gave him some black coffee to help sober him up and then I encouraged him to talk about his feelings and what it was that made him behave like a deadbeat when, as a young man, he had his whole life before him. It took a while but I am a patient man and eventually he opened up a little bit and I listened to what he had to say. He told me that nobody had ever listened to him before or taken any interest in him. In fact for most of his young life he had been bullied and abused. Using drugs and alcohol was his way of deadening the emotional pain.

'I told him that he could either carry on feeling sorry for himself and running away from reality, eventually ending up in jail – a failure, a nobody with a wasted life, or he could put the past behind him and concentrate on building a decent life for himself and be *somebody* – somebody to be respected and trusted. But that would have to be earned and he would have to make some big changes.

I let him sleep on my couch, gave him breakfast the next morning and my phone number in case he wanted to get in touch.'

Kurt paused, poured himself another half glass of wine, took a few sips and continued.

'He was not sure at first what to make of me, you know. He was very mistrustful. Asked me what was in it for me; he didn't want me taking over his life, watching his every move. Why would I want to be bothered with his problems?

'I told him I had also had a troubled past and I knew what it was like to feel alone and rejected. I had almost given up on myself when I was offered a lifeline—the chance of a good job with a reputable security firm. That was more than twenty years ago and I have never looked back. I believe that everybody deserves a second chance, Robbie.'

Robbie said Kurt was a very understanding, caring person. 'A perfect role model,' he added.

'I certainly tried to be,' Kurt agreed, 'and everything I had told him he took on board and made an effort to help himself. That took some doing but I supported him as much as I could and we got him through it. When he told me he was applying for a job in the police force, I could not have been more delighted. We became very good friends. He was instrumental in getting me this job with Ciba-Geigy when my last employer hit the skids. I began as a courier – that was almost four years ago and now I am head of security! I did not know at the beginning that Fritz would turn out to be gay, of course, and now I am pretty sure that all those mixed up emotions on top of his other troubles were the reason he turned to drink and drugs —to blot out the reality. He did seem somehow different, but not in any obvious way apart from his stunning good looks, and although I have been gay all my life, I certainly did not single him out for the purpose of forming a relationship. Nothing was further from my mind.' Again he paused, stroking his moustache thoughtfully. 'No, it evolved in a very natural sort of way, as if it was meant to be.'

'What an amazing and inspiring story,' Robbie said, 'and how wonderful that the two of you have found happiness.'

Kurt smiled. 'We are very happy,' he agreed. 'Fritz and I, we are soul mates... we live for each other.'

The waiter came to clear away their dinner plates and asked if they would like a dessert. Robbie could not resist the Black Forest gateau and Kurt decided to join him.

'I have heard you go motor racing,' Kurt mentioned as the waiter left.

'I used to, yes,' replied Robbie, 'until one reckless driver caused a crash and wrote my car off—nearly wrote me off as well.' He told Kurt what had happened during the practice laps at Silverstone.

'You were very lucky to survive that,' Kurt said.

'I was extremely lucky. They said I was just inches away from having my head severed!'

'Whoa... really? So have you given it up now?'

'I had to, yes. The cost of replacing the car was more than I could afford, even with the insurance, and Anna didn't want me to continue. She had always been against it and hated it. She was there at the time and saw it happen; in fact she thought I had been killed. So...' Robbie shrugged, 'it wouldn't be fair.'

'But you miss it?'

'I do, yes, but it probably all happened for the best. How about you? Are you a sporting man?'

'I like tennis and play a bit now and again. Fritz is very powerful and always beats me. But golf is my game, really.'

Robbie smiled. 'You would get on well with my dad—he plays golf at every opportunity. My mum reckons she was the original golf widow!'

They laughed. 'Yes, there are a few of those about,' Kurt agreed. 'And what football team do you support?'

'Middlesbrough FC in England and Stirling Albion in Scotland,' Robbie replied. 'If they are doing well,' he grinned.

'And mine, of course, is FC Basel,' Kurt added.

'My friend, Marcel, is a Basel supporter,' Robbie added. 'He has promised to take me to a game.'

'Marcel?' I am sure I have heard that name before...'

'Very possibly. He is Anna's sister's boyfriend. A little bit crazy,' he twirled his index finger near his temple to stress the point, 'but a charming fellow and a very good friend.'

'He is French?'

'Yes, do you know him?'

'No, but I know of him. He works for the local Ferrari dealer, yes?'

'The very same, yes... Anna's dad.'

Robbie smiled, not really surprised that Marcel's reputation went before him. However, he did not elaborate further on the family connections. Kristina would no doubt have plenty of details for anyone who was interested, anyway.

The two of them completed their meal with a carafe of fresh coffee and Kurt picked up the tab. Robbie offered to pay for his half but Kurt would not hear of it.

'My friend, I invited you and you have done me a great honour in joining me this evening. I will not hear of it. You can perhaps buy me a beer on another occasion?'

'Of course. I will be glad to, thank you... and thank you, Kurt, for everything you did to help me get the job at Ciba-Geigy. I want you to know how much I appreciate it.'

'It was nothing, my friend. And I want you to understand that it is a pleasure to know you. But Kristina was the one with all the inside information.' He lowered his voice. 'There is not much that she does not know,' he confided. 'She likes to find out everybody's business. A word of advice... she can be a trouble maker so just be careful what you tell her.'

'I keep out of her way as much as possible,' Robbie answered. 'Between you and me, I think she is a bit of a nutter. She is always hovering about and makes a beeline for me if she spots me. She seems to fancy me and, well, she's okay but not my type, you know, and anyway I am in love with Anna.'

Kurt nodded and raised a warning forefinger. 'Just remember, be careful.'

Chapter 14

When Anna had been with Crossair for three months, to her utter delight she was offered a trip to three capital cities at a greatly reduced price. A three-day stopover break with Crossair at a fraction of the usual cost for herself and her partner.

She couldn't wait to tell Robbie, who had neither been to Paris nor Rome and the joy of it for her was that she could relax from her duties and take in the sights with the rest of the tourists.

Robbie phoned his parents from the payphone in reception at work a few days before the trip. His mum answered the phone. She listened as he explained that he and Anna would be making a flying visit as they had booked a three day mini-break taking in London, Rome and Paris.

'Och, Robbie, that has made my day! I am so excited… I am that! Now then, when will ye be coming, d'ye think?'

'It will be next Wednesday. Is it okay if we stay overnight with you and Dad?'

'Next Wednesday? Och! As soon as that? Pairfect… and o'course ye can stay o'ernight. Anna can have Sophie's wee room.'

'Great. Thanks, Mum. Is Dad all right?'

'Aye, he's fine, so. 'I'll tell him the news when he's hame frae the golf course!'

Robbie laughed. 'See you next week then!'

'Aye—and listen, laddie, when ye get here, ye're going tae hae one big surprise!'

'Really? What?'

'If I tell ye, it winnae be a surprise now, will it?' Fiona answered. 'Wait and see. Take care now and love to Anna.'

Robbie laughed, said his goodbyes and hung up the phone, unaware that Kristina had heard every word of his part in the conversation.

As Anna and Robbie turned into his parents' road in Richmond, time seemed to have stood still. They both had fond memories of their walks to the park with Lucy—and that first meeting, when Robbie had arrived home covered in soot seemed like only yesterday. Unusually, nobody was watching through the lounge window for their arrival and Robbie was forced to ring the front door bell. After several seconds, the door opened and Fiona stretched out her arms to her son and her beloved Anna, both of whom she had missed so much.

Robbie instantly had a feeling that something was going on and asked his mum if everything was okay.

'Och, of course, okay. And why shouldn't it be?' she retorted, stepping back and looking behind her, anxiously.

'I know you... you're hiding something,' Robbie replied.

'Aye, laddie, I am,' she agreed, her face now wreathed in smiles. 'Come along in both o'ye and see who's here just now!'

A well-built woman in her thirties sat in an armchair just inside the lounge, legs crossed at the ankles, her round face also a mass of smiles.

G'day, cuz,' she greeted him.

Robbie was confused.

'Cousin Martha, all the way from Brisbane,' she enlightened him, heaving herself out of the low chair and hugging him to her bosom almost to the point of suffocation.

Still smiling, Fiona trotted off to put the kettle on, leaving Robbie and Anna at Martha's mercy.

'Oh yes, of course,' Robbie said, when at last able to breathe again. 'Dad's sister emigrated to Australia,' he explained to Anna who was then introduced to Martha and also similarly deprived of oxygen for several uncomfortable seconds.

'Sorry, Martha, but it came a bit out of the blue— Mum said she had a surprise for me but of course gave me no clue!'

'No worries, cuz,' Martha replied. 'Now how were you to know who the heck I was when you've never even met me?'

The front door opened and Mike entered. He was back in good time and delighted to see Anna and Robbie again.

'You're both looking well,' he observed, 'and from what I hear, enjoying your new jobs.'

Fiona had decided on a roast dinner with Yorkshire pudding and apple tart and custard to follow.

'We are a truly international gathering,' Mike said as they sat down to their meal. 'Swiss, Scottish, English and Australian!'

'I'll drink to that,' Robbie said, raising his glass of beer.

'Aye, lad, and mebbe we'll have a drop of The Old Grouse later!'

'What is Brisbane like?' Anna asked Martha.

'Queensland, the capital, is fair buzzing,' Martha told her. 'Our apartment is in Kangaroo Point – a busy little suburb about twenty minutes' drive away from Brisbane – the main cosmopolitan hub for arts, culture and eating out. Right on the riverside, it's wedged between the ocean and rugged national parks and I can tell you for sure that no other area of Brisbane can match Kangaroo Point for its location and natural beauty.'

Now Brisbane, on the other hand, has the Queensland Museum and Science Centre, and the Queensland Gallery of Modern Art, and looming over the city is Mount Coot-tha, the site of Brisbane Botanic Gardens.' Martha clapped her hands. 'Now that's something else!' she declared proudly.

They chatted long into the night, exchanging information and both Martha and Anna declaring how much they would like to visit each other's countries.

'We do not operate long haul flights yet,' Anna said, 'but the day will surely come!'

200

'Yeah – and come in summer – we'll get the barbie goin' and crack open a few tinnies!'

Anna and Robbie had planned to visit the Tate Gallery (now Tate Britain) the next morning as there was an exhibition of Impressionist art on and they took Martha along with them, leaving her to make her own way back to Richmond while they carried on to the airport for their flight to Rome.

Before they left the house, Fiona had a quiet chat with Anna.

'Ah can see ye're looking after my wee laddie well, hen,' she said, taking Anna's face in both her hands and smiling lovingly into her eyes. 'I hope he's nae trouble to ye and minds his manners, aye!'

'He does,' Anna assured her. 'He is the perfect gentleman. And I am pleased to see you are looking so much better, Fiona.'

'Aye, I'm no so bad noo and I wanted tae tell ye,' Fiona said, 'that ever since I met ye that day in Richmond Park and brought ye hame wi' me for a wee chat, I have never touched one drop of the liquor... not one wee droppie!'

Anna was so pleased to hear that Fiona was doing well that she hugged this lovely lady, Robbie's mum, to whom she had become so attached and loved dearly.

'I knew you could do it,' she told her, 'and Robbie and I are so proud of you!'

The next capital on the itinerary was Rome, where there was so much to see and so little time available. For Anna, being a Catholic, the visit anyway had a more spiritual significance but no one could fail to notice the prevailing atmosphere of respect and dignity, especially so in Vatican City, the Basilica and St Peter's Square. Michelangelo's sheer beauty and detail of the Sistine Chapel ceiling literally took Robbie's breath away. Both he and Anna were in awe of the Vatican itself. They wondered whether the citizens took it all for granted, as can often be the case and yet it was apparent that there was a certain pride in the Vatican, being the revered seat of a spiritual kingdom: the Roman Catholic Church.

They visited The Colosseum and again were fascinated at the way in which the architecture of the building had evolved over the centuries and they were truly amazed by the enormity and grandeur of it, even as a ruin. Vespasian's decision to build the Colosseum on the site of Nero's lake was seen as a populist gesture of returning to the people an area of the city which Nero had appropriated for his own use. In contrast to many other amphitheatres, which were located on the outskirts of a city, the Colosseum was constructed in the city centre; in effect placing it both symbolically and precisely at the heart of Rome.

With time running short, they managed to see the Arch of Constantine, erected in the fourth century; the Roman Forum (plaza), surrounded by the ruins of several important ancient government buildings, and then hurried off to see the Trevi Fountain. Unfortunately, workers were cleaning the marble and the structure was covered with green netting, so that was disappointing as they had wanted to make a wish together.

There was so much to see and do in Rome that they were in danger of being late for their flight to Paris. Anna was stressing about it so Robbie said they would take a taxi to the airport. The driver was not only very rude but also charged more than double the normal fare – something like the equivalent of £65 and Robbie was ready to thump him.

'For God's sake, leave it, Robbie!' Anna shouted, dragging him out of the taxi.

'I'm not letting him get away with that!' Robbie replied, trying to fend her off but Anna used all her strength and pushed him out into the street.

'Just leave it, will you? We will miss our flight!'

In his rage at being cheated, Robbie kicked the taxi's headlamp as it drove away, aiming well and smashing the glass and bulbs.

'You stupid idiot,' Anna grumbled, 'they will send the Mafia to kill you now!'

'He should be reported for that,' Robbie retorted. 'It's daylight robbery.'

'Look, even if you report him nobody will do anything about it,' she replied. 'It is not worth losing your temper over. Now come on, otherwise we will be spending the night here!'

About three hours later, they were touching down at Charles de Gaulle Airport where they were booked into a

203

hotel for the night and would have most of the following day to spend sightseeing in Paris. However, they had been told that the Eiffel Tower's dramatic night lighting was spectacular and after dinner, they decided to go along. Lit by more than three hundred spotlights arranged along its girders, the tower took on a gold sheen as soon as night fell. Cones of light revealed the structure in a new light, both from the lower and second levels, where the tower's curved silhouette served up an unbeatable view. Visiting the Eiffel Tower at night also allowed observation of the light beam emitted by the beacon at the top of the tower, its fifty-mile range illuminating the clouds and the city in its hypnotic sweep.

'Wow!' Robbie breathed, 'I never knew it could look like that!'

'It is fantastic,' Anna agreed. 'So romantic!'

They climbed as high as the second level and that was enough for them both. Hand in hand, they descended, the magic of the tower's lights reflecting in their eyes, and then strolled through the streets back to the hotel.

The following day they had planned a visit to the Musée d'Orsay, a museum and art gallery on the Left Bank, housed in what was the Gare d'Orsay, a Beaux-Arts railway station, dating back to 1898/1900.

Robbie particularly wanted to visit the Musée d'Orsay because they held a collection of paintings by his favourite artist, Alfred Sisley, an impressionist landscape painter who was born and spent most of his life in France but retained British citizenship. Born in Paris in 1839; he died in 1899 at Moret-sur-Loing, and he was the most consistent of the Impressionists in his dedication to painting landscape en plein air.

His works were permanently exhibited at the Musée d'Orsay in Paris and Robbie was excited to see his favourite painting on show there, a winter scene.

'Anna!' he called trying not to attract too much attention to himself. 'Look… look what I have found!'

'Ah, is that it? The painting you have always admired?'

'Yes, my absolute favourite. Wow, it's amazing to see the real thing—I have seen so many photographs of it.'

To Anna it was just a snow scene—well painted, but not to her taste. She preferred the immediacy of works by Edgar Degas, Paul Cézanne and her favourite of all was Claude Monet, but she could see that Robbie was deeply moved to be in the presence of the work of an artist he greatly admired in such a prestigious gallery and she was keen to add her own praises.

They moved on to the sculptures and frescoes which again reminded them of the Sistine Chapel and finished in the room housing the neo-impressionist work – the name given to the post-impressionist works of Georges Seurat, Paul Signac and their followers who, inspired by optical theory, painted using tiny adjacent dabs of primary colour to create the effect of light.

'Right, can we just go back to the Alfred Sisley room?' Robbie asked.

'Sure, if you want to have a last look.'

Robbie did want to have a last look at his favourite painting, but there was something else of importance on his mind.

'Come on then, and we'll have lunch somewhere afterwards.'

As they stood in front of the winter scene, Robbie slid his arm around Anna's shoulder and held her close. She responded by laying her head against his shoulder.

'Anna?' he said softly.

'Robbie?' she replied.

He waited a moment until she tilted her face to look at him.

'I love you so much,' he said. 'I have loved you since the evening we met and I want to spend the rest of my life with you.'

She gazed into his eyes but said nothing.

'Anna, will you marry me?' he asked.

'You are not romantic enough,' she pointed out. You should be down one knee!'

'What? In here? With all these people?'

'I don't see why not.'

'Are you serious?'

'It is a serious matter, darling… better get it right, don't you think?'

Deeply self-conscious and blushing to the roots of his hair, he dropped down on one knee, caught her hand and asked her again. 'Anna, will you marry me?'

He was completely unprepared for her reply – shocked by it, in fact.

'You had better get up; people are staring at us. I will have to think about it. Let's go for lunch; I am very hungry.'

Think about it? She would have to think about it? Robbie felt bitterly disappointed and humiliated. He had been so sure that she would accept immediately but now had serious doubts about her feelings for him.

'How long are you going to be thinking about it?' he asked.

'As long as it takes—and please don't rush me. I will tell you as soon as I have made my decision!'

He picked at his lunch, his appetite having vanished with his hopes and afterwards they looked around the shops and admired the Parisian architecture down through the ages. The Louvre was obviously a huge attraction for visitors and they went to look at the building but did not go inside. For one thing, Robbie was now running out of money after the taxi fare scam and time was also in short supply as they had a very early flight back to Basel so they needed to get back and have a few hours' rest before their journey home.

Anna kicked off her shoes in the hotel bedroom and dropped onto the bed.

'I don't know about you, Robbie,' she began, 'but I am exhausted. I think I am going to have a bath and a few hours' sleep.'

Robbie was still upset and didn't feel like conversing, so merely agreed with her that it would be a good idea; that travelling could be extremely tiring.

207

While Anna was in the bathroom, he packed his bag with all but the clothes he needed for the next day and then laid down on the bed, head resting in his clasped hands, staring at the ceiling, still struggling with his emotions.

'Ah, that was very relaxing,' Anna commented, returning to the room from the en-suite. 'I have left it all warm and sweet-smelling for you to go and have yours now,' she said, smiling. 'What are you thinking about?'

He knew it was pointless to mention marriage again yet; she would probably keep him waiting for days—weeks even! A true Aquarian, Evelyn had said. True words, too.

'Nothing in particular,' he replied. 'I think I shall have a shower.'

'Don't take too long, then!'

He slid off the bed. What was she grinning at? His discomfort? Well I'm glad you think it's funny, he thought as he disappeared into the bathroom and locked the door.

It was still steamy in there in spite of the extractor fan but not so much that he could not see the message written right across the mirror. In bright red lipstick she had written her answer to his earlier proposal. *YES, DARLING, I WILL MARRY YOU*, it said.

His heart leapt in his chest; he might have known she would tease him, something she loved to do. The dream had come true; his beloved had agreed to marry him and he was about to rush back into the bedroom, take her in his arms and tell her that she had made him the happiest man on the planet.

He hesitated, hand on the doorknob. No, dammit, she could wait... two could play at that game... he would string her along for a change!

He took his time in the shower, shampooing his hair and rinsing off the resulting foam. After drying himself with the luxurious, soft cotton towels, he put on his bathrobe. Stroking his face, he decided a shave would not go amiss and instantly regretted it as he could not see himself clearly in the mirror for the lipstick. He tried rubbing it with a damp flannel, but that only made it worse. He was just squeezing some toilet cleaner on to a wad of toilet roll when there was a knock on the door and he heard Anna's voice.

'Are you all right in there, Robbie?'

He grinned to himself. She was becoming impatient.

She knocked again.

He opened the bathroom door a few inches.

'Did you call?' he asked. 'What's the problem?'

'Yes, I... nothing. You just seemed to be taking a long time...'

'Oh. Sorry. I won't be long now.' He closed the door and locked it again.

He managed to finish shaving and then thoroughly cleaned his teeth before clicking off the light and returning to the bedroom.

Anna was in bed, sitting up, smiling.

'You are looking very pleased with yourself,' he observed, removing his robe and getting into bed beside her.

She did not know quite what to say. He could not have missed her message, surely, even though there had been a fair amount of condensation? Was he teasing her? She had quite expected him to come tearing out of the bathroom and sweep her up in his arms.

'Did you notice anything in the bathroom?' she asked.

He frowned. 'Like what? It was obviously a bit steamed up in there; otherwise no. Should I have done?'

She looked closely at him, detecting no signs of mischief or playing the fool. In fact he still looked disappointed and dejected.

'I guess not,' she replied.

'Okay, sleep well, then.' He kissed her goodnight and put the light out.

'You too. Goodnight.'

As she lay there, thinking that her message would be clear and readable again by morning, Robbie's voice filtered through the darkness.

'By the way, we'll have to be up even earlier than planned—we're going to have a hell of a job cleaning the lipstick off that mirror!'

Chapter 15

When they returned from their three day trip, Anna and Robbie went to a custom jeweller in Basel, called *Meister*, where The 'M' engraved in every piece of jewellery and in every ring was the guarantor of supreme quality. In the *MEISTER* Manufactory, every piece of jewellery and every ring was individually and painstakingly designed and crafted by hand for their customers and no two were alike. They came with full provenance to provide proof of ownership and to satisfy insurance requirements.

Robbie and Anna had taken some time to present their design to the jeweller. It was to be crafted from white gold and would have diamonds surrounded by tiny rose petals. It would be ready, the assistant said, in time for their forthcoming holiday to the romantic city of Salzburg.

As they left the shop, Robbie noticed Kristina lurking in a nearby doorway.

'Don't look up straight away,' he told Anna, 'but we are being watched. Kristina is just a few doors away, up the street.'

'What? Are you sure?'

'Yes. She is stalking me now… I told you, she is a menace.'

'But she could have a legitimate reason for being here,' Anna pointed out.

'She should be at work!'

'Ha, like you?'

'I have permission; I bet she doesn't.'

'Oh, Robbie, put her out of your mind. She is just a jealous, rather sad woman.' She linked her arm with his. 'Perhaps we should find her a suitable man and then she will leave you in peace.' Anna looked up and saw the tall figure of Kristina hurrying away in the direction of Ciba-Geigy. 'Is that her?'

'That's her. And by the time I get back to work, the whole factory will know we have been seen at the jewellers!'

Kurt already knew when he opened the gates to admit Robbie back into work later.

'I am guessing you two have been to order your engagement ring,' he said, smiling. 'Meisters, no less. Nothing but the best, uh?'

'Kristina!'

Kurt nodded, wagging a warning finger. 'Remember what I told you, my friend, and be very careful... very, very careful.'

It was late June – the prettiest time of year in the Austrian mountain regions and Robbie and Anna were preparing for their holiday. Robbie looked worried as he rummaged in the drawer where he kept his personal and family items.

'Anna, have you seen my coins and Granddad's medals?' he asked.

'Not since you put them in your drawer, no. What on earth do you want to take them to Salzburg for?'

'I don't. Marcel has asked me if he can have a look at them and when I went to get them out to show him, they weren't there!'

Anna pulled a face. 'Maybe you have put them in another drawer by mistake? They must be there; they would not have just vanished!'

'Exactly. So where are they?'

'Excuse me – you are not accusing me of taking them, are you? Why would I want them?'

Robbie shook his head. These items were precious to him and the fact that they were missing was making him anxious. 'No, of course I am not accusing you, Anna. But could someone else have had access to them?'

'Marcel or Evelyn, you mean? Of course not... and again – why would they want them?'

Robbie shrugged. 'I don't know.'

'I don't know either,' she snapped. 'Do you want me to ask if we can search their room?'

'Of course not, Anna. Please don't be like that. I am merely trying to find out what has happened to them. It is a complete mystery.'

'I am sure they will turn up; none of us will have taken them, that is for certain. Now can we change the subject?'

With Robbie's coin collection and the medals still missing, Robbie and Anna were to fly to Salzburg the following afternoon. He was discussing his holiday with a colleague as they came down to reception from the lab.

'You are in for a treat,' Maryse told him. 'Especially as you have not been before.'

213

'Yes, everyone says it is like going to heaven,' Robbie replied.

'Good description. Are you good for getting to the airport?' Maryse asked.

'Yes, Anna's sister and her boyfriend are dropping us off. They are going to spend a few days with their other sister near Lugano. They did think of coming with us but Marcel cannot get enough time off so they are having a long weekend away instead.'

'Well, enjoy yourselves,' Maryse said, 'and I'll see you when you get back.'

'Have a lovely time, Robbie,' Kristina said as he was leaving. 'Don't forget to send me a postcard!'

'Thank you,' was all he said to her.

'I used to have a friend in Lugano.' She nodded, the blonde curls bouncing and bobbing. 'It was nice there, by the lake. Really romantic.'

For God's sake, he thought, does she miss *nothing*?

They arrived and booked into the pension where they had requested full board and, if they happened to be in, afternoon tea which, in Austria was a speciality and Robbie was naturally delighted to be having coffee and cakes in the afternoon. The pension was central to the Old Town and Altstadt, encompassing some of the oldest buildings and monuments in the Alps and, perhaps more importantly, Altstadt was the birthplace of child prodigy Mozart, and was preserved as a museum displaying his childhood instruments.

This, then, was the romantic city of Salzburg—famous for one of the greatest and most prolific classical composers of the eighteenth century, Wolfgang Amadeus Mozart and, in later years, the setting for the most popular musical of the sixties, *The Sound of Music*. There was a Sound of Music tour that included a visit to the Family von Trapp home and Robbie and Anna were undecided whether to go on that or the Alpine. They plumped for the Alpine tour as they thought it would be more scenic and beautiful than the Sound of Music tour which was too commercial for their taste. They were not disappointed and were treated to some of the most breathtaking scenery, all conducted by a knowledgeable and experienced guide. They were given enough time at each stop without having to rush and the whole thing was easy-going, unlike some of the tours that adhered strictly to their itinerary, every moment being precisely scheduled.

They became friendly with a couple from Philadelphia, Hugh and Doris Harris. Hugh had recently retired from the steelworks on the blast furnaces and they were now fulfilling their dream of travelling around Europe. They were especially fond of the architecture, art and culture of the major cities.

'Harris,' Robbie said, 'does not strike me as a name associated with America.' He smiled, 'In fact, it belongs to my own country of birth... the home of Harris Tweed!'

'Scotland!' Hugh said, removing his baseball cap for a moment, allowing his greying curls to spring free. 'You're Scottish folk, uh?'

'I am,' Robbie confirmed. He touched Anna's arm. 'Anna here is Swiss… well Swiss with Italian and French ancestry to be precise.'

'I was born in Switzerland,' Anna explained, 'but my father is of Italian descent and my mother is French.'

'And your husband is Scottish! That sure is an interesting mix,' Hugh remarked.

'Fiancé,' Anna gently corrected him. 'We are engaged.'

Doris just smiled, looking slightly bemused.

When Robbie looked at the couple, Doris with her bright blue eyes and longish light-grey hair, and Hugh – a curly-haired guy and of medium build but strong – he saw himself and Anna in their own retirement—possibly touring America, who knew? It was an interesting thought, anyway.

'Where are you staying?' Anna asked.

'At the Hotel Goldener Hirsch in Old Town,' Hugh replied. 'Boy, there is some history in that building and you know, the atmosphere of the place is amazing!'

Anna and Robbie exchanged glances. The Goldener Hirsch was five-star luxury, a refined, traditional hotel, centuries old and within five minutes' walk of Mozart's birthplace and the summer Salzburg Festival.

The four of them enjoyed the rest of the Alpine Tour together and as they left the coach after their return to the city, Hugh shook hands with Robbie and thanked him for his and Anna's company.

'It's been great to have you two around,' he said, 'and I'm sure I speak for Doris here when I say that it's been a real pleasure to meet you!'

'Thank you,' Robbie said. 'We feel the same.'

Anna smiled.' It has been an honour,' she added, 'and I hope we may meet up again before we leave this beautiful city.'

The next day, Robbie and Anna visited the place where Mozart was born in 1756 in the Hagenauer Haus at No. 9 Getreidegasse. His birthplace was one of the most visited museums in Salzburg and there was a considerable delay with so many people queuing to get in. However, they were eventually admitted and were fascinated by the preserved rooms where some of his instruments, including his piano, were still displayed and where he had practised for hours as a child.

'It is very sad that his life was so short and although a genius, he died a pauper,' Anna murmured.

'Yes,' Robbie replied. 'Why was that?'

'Put simply, he lived beyond his means.'

'And was he poisoned?'

It was suggested that he was poisoned by his colleague, Antonio Salieri, but that was unlikely to be anything but rumour as his symptoms were not consistent with poisoning. It was said he had a fever and also that he had syphilis and may have accidentally poisoned himself by taking large doses of mercury in an attempt to cure himself.'

'Really?' Robbie raised his eyebrows, surprised to hear that.

Anna nodded. 'Oh yes. It was entirely consistent with his lifestyle.' She sighed. 'Whatever the cause, it was still tragic—for his family and for the music world.'

A few tickets were still available for a concert of Mozart's music being held the following evening at the concert hall in the Hohensalzburg Fortress and Robbie felt compelled to buy two tickets which also included dinner and promised to be a very special night out.

Before returning to their pension, they decided to stay and have a meal. For his dessert, Robbie ordered a kind of chocolate covered rock cake. The food apparently lived up to its name because as he took a bite, he cried out with pain and spat the mouthful back onto his plate.

Anna was disgusted. 'You filthy pig!' she scolded. 'What are you playing at? Where are your manners?' She looked around anxiously, hoping no one else had witnessed it.

'Well, I am sorry,' Robbie replied, holding his palm to his upper jaw, obviously in some pain, 'but a tooth has just broken off...' he fished about on his plate and held the molar out for her to see. 'What was I supposed to do, swallow it?'

'No, of course not, but you could have been a little more discreet about it. Ugh, for goodness' sake, get rid of it!'

'Thank you for your sympathy, my love. Much appreciated.' He pushed his plate away, unwilling to risk any further damage by eating the rest of his dessert. He probed the sore spot with his tongue. What was left of the tooth was rough and painful, and he would have to seek emergency treatment.

'Will I be able to see a dentist tomorrow, do you think?' he asked Anna.

'Are you in pain?'

He nodded.

'Then you will have to.'

They did not wait for coffee; Robbie paid the bill and collected their coats.

'I think the chef should pay for my treatment,' he grumbled as they left.

Robbie's mouth was no better the next morning and he asked the proprietor of their pension if she could recommend a good dental practice. She told him of one that she had been to herself and was kind enough to contact them, explaining the problem. As he was in pain they booked him in for treatment that same morning and although still a bit sore when the injection wore off, he was considerably more comfortable and able to eat normally again.

'But you will have to be careful with it—and watch what you are eating this evening,' Anna reminded him.

'Well I will not be having a rock cake dessert again, that's for sure,' he replied. 'I never knew they were real rocks!'

Anna simply rolled her eyes and said no more.

They were looking forward to their evening of Mozart later. Both liked contemporary music of course but spending time in the city where one of the most prolific and famous classical composers once lived and worked was almost like being in the great man's presence, and some kind of tribute to him could be found wherever you went in Salzburg.

The joke 'If it's baroque, don't fix it' was a perfect maxim for Salzburg: the legendary Old Town nestling at the feet of steep hills looking much as it did two hundred and fifty years ago. Standing beside the fast-flowing Salzach River, your gaze rose inch by inch, past graceful domes and spires to the vast and mighty clifftop fortress and the mountains beyond. A breathtaking backdrop! When Archbishop Gebhard built Hohensalzburg Castle in 1077, he changed the Salzburg skyline forever.

Tonight's *Dinner & Best of Mozart Concert* was taking place in Hohensalzburg Castle's impressive concert hall. There were many other venues for Mozart dinner concerts and all were popular. Some had limited space; here there was room for a full orchestra. The hall was lit by candles, and orchestra members and waiting staff alike were dressed in period costume.

Anna and Robbie were just about to take their seats when they heard a familiar voice with an American accent.

'Hey, Doris! Look who's here! Well, who'd a thought we'd bump into you again so soon?'

Anna gave a little squeal and clapped her hands as she was wont to do at such times.

'How wonderful to see you!' she said, giving Doris a hug and kissing her cheek.

220

'Hi,' Robbie shook Hugh by the hand. 'Well this is a nice surprise!'

They all sat together for dinner and the concert. The food was of the highest quality and the music included some of Mozart's best known works, including his *Eine Kleine Nachtmusik*, a piano concerto and his harp and flute concerto. Anna was particularly taken with the arias from his popular operatic work, *The Magic Flute*, and also featured was a rare cello solo, played by a very young and talented cellist and Robbie was very impressed with his performance.

When the evening was over, Anna and Robbie said their goodbyes to Hugh and Doris and wished them bon voyage on their European tour.

'And you two enjoy your lives together, same as we have,' Doris said, taking hold of Hugh's arm and hugging it close to her.

Hugh smiled beneath the peak of his baseball cap. 'Me an' my Doris fell in love at High School in Pennsylvania and we been together ever since. My folks was against us marrying and so was hers... kinda tough, that was y'know, us havin' to wait till we was of age and emancipated. I started with work experience at the steelworks and Doris, she did waitressing and anything she could to bring in a few extra dollars. We didn't have much, but two things saw us through: determination and our love for each other. Eventually we got a nice home together, raised a family and earned the respect of our families again, for they all said it would never last. We worked danged hard and saved and one day, we said, we would take a tour of Europe

221

and…' he spread his arms, '… here we are, livin' our dream! Go for it, kids… make it happen, cos it sure as hell won't happen on its own!'

On that note they parted and went their separate ways; Hugh and Doris hailing a taxi to their hotel and Anna and Robbie walking hand in hand back to their modest pension.

It was a full moon that night, though only glimpses of it could be seen through the cloud that dominated the night sky. The couple strolled over the river bridge, still feeling very much under the influence of the extraordinary musical romantic evening. They stopped for a moment and Anna rested her head against Robbie's shoulder. The light from the moon played hide-and-seek through the clouds, one moment flooding her white, half-sleeve button-through blouse and mauve-and-black floral full length skirt in an aura of magical light; the next casting a slightly understated, regal look.

'Thank you for that beautiful experience, darling,' she whispered. 'I would not have missed one moment of it.'

He took her in his arms and kissed her. He was full of desire for her, as he had been for many months. He sensed that Anna now felt the same need as she responded with an urgent, unmistakeable passion. With reluctance they drew apart and at that precise moment the clouds also parted, allowing the moon's full face to shine down on them, reflecting and shimmering in the shadowy flow of the river.

'Come!' Robbie said. 'The night is not over yet… the best is still to come, my love.'

Anna snuggled up to her lover; both his arms enfolding her protectively as he slept. She smiled, reflecting on the night of love they had just shared, at last consummating their relationship, both surrendering their virginity. She had often wondered what the first time would be like... would it be painful? Would she be anxious? Her sister, Evelyn, had told her she would know when the time was right and the more relaxed she was, the better the experience would be.

They were now resting in the quiet darkness of their room, completely at peace in the calm aftermath. She almost giggled aloud, remembering the fact that both had kept most of their clothes on – in fact she was still wearing her blouse and Robbie his shirt, both now in a crumpled state. It had not happened this way for reasons of modesty, nor had it been the fact that their passion could not wait for them to undress; it was simply the way it had happened, quite naturally and in a way that, for them, seemed right.

She gently traced the features of his face with her finger, playfully tickling him under the chin.

'Are you awake or pretending to be asleep?'

Robbie opened his eyes. 'Tell me it is not a dream,' he said.' Tell me that I have experienced the most magical moments imaginable... beyond my wildest dreams.'

'For me, too,' she replied.

She kissed him. 'I love you so much,' she murmured, as he began to remove her top and then what remained of her undergarments. Now there was more urgency; she laid bare his chest, slipping his shirt from his body and for a moment or two they lay closely together, skin against skin,

223

caressing and kissing until once again they were lost in their own world—a world of love and the sheer undiluted joyfulness of being in love and expressing and sharing their passion for each other; not just demonstrating their love through sexual attraction but reaching far deeper as their two souls became one.

When Evelyn and Marcel returned from their weekend with Silke in Lugano they had a shock. An intruder had gained access to their apartment and trashed it. Drawers had been opened and emptied, furnishings were slashed, kitchen cupboards were open and their contents had been strewn across the floor and counter and there was a muddy trail indicating that the culprit had entered wearing muddy Wellingtons.

Marcel looked around him in bewilderment. 'What the—'

'Oh my God, nooooo!' Evelyn shrieked. 'I don't believe this…' she broke down in tears, '… it's like a nightmare!'

Marcel comforted her with a hug, kissing her hair. 'Don't touch anything,' he warned. 'Ssh, I will call the police.'

It was the last full day of their Salzburg holiday for Anna and Robbie and they were looking around the shops for small gifts and souvenirs to take home.

'How about that for Marcel?' Robbie asked, pointing to an authentic Austrian beer stein with a pointed lid.

'Perfect,' Anna agreed. 'And I thought we might get Evie one of those cowbell pendants.' These were miniature, silver cowbells fixed to a silver chain. 'You know how she loves her quirky jewellery.'

They finished their shopping and went for a coffee. They agreed that this holiday had been the most memorable time ever, for both of them. Salzburg would always be special for them. While they were chatting, Robbie suddenly stopped mid-sentence and stared at Anna, frowning as a thought came to him.

'Oh no,' he said. 'I should have been more—'

'What? Been more what, Robbie? What is wrong with you?'

'Anna, I… you do know you could be pregnant?'

She laughed. 'No, I cannot, but that is no thanks to you; you are right, you should have been more…' she nodded, still smiling, mostly at his horrified expression.

'But?'

She put him out of his misery. 'Robbie,' she spread out the fingers of her left hand, 'I have an engagement ring on my finger, a very beautiful engagement ring, too,' she added, digressing slightly. 'I knew it was only a matter of time until the moment came when we would make love. I wanted to be prepared for that moment and ever since we got engaged, I have been taking the precautions.'

Robbie sighed with relief. 'The pill?'

She nodded. 'Better now?'

'Don't get me wrong,' he explained, 'I would really love to have a family when the time is right, but now would be a disaster for both of us.'

'Of course! For a start we are not married. I know that is not a necessity these days, but it is important to me. And then there is the question of our careers and also we should have some fun together, just the two of us, before we take on the responsibility of having babies. There is plenty of time to do that.'

They left the coffee house and with arms linked, each carrying a bag of small gifts, they made their way back to the pension to begin packing for home.

Chapter 16

'So what did the police say?' Robbie asked, when Marcel and Evelyn were describing the carnage that had greeted them on their return from Silke's.

'They were as baffled as we were,' Marcel replied. 'There was no forced entry, nothing was stolen as far as we could tell, there were no fingerprints… nothing. Just this mindless vandalism.' He shrugged.

'There was only one thing,' Evelyn added 'The intruder wore muddy boots and left a trail of footprints across the kitchen floor and down the stairs, so that could provide a lead but it is not much to go on unless they can match the boots.'

Anna and Robbie looked around the floor.

'Well, we have cleaned it up now,' Evelyn explained. 'The police took photographs and forensic samples and then said it was okay for us to go ahead and clear up whenever we were ready.'

'Yes, yes of course,' Robbie agreed, 'I was just trying to picture it my mind's eye.'

'The footprints were all over the apartment.' Evelyn pointed to the kitchen. 'But of course they looked a lot worse on the tiled kitchen floor.'

'They suggest he was a big guy,' Marcel pointed out, 'size 44 boots, they thought, and carried some weight, judging by certain marks left on the carpet.'

Anna shivered. 'This is horrible,' she said. 'I don't feel safe here anymore.'

Robbie agreed that it was unnerving. 'What I can't understand is how he got in. There were no windows left open?'

'Absolutely not,' Marcel replied, 'and in any case, we are on the second floor... he would have to be Spiderman!'

'The lock was not tampered with at all?'

'No. There were no scratches around the lock or any evidence at all that the lock had been picked or forced in any way.' He shrugged again. 'It is a mystery.'

Anna asked, 'Have any of you given or lent your key to anyone else for any reason?'

They all shook their heads.

'Think about this for a moment. It may be important. It does seem obvious to me that whoever entered our home did so by using a key. There is no other explanation.'

There was no response. All of them were completely baffled by it.

'Well,' Anna said, folding her arms in a determined fashion, 'as I said, I do not feel safe now and I suggest we get the lock changed first thing tomorrow.'

'I will do that,' Robbie said. 'As soon as the shops open in the morning I will go and buy a five lever deadlock.' He frowned, looking around the apartment. 'You know, I can't help thinking that it must be the same person who was responsible for taking my grandfather's medals and my gold sovereigns.'

'But we do not know that they have been taken. They are most likely still here, just in a different place!'

However, Robbie knew that he had not taken them out of his drawer since he put them there when he moved in and was convinced that they had been stolen. He recalled that he had mentioned the medals and coins to Kurt once when they were talking. But Kurt's partner was a police officer. And surely it was not something that Kurt would even dream of doing? And in any case, how would he have achieved it?

However, Robbie felt suddenly uneasy. Kurt would definitely know how to pick a lock… and he certainly wore large boots. But no, the very idea was preposterous and he dismissed it from his mind. Then he remembered the time his key was missing from his jacket pocket.

'And that was very odd, come to think of it,' he said aloud, 'when my key went missing from my jacket pocket and Kristina found it on the floor. She said the maintenance man had slipped and pulled the coats down…'

'Yes,' Anna agreed, 'but she found it and gave it back to you; it's not as if it went missing and was never seen again. I don't think it was anything to do with her, but perhaps you will be more careful in future and keep your belongings in your locker… you men are too careless!'

Robbie changed the lock straight after breakfast the following morning. It came complete with two keys and he had two more cut so that they had one each.

'Please keep your keys safe at all times,' Anna warned the others, and do not lend them to anyone or leave them lying around.' She shot a glance at Marcel who was more inclined to be casual about such matters.

When Robbie returned to work the next day, Kurt was all smiles and greeted him as an old friend, extending his hand.

'Is good to have you back with us, my friend. I hope you have had a most enjoyable holiday?'

Robbie shook Kurt's hand vigorously. A pang of regret rose within him for even thinking that he could have had anything to do with the recent incidents. It was unthinkable that Kurt could stoop to such depths and anyway, what would be his motive?

'We had a fabulous time, Kurt, thank you.'

Kurt grinned. 'Your girlfriend has missed you—I swear she has been crossing off the days until you came home.'

Robbie pulled a face. 'Uh, I was hoping she had either moved on or better still, got married!'

'No, sorry—she is still here, large as life and waiting to see you again.'

Robbie sighed. 'See you at lunchtime, Kurt.'

As he entered the building, Kristina's eyes narrowed and her smile was one of smug satisfaction. Time I stepped up the action, she thought to herself.

'Robbie! You are back, thank goodness.' She almost threw herself at him, taking him by surprise and he had to fend her off.

'It has not been the same here without you,' she pouted. 'I have missed you so much!' She took a letter tray full of messages from a shelf near her desk and held them up.

'You have all these reports to go through and log into the system,' she told him. 'I have kept them all in date order for you. If I am free later I will come and help you with them; it won't take so long with two of us.'

'I can manage, thank you, Kristina,' Robbie replied, 'and in any case, I will need to study them.'

'It's no trouble,' she insisted.

Outwardly calm, he took the tray from her, turned quickly and without another word, went through the door leading up to the laboratory, but he had an uneasy sense of being preyed upon and for the first time, felt threatened by her. He just caught her parting words as the door closed behind him.

'I expect you are still engaged to the flying waitress?'

'Bloody crackpot,' he said quietly to himself as he reached the top of the stairs.

'Hallo, Robbie,' Maryse greeted him with a peck on the cheek as he entered. 'Good holiday?'

'Yes, it was amazing,' Robbie replied.' We had a wonderful time.'

'And now you have to pay for it,' she said, nodding to the pile of work he was carrying.

He smiled. 'Yes, but I am happier when I have plenty to do and I find all this very stimulating. I will soon catch up with it.'

Robbie left the work on his desk and went to report to the professor.

Professor Martie shook his hand, clearly pleased to see him again.

'Now I know you have a bit to catch up with,' he said, but come and see me when you are up to date. I have some new studies to work on that I believe you will find more interesting than the plastics you are currently researching. If you are interested, you will be working closely with me and Monsieur Jaffra.'

'Oh, really?' Robbie was all ears. 'That does sound interesting.'

The professor smiled warmly. He had a very engaging manner, but his kindly blue eyes concealed an authority and steely discipline that anyone who valued their position here would never question or disrespect.

'But,' he tapped his nose with an index finger, 'it is top secret, you understand, and what happens in this room stays in this room. We do understand each other?'

'Of course, sir. Absolutely.'

The professor nodded. 'Then go and carry on with your work and come and see me in a day or two, okay? And remember…' he tapped his nose again.

Wow! Life was getting better by the minute. Even now, Robbie sometimes wondered whether he was dreaming and would wake up and find himself stuck halfway up an old Victorian chimney like an urchin straight out of a Dickens novel.

When he left the laboratory four hours later, hoping to catch Kurt and have lunch with him in the canteen, he found Kristina still hanging around, quite obviously waiting for him.

'Are you going to the canteen for lunch, Robbie?' she asked, smoothing her skirt down over her hips.

Damn the woman! 'Er, no, I have to pop out for something,' he replied.

'Oh, I see.' She smiled, nodding. 'It looks nice out there today. I could come with you if you want some company?'

'Thank you,' Robbie said politely, 'but I have some business to attend to.'

'Something I can help with?'

'No, so if you'll excuse me…'

'Perhaps tomorrow, then.'

'Tomorrow what?'

'The canteen. I am dying to hear all about your holiday and I have not seen you all morning!'

Tutting to himself, Robbie turned, heading out through the automatic doors, making for the main gates and, once out of sight, doubling back to a side entrance which was also a shortcut to the canteen.

Spotting Kurt at a table, Robbie threaded his way through the busy staff dining room, aware of the clattering of plates and cutlery and the buzz of conversation. Reaching their table, he touched Kurt on the shoulder.

'Sorry I am late, Kurt. I was held up.'

Kurt noticed the tension in Robbie's expression.

'Tangled up, more like,' he grinned,' in the blonde spider's web!'

'Oh, don't,' Robbie groaned. 'I have just had to tell her a lie – that I was going out for lunch today—'

'Don't look towards the door,' Kurt interrupted, leaning forward towards Robbie, 'but I do not think she believed you!'

Ignoring Kurt's caution, Robbie was compelled to turn and glance back at the canteen entrance.

Kristina stood just inside the room, partially hidden by a vending machine, a useful commodity for those who preferred a quick drink and a snack to keep them going.

'God, she gives me the creeps,' Robbie muttered. 'Now what do I do?'

'Just ignore her. It is none of her business what you do.'

'But I told her I was going out on business.'

Kurt shrugged. 'So you changed your mind.' He reached across to the next table. 'Excuse me, may I?' he asked the occupant, taking a spare knife and fork lying on the table. 'My colleague – he forgot his utensils!'

Robbie looked bemused, not for the first time wondering where all this was going to end.

'Here...' Kurt handed him the knife and fork and pushed his plate towards him. 'Help yourself,' he indicated the ample helping of rösti and salad – there is far more than I can eat, anyway – and don't even look in her direction!'

Robbie was impressed by Kurt's initiative and also touched by his actions and began to relax. He told him how much he and Anna had enjoyed their holiday in Salzburg, about the American couple they had met, the wonderful Mozart concert and how special it had all been.

'Then we arrived home to find that our apartment had been vandalised, so that rather took the edge off it.'

Kurt did not seem surprised. 'Well, you know Fritz is not supposed to discuss police business with anyone, including me, and he doesn't, but I did wonder, because I knew he had been called out to a case of malicious damage in your street. And then I took a telephone message for him at home from Marcel—he is the guy you have mentioned, who lives with you?'

'Yes.' Robbie was thoughtful. 'Look, Kurt, I know this is very irregular and I don't want to get Fritz into any trouble, but could you ask him if there is any news? Anna has been very nervous since we got back.'

'I will ask him if there is anything he can tell me, but they will be doing all they can to find the person responsible. You have of course had the lock changed?'

'Oh yes, I did that the morning after we got back.'

'Good—because it does sound to me as if the intruder somehow obtained a key.'

Robbie mentioned the time when his key went missing from his jacket pocket and how Kristina had found it on the floor.

Kurt was perturbed. 'Remember what I said, Robbie – be very careful.'

'Anna dismissed it as coincidence and I have to agree there is absolutely no reason to suspect that Kristina was involved.'

'Even so… that woman is trouble!'

Robbie was relieved that Kristina was on the phone when he returned from lunch and swiftly crossed to the door leading to his laboratory, cringing as, just about to turn the door handle, he heard her hang up the phone.

'And was your business in town successful?' she asked.

'It went as planned,' he replied before disappearing up the stairs.

Robbie strongly suspected that Kristina was involved both in the earlier theft of his property and now the vandalism of his home. He decided to go to the police station and tell them of his suspicions, particularly as Kristina was now openly stalking him without even attempting to hide the fact.

He asked if it would be possible to speak to Fritz as he had some information that he thought would be useful to his enquiries.

Fritz was one of the officers working on the case and took Robbie to one of the interview rooms.

'What makes you think Kristina is responsible?' he asked Robbie. 'Do you have any evidence that it was her?'

'No, I'm afraid not. I just feel she is in some way involved. I don't trust her.' He explained to Fritz about the key episode and how she had begun stalking him and was now turning up practically everywhere he went. 'I have a strong hunch that if you were to search her home you would find my gold sovereigns and Grandfather's medals,' he said.

'Robbie, we would need a search warrant to do that and it certainly would not be granted on the basis of a mere hunch and that you mistrust her. We will need strong evidence.'

'I am just wondering if she has alibis for the times that these incidents took place?' Robbie asked.

'But we do not know the exact day or time of either incident,' Fritz pointed out, 'especially the first. The second can only be narrowed down to the three days that your room mates were absent. Therefore whether or not she has an alibi is irrelevant.'

Robbie sighed. He had expected a little more cooperation from Fritz but he was getting nowhere.

'Look,' Fritz said, understanding Robbie's frustration, 'I can see how troubled you are by all this. I can do nothing officially without sufficient evidence but I will try to make a few discreet enquiries about her movements. If anything should come to light I will of course inform the inspector who will then decide whether any action should be taken; otherwise, I am sorry, but my hands are tied.'

Chapter 17

Anna nudged Robbie while they were out shopping in the town one Saturday morning.

'Isn't that Kristina just across the road there?' she asked.

'What?' Robbie's head swivelled in the direction of Anna's gaze. 'Where? Oh, God, yes it is; you can't mistake her! What is she playing at? I am going over there to give her a piece of—'

Anna pulled at Robbie's sleeve. 'Leave it, Robbie. It is far better if you ignore her. She wants you to make a scene, especially as I am with you as well—she is an attention seeker, don't you see that?'

'Of course. She is also obsessed with me and it's beginning to interfere with my life. I think she is off her rocker actually, but this has got to stop. I am getting really pissed off with it!'

Anna had found the situation amusing to begin with but it was getting so bad now that even she agreed that something should be done about her.

'I will have a word with Martina,' she told Robbie. 'She and Fritz between them ought to be able to warn her off.' She gestured with her hands palms upwards. 'Look, for now, can we just try to ignore her and finish our shopping?' she appealed. 'So is it going to be cold in

Scotland, do you think? I am wondering whether to buy some new sweaters.'

'It's all right saying ignore her,' Robbie replied, but it's not easy when she is always bloody well there, creeping about, following us—'

'Robbie! Leave it, will you!'

'Sorry, my love. Erm, probably not too cold,' Robbie replied, 'but almost certainly wet. It does rain a lot in Scotland!'

'I thought that was Ireland?'

'Aye, there's a saying that you know it's summer in Ireland when the rain gets warmer!'

'Is Irish rain for real though, or just myth?'

Robbie grinned. 'More real than myth, I would say, but it's not just Ireland. In the Scottish Highlands there is an old proverb that goes, 'today's rain is tomorrow's whisky'.'

'Oh, okay, waterproofs and mollies for Scotland, then?'

'Mollies?'

Or perhaps I mean trollies? You know, to keep the rain off.'

Robbie creased with laughter. 'You... ha ha hah... you mean brollies, sweetheart,' he spluttered '... they are actually properly called umbrellas!'

'I know very well what is an umbrella, I was trying to think of the colloquial word for it.' She also laughed at her mistake.

Robbie was amused that she knew the English meaning of colloquial but not a simple everyday word like brolly. He caught her up in his arms and hugged her.

'I do love you so much! And if you need an extra sweater, we can buy you an authentic Fair Isle hand-spun, hand-knitted one in Scotland.'

'What? They still make them by hand?'

'In some of the villages, yes. It is quite a lucrative cottage industry.'

The deep, jealous green eyes of Kristina watched every step and movement made by Anna and Robbie as they made their last minute purchases for their forthcoming holiday. Robbie was going to show Anna his birthplace and home town where he spent his early childhood.

Their plane touched down smoothly at Edinburgh airport and after all the usual formalities, they left the airport building and made their way to the short stay car park where their hire car was ready and waiting.

Anna immediately fell in love with the little Fiat Uno and clapped her hands.

'A red Italian car, Robbie,' she chirped. 'Marcel will be impressed…'

Robbie's expression conveyed his thoughts perfectly.

She laughed. 'He does not have to know that it is not a Ferrari!'

'Come on,' he said, taking her arm, 'you and your sister are both incorrigible!'

'Well, Evie is definitely a true Aquarian.'

'Strange that you were both under the same star sign.'

'Yes, same sign but she in January and me in February.'

'Evie says the same about you—that *you* are the true Aquarian. And you know what Marcel says?'

'Go on…'

'That you both saw us coming!'

Their holiday was off to a happy start as their laughter drifted through the open car windows and Robbie, after a quick look at the map, drove out of the airport and followed the sign to the M9, on their way to the village called Bridge of Allan, where a friend from his schooldays, Alastair Harvey, ran a guest house with his wife, Flora. On the way there, Robbie told Anna a little bit about the place.

'Bridge of Allan is one of Stirling's hidden gems,' he told her, 'and is home to Stirling University, less than three miles from the city centre.'

'It's a spa, isn't it?' Anna asked.

'Yes, right by the Allan Water, and really very charming. It is overlooked by the National Wallace Monument and within sight of Stirling Castle perched at the top of the cliff.'

'It sounds delightful.'

'Oh, you are going to love it, believe me!'

'And it must be exciting for you to come back to your roots if you have not visited since you were a child?'

'I have been back once or twice, but not for a few years now and I am feeling very nostalgic,' Robbie admitted.

After about forty-five minutes of motorway driving, they took the exit for Bridge of Allan and were soon skirting the golf club on their way to the B&B just a short distance away. Robbie spotted it and pointed to the attractive stonework of the building just ahead of them.

'It looks just the same as it always did,' he remarked.

Alastair was pinning a notice on the information board in the hallway as Anna and Robbie entered and immediately came forward to greet them. A few months older than Robbie, he was taller and less muscular, with dark curly hair and brown eyes. He called upstairs to his wife, Flora.

'She'll be down in a minute,' he said, smiling. 'Always a job to be to doing in this business!'

'It must be your busiest time, too?' Robbie asked.

'Aye, we have only one room unoccupied this week so far, but you know, we have a pretty steady flow in the wintertime as well—and a lot of folk who visit in summer want to come back for Hogmanay!'

As they chatted, waiting for Flora to appear, Anna was relieved that she could understand pretty well most of what he was saying. She had expected conversation with a Scot on his own ground to be difficult but in fact it was not a problem. Flora, on the other hand, spoke with a slightly stronger accent.

'Och,' Flora said, 'will ye look at the state ye've found me in!' She untied her apron and patted her hair, allowing Robbie to hug her and she in turn then hugged Anna as Robbie introduced 'my soon-to-be-wife, Anna'.

Just a year younger than her husband, Flora, a homely, welcoming person who struggled with her weight, also had dark, curly hair and unusual but attractive almost turquoise eyes.

'And have ye fixed a date for the wedding yet?' she asked.

'No,' Robbie answered, 'but it will be soon. We see no point in waiting.'

'And did ye have an engagement party?'

Anna shook her head. 'Just a special meal out to mark the occasion.'

Flora looked at Alastair, her eyes twinkling like jewels with delight.

He grinned back at her.

'I suspect a party to celebrate the occasion is on the cards,' he told Anna. 'I hope you've brought your party frock!'

'No. But he will buy me one,' she replied, giving Robbie a playful poke.

Robbie pulled a face. 'Aw. Are you sure?'

'Aye that's right enough,' Flora agreed, 'and don't be forgetting the shoes and all the accessories now.'

'Come on, Robbie, I'll show ye up to ye're room,' Alastair said, picking up one of the bags and leading the way, 'else these two will hae spent all your money afore the holiday's even begun!'

Alastair unlocked the door and pushed it open for Robbie to go in ahead of him.

'Wow, a room with a view,' Robbie said, looking through the large picture window onto the lovely Ochil

Hills that offered some shelter in winter from the north and east winds. 'I'd forgotten how beautiful the hills are, and yet nothing has changed... they look just the same as always.'

Alastair nodded. 'Timeless. We knew it had to be this room for your visit.'

'Anna will love it,' Robbie said, looking around the spacious room which was welcoming but understated. Alastair and Flora did not go in for glamorous, ultra-modern décor and swish furnishings but preferred clean, wholesome and functional.

'Course, we cannae compete wi' the Matterhorn and we've no edelweiss on the terrace but it's no easy to beat the Ochils when the bonnie heather blooms at their feet!'

After dinner and a brief catch up with Alastair and Flora, Anna and Robbie left their hosts attending to fellow guests residing at the six-room guesthouse and went out for a walk. Breathing the pure, cool air helped them to shake off their travel weariness. Strolling hand in hand down the quiet street, they found a gift shop still open and went inside to have a look round and stayed for a coffee.

'Are you always open as late as this?' Anna asked.

'Sometimes,' the lady proprietor replied, 'depending, aye...'

Anna wondered 'depending, aye' on what, but did not ask.

'And such a lovely evening,' the woman said, clearing away their cups as if hinting that staying open late did not mean all night.

Close by, presiding over the town and visible against the skyline for miles around, was Stirling Castle, where Robbie planned to take Anna during their stay. He was excited about visiting his old haunts again and pointed out the castle to Anna.

'There she sits, the pride of Stirling. I can't wait to take you there and to the Wallace Monument—'

'Brigadoon!' Anna cut in, 'Robert the Bruce and bagpipes!'

Robbie laughed at Anna's memories of the show they had seen in London. 'Yes... wow, all that seems a long time ago now! You were quite impressed with that weren't you?'

Anna smiled, linking arms with Robbie. 'Yes, I was, but...' she looked around her at the breathtaking scenery, the castle taking centre stage. '... I had no idea how stunning it would be in reality!'

'No, you really have to experience it to appreciate its full glory.'

They were lucky with the weather and although in midsummer the nights barely turned darker than twilight, they could also be chilly. Although Robbie was anxious to take Anna to Stirling Castle, they decided to go to Callander the next day to buy that sweater that Robbie had spoken of. There were so many to choose from in the Woollen Mill, but she decided on a colourful design and Robbie also bought her a Cameron Tartan scarf. She joked that she would have to keep them both out of Evie's clutches.

Callander was a small town in Stirling, a popular tourist stop to and from the Highlands, on the River Teith and located in the historic county of Perthshire.

Anna bought Robbie a wallet from a gift shop and then they moved on to look at ladies' fashions as Anna also wanted to buy a dress to do justice to the party that Flora was organising for them.

She emerged from the fitting room in a dark red, three-quarter length, full-skirted dress with a tight fitting bodice embroidered with tiny, mauve, thistle emblems.

'Well?'

'Anna, you look gorgeous in all of them.'

'Well, I cannot buy them all. Do you have a preference?'

'It's hard to choose...'

'Oh, you men are hopeless!' She looked at the assistant who was standing aside patiently, offering assistance if asked but otherwise remaining neutral.

'What do you think?' she asked her.

The assistant stepped forward.

'May I ask... it seems to be for a special occasion?' she asked.

'Yes,' Anna and Robbie answered in unison.

'Our engagement party,' Anna added.

'Oh, I see; so it's very special.' Taking a full length garment from the half dozen now adorning the fitting room area, the assistant draped the gown across her arm, extending it towards Anna. Made from royal blue silk, its movement caught the light.

'Perhaps Madam would like to try the silk?'

Anna had fallen in love with this one the moment she saw it but had not tried it on as the price tag was, she considered, a little excessive. However, she allowed the assistant to help her into the full length, off the shoulder, loosely pleated sheath with a flare at the ankle to aid walking. Zipped in and feeling like a celebrity in such a fabulous creation, Anna emerged from the fitting room for Robbie's response.

The sight of her took his breath away.

'Anna, you look absolutely stunning,' he breathed.

'I feel like a million dollars,' she replied with a smile, stroking the soft, rich fabric, 'but it is really more than we planned to pay.'

'If I may be so bold, Madam, with your blue eyes and hair colouring, it could have been made for you.' She paused for a moment and then excused herself to go to the counter, where she appeared to be writing on a pad. She then opened a drawer and took out a fine cashmere stole of pale turquoise with a royal blue fringe and returned to the fitting room.

'If it will help, I can offer you a ten percent discount on the gown—it is, after all, approaching the end of the season.' She held out the stole for Anna to look at. 'And if that is of interest to you, please also accept the stole with our compliments.'

It was still more than Anna had bargained for, but the dress was exquisite and the stole added the perfect finishing touch. She found herself unable to resist and left the shop with a feeling of walking on air.

They rounded off their trip to Callander with a meal. Robbie went for his favourite Haggis while Anna, wrinkling her nose slightly at the smell and sight of it, played safe with poached salmon and a side salad.

The next day dawned sunny and promised to be warm and Anna and Robbie set off for their visit to Stirling Castle. Robbie's rucksack was half filled with freshly made sandwiches cut from home baked bread, together with generous slices of rich fruit cake and a flask each of tea and coffee.

'Just a snack in case ye feel a wee bit peckish,' Flora explained.

Robbie thanked her, grateful for her generosity and thinking to himself that if she called this a snack, it was no wonder she was overweight.

Dominating the skyline for miles around, Stirling Castle was an outstanding example of Renaissance architecture. At the heart of the old town of Stirling, the medieval castle sat on a craggy volcanic rock. Visitors could look out from its high stone walls to the battlefields of Stirling Bridge where the great medieval armies clashed to decide the fate of nations. Home to generations of Scottish monarchs, including Mary Queen of Scots, the Castle was and is today, an enduring and powerful reminder of Scotland's colourful and fascinating history.

The couple spent the morning looking around the castle. Anna enjoyed hearing about the history of the place and its surroundings and for Robbie it was a nostalgic journey down memory lane. They found a low wall away from the main visitor attractions where they could eat their 'wee snack' in relative peace. Robbie thought how attractive Anna looked in her aqua blue sweatshirt and short black skirt; her hair was loose and free, just how he liked it. He thought himself blessed.

A short bus ride away, on the Abbey Craig outcrop was the National Wallace Monument, a 19th-century tower. It overlooked the site of the 1297 Battle of Stirling Bridge, where William Wallace defeated the English. Unfortunately, as with the Trevi Fountain in Rome, the monument was undergoing restoration so they were unable to appreciate its full significance. The Battle of Bannockburn Experience had interactive 3D displays on the history of the 1314 conflict. Robbie had told Anna about the Battle of Stirling Bridge and it was quite an experience for her to actually visit the site.

They eventually made their way back to the car and finished off the last of Flora's tea—not so fresh now, and no longer hot, but warm and wet at least.

'Robbie, this has been a wonderful day,' Anna said, taking his hand. 'I have loved every minute of it—thank you so much for bringing me to see your homeland.'

Robbie kissed her cheek. 'I have one – well, two more places to show you, actually, before we go back to the guesthouse.'

They drove a short distance before he stopped the car near a stone wall, behind which was a stone-built primary school. They left the car and walked towards it for a closer look. Robbie thought it looked pretty much the same as he remembered it when he had briefly attended the infants' class before they moved to England. The high arched windows and heavy green doors seemed to call to him across the playground, 'Quickly now… laddies in one line; lassies in the other…' and he heard the old school bell in his head, signalling the end of playtime.

'Wow!' Anna exclaimed. 'It looks like time has stood still.'

'It has,' Robbie replied. 'Nothing has changed! Except perhaps the toilet block has been modernised.' He pointed to a low stone building, *Boys* painted on one red door, *Girls* on the other. 'It used to be an old shack. Thank heaven for modern sanitation uh?'

'And the second place?' Anna questioned as she waited for the car door to be unlocked.

'We won't need the car.' Robbie took her arm and gestured ahead. They walked for about a hundred yards and turned a corner. There, built from the same Stirling stone, was a row of small identical cottages; two upstairs windows and two downstairs, beneath grey slate roofs.

'Ours was the second from the end,' Robbie said. 'They have been modernised as well, but they don't look that different from when I was a boy!'

'What a charming little place,' Anna said as they walked back to the car.

'Aye,' Robbie agreed, 'we could have done a lot worse, that's for sure!'

The following day had been earmarked by Flora and Alastair for the engagement party. All the guests currently staying at the guesthouse had been invited and Flora, who knew most people in the village and surrounding area, from business owners and their staff to local parish councillors and school teachers, had also invited an eclectic mix of people, some older, some younger and most in between, to ensure the celebrations went well.

When lunch was over, Flora and her staff turned the guesthouse kitchen into a mini food factory and by late afternoon the dining room tables and chairs had been rearranged to form a ballroom with a buffet and bar area at one end and chairs lining the walls. A small make-do stage to accommodate a local DJ had been erected in one corner beneath a large '*CONGRATULATIONS*' banner and several heart-shaped balloons bobbed from the ceiling.

Guests began arriving from seven-thirty p.m. and although they felt it a great honour, both Robbie and Anna felt nervous at the prospect of meeting a roomful of strangers.

'It feels somehow surreal,' Robbie commented, already feeling uncomfortable in his smart trousers and missing his regulation jeans.

'Yes, I know what you mean,' Anna agreed, fixing her jet earrings to match the necklace around her throat, 'but such a kind gesture and completely out of our hands.'

'And if I know Alastair and Flora, a night to remember.' Robbie looked at his fiancée with love and pride. 'You look absolutely fabulous,' he told her.

'Thank you, kind sir,' she replied with a smile and slight bow of her head. 'You may take me to the ball!'

A hush fell over the room as the couple entered, accompanied by Alastair, and all eyes were on Anna who looked like a movie star. Robbie felt his heart would burst.

Alastair, who had decided to give his kilt an airing for the occasion, cleared his throat. 'First of all,' he began, 'I would like to introduce ye to a childhood friend of mine who lived right here in Bridge of Allan when we were schoolboys together – aye, a few years back now, but some of you will already know of him – and also his charming young lady from Basel in Switzerland. Please welcome Robbie and his fiancée, Anna, and enjoy this occasion in their honour, to celebrate their recent engagement.' He paused as the young couple were politely applauded and then nodded towards the DJ.

'Andrew here will keep ye entertained with whatever music ye want him to play—just remember it's an engagement party and no a wake! Ma wife, Flora, has provided enough food to feed a regiment and there's even room to do the Highland Fling if the fancy takes ye!'

As the celebrations commenced, Robbie explained to Anna what the Highland Fling was and said no, he was definitely not going to give a demonstration.

'Besides,' he added, 'it should be danced wearing a kilt.'

Anna looked a little crestfallen but didn't pursue it. Then Robbie remembered a detail from Brigadoon that had really interested her. Hm, he thought, and slipped out to have a quiet word with Alastair.

Andrew did a fine job, mixing a few requests in with some modern hits of the time and also threw in a few traditional Scottish ballads to pay homage to his country. The food disappeared, the ale and whisky flowed and dance steps were seen that hadn't been performed in years, as well as some that would have been better not even attempted.

Around eleven p.m., a few people were beginning to make a move and Alastair made another announcement.

'I know that some of ye have work tae go to in the morning,' he said, 'and I fully understand if ye need tae be leaving soon, but if I could just ask ye all tae bear wi' me for just a few more wee minutes, while we sing Auld Lang Syne? Och, and any of ye who want to stay on for a wee while longer afterwards are most welcome.'

Anna glanced around the room, unsure of what was happening as people began crossing arms and holding hands.

'It's traditional,' Robbie whispered, 'more usually at Hogmanay, but at any time, really… don't worry about singing the words, just listen.'

Then, perfectly on cue, a lone piper was heard, the distinctive, haunting sound increasing as he approached the room and then stopped in the doorway, playing the original folk song tune set to Robbie Burns's poem of 1788, while the gathered guests sang the lyrics of Auld Lang Syne.

Anna was surprised, delighted and a little overcome by this unexpected rendition on the bagpipes, especially to see it all taking place live in front of her very eyes and not on a cinema screen as it had the first time.

She stood, transfixed, as the piper retreated.

'Are you all right?' Robbie asked her.

'Yes, I am fine,' she answered, 'just blown away by it all. Wow! That was so special! What a night!'

'A night to remember,' Robbie said. He squeezed her hand and gave her a sexy wink. 'And it's no over yet, hen...'

One more thing that Robbie had planned to do during this visit to his old town was to visit Pitlochry. It was the salmon spawning or breeding season and he was keen to go and watch the fish travelling upstream to lay their eggs on the gravel beds. However, he was not sure whether it was something Anna would fancy doing on her last day here. And this morning it was raining.

'Why not?' she asked when Robbie broached the subject at breakfast. 'It is not harmful surely... it is a natural phenomenon. And the fish jump, don't they? I would love to go and watch them.'

So they took the little red Uno on her last trip before the airport run, to the Pitlochry Fish Ladder that allowed the salmon to travel upstream and made the whole process much easier for them.

Robbie had not seen the fish ladder before but had previously watched the salmon jumping against the current, using the power of the weirs and waves to help them spring high above them, covering each layer until they reached the spawning beds. His scientific mind was fascinated by the natural instincts in force that prompted this behaviour and also that the flesh of the salmon turned red after spawning and then the fish died, thus making way for the next generations that would continue to travel upstream to spawn, untaught and aided by a ladder or not.

They spent some time watching the salmon before taking a walk around the immediate area.

'It is a very beautiful place,' Anna observed, 'even in the rain. 'You could just sit and look at the scenery and never be bored with it.'

'Right,' Robbie replied, as they rested for a few minutes on a stone wall near a wooded area. The fine rain was now easing off and the clouds were beginning to disperse.

'Stirling and its surrounding area is one of my most favourite places on earth and that is why I wanted you to see it too.' He pointed to a low, stone building with red doors, not far from where they were sitting.

'That is the Blair Athol Distillery that produces Blair Athol single malt whisky. It is aged for twelve years; they use it in Bell's whisky. My dad drinks Bell's sometimes if he can't get his Famous Grouse.'

Anna smiled with fond thoughts of Mike. 'He would like to be here now… a stone's throw away!'

'Oh, he has been inside the distillery many times,' Robbie told her. 'Some of his old chums used to work there!'

'And provided him with a few samples, I imagine,' Anna said, still smiling.

'Aye, there would always have been a wee dram or two waiting to be tested, it's true!'

Robbie stood up and helped Anna to her feet.

She brushed her skirt down and smoothed the damp creases.

'I hope the salmon ladder wasn't too boring for you,' he said. 'Thanks for coming with me to watch.'

'It was interesting,' she replied. I have enjoyed it and the scenery is so beautiful, I would not have missed any of it.'

'I am glad.' He kissed her and, taking her hand, led her safely across the stony pathway and back to where he had parked the car.

'So now we have to go and pack our bags and tomorrow we will leave behind your homeland and return to mine,' Anna said on reaching the car.

'Yes—and both are equally beautiful... don't you think so?'

'I do, yes, and I hope we will come to Stirling again – it already feels like my second home!'

When they arrived back at the guesthouse, Flora was busily preparing the casserole she was planning for the guests' main course that evening.

'Can we help?' Anna asked.

'Och, I'll no hear of it,' Flora replied, indicating her helpers who were cleaning and chopping a vast array of fresh vegetables. 'The lassies'll manage fine. Why don't ye take ye're tea oot on the terrace and have a few more minutes wi' the hills? I've made some traditional ginger nuts, she winked, 'wi' just a wee drezzle o' whisky tae bring oot the flavour!'

It was peaceful in the garden with the hills providing the magical backdrop – magical in that they were constantly changing – some days carrying a purple haze; other times shrouded in mist. They could be mean and moody, especially in the harshness of winter and they were also warm and welcoming. At all times and in all seasons, they were solid and dependable.

As Robbie sipped his tea, reflecting on past memories and the pleasures of this latest visit, Anna, beside him, suddenly cried out in pain.

He put his cup down and turned to her. 'What is it, my love? What's happened?'

Anna's hand was clamped firmly across her mouth, her brow furrowed and her eyes half closed. She manoeuvred her tongue around her mouth and, using a tissue, deposited a large, broken filling into it.

'Oh, my God! That has left such a huge cavity and it feels so sharp,' she spluttered, again holding her mouth.

'Is it hurting?' Robbie asked, recalling his own experience in Salzburg.

Anna nodded.

'I will go and ask Flora for a painkiller; that might help.'

The pain did ease a little and it was fortunate that Flora's casserole virtually melted in the mouth and so did not need much chewing at dinner later. Brushing her teeth before bed, Anna was especially careful, treating the area very gently, not wanting to start the nerve throbbing again.

'I hope you are able to get some sleep,' Robbie said as they settled down for their last night in Stirling. He kissed her goodnight. 'Wake me if you need to.'

'I will be all right,' Anna answered, knowing that she would need to make an emergency dental appointment as soon as she was back home in Basel.

Chapter 18

It was mid-afternoon when Anna and Robbie arrived home. It had turned noticeably cooler in Switzerland and Anna smiled to herself at the thought of snuggling into her Fair Isle sweater, so lovingly made by the craftspeople of Scotland. Her smile quickly turned to a frown of puzzlement as she struggled to unlock the door.

Robbie, right behind her with the suitcases, asked her what was wrong?

'This lock, Robbie… it seems very stiff, I can't…'

Robbie put the cases down. 'Let me have a look? Perhaps it just needs oiling.' He took the key from Anna and encountered a similar problem but using considerable force, managed to unlock the door. He noticed some scratch marks all around the lock.

'I think somebody has tried to force entry with the wrong key,' he said, 'and it has damaged the mechanism.'

'But who would do that?' Anna asked. 'Evie and Marcel both have keys for the new lock you fitted.' She shook her head. 'I think you were right first time – it needs some oil.'

For some reason, Robbie thought of Kristina. He found himself glancing up and down the street, half expecting to see her tall form observing them from a shop doorway. He pushed his suspicions to the back of his mind. She would still be at work; he was being paranoid now.

'I expect you are right,' he replied. 'I'll just have a word with Marcel when he gets home, in case there has been a problem with the keys.'

Tomorrow being Saturday, Anna was not sure whether she could get an emergency dental appointment, especially at such short notice, but she rang the dentist soon after arriving home and, as she was in pain, was given an early afternoon appointment.

'Is Evie going with you?' Robbie asked.

Anna shook her head. 'I will be fine, darling. It's only a filling!'

'You are sure you will be okay to go on your own?' Robbie asked. 'Or shall I cancel the match and come with you? You know you react to the anaesthetic sometimes.'

She kissed his cheek. 'I shall be fine. You go to the football with Marcel as planned. I shall rest when I get home and I expect Evie will be here anyway.'

'I am sure Evie would go with you—'

'Robbie,' she cut him off, 'I do not need anybody with me to have a tooth filled! And anyway, I think Evie is working today until lunchtime.'

'Okay, I just thought...'

'No. End of story. Now let's get unpacked.'

The two unpacked and Robbie loaded the washing machine while Anna went to see what was in the fridge and had a pleasant surprise to find it well stocked.

'My God,' she said, 'they have been shopping... there is food in the house!'

Robbie grinned. 'That's unusual, uh?'

'It is what you Brits call a *bloody miracle*!' Anna laughed.

They shared an affectionate hug, happy to be home again after their lovely stay in Scotland that had turned out to be rather a special holiday.

When Marcel came in from work he and Robbie shared a man hug, genuinely pleased to see each other again.

'So did you two have a good time?' Marcel asked. 'And was it raining all the time?'

'No,' Anna replied. 'In fact it rained very little; the weather was perfect.'

'We didn't need a molly, or even a trolley,' Robbie teased, ducking to avoid Anna's sharp left hook.

Marcel shrugged, not understanding the joke.

Thinking of more serious matters, Robbie asked if Marcel had been having any trouble with the door lock.

'Ah, *oui*, the door, Marcel nodded. 'It has been very stiff, you know? Once we thought we were locked out but eventually we managed to turn the key. I put some oil in the lock, which helped a bit, but it is still, you know, a bit tricky.'

'Yes, we noticed it straight away,' Robbie replied. 'It was fine when we left. I believe someone has been trying to force the lock using the wrong key. That's what happens – and sometimes it can jam the works up altogether.'

Marcel looked puzzled.

'Make it seize up?' Robbie explained.

Marcel nodded. 'Ah, *oui*. It is seizing up, for sure.'

'Marcel, have you noticed a strange woman hanging around here lately?'

He shrugged. 'Strange? How you mean strange?'

'Well, I mean behaving strangely, really. You know Kristina, who works with me—'

'No, I do not know the lady, only what you have told me about her. She is trouble, yeah?'

'So you haven't noticed a tall, attractive blonde hanging around the area?'

'No, my friend, you think I would not notice an attractive blonde, uh?'

'A *very* tall attractive blonde,' Anna added.

Their line of enquiry was getting them nowhere and Anna said she would get in touch with Martina later to see if either she or Fritz had anything to report.

When she came home from work, Evelyn greeted her sister and Robbie as if they had been away for a year instead of a week and was keen to hear all about their holiday in Stirling.

When asked if she had seen Kristina hanging around, she said no but she had seen her in the town a couple of times going into the cake shop.

'Well, she is always going to the cake shop,' Robbie said, 'so I don't think we can read anything into that.'

After a dinner of steak and fries with salad, followed by strudel, Anna left her companions with their coffee and went to phone her friend, Martina. They chatted for a few minutes about the holiday, there was apparently nothing unusual to report on Kristina, and Fritz had seen nothing to raise his suspicions either. Kurt had said she had been at work every day on time and also left as normal.

They arranged to meet for lunch during the coming week and Martina wished her friend luck at the dentists in the morning.

'Bis bald!' (see you soon) they said and rang off.

'So our friend Kristina has apparently been keeping a low profile according to Martina,' Anna said, joining the others for coffee.

'Let's hope she has found someone else to fix her attentions on,' Robbie said and with a passion added, 'and I wish them luck!'

'See you boys later!' Anna called as Marcel and Robbie set off for the Basel football Stadium where Basel were playing a Europa Cup match against Middlesbrough FC that afternoon. 'May the best team win!'

'Basel, of course!' Marcel said.

'Middlesbrough!' Robbie countered. 'They are in good form.'

'Huh, you think so? No chance, *mon ami*. Good luck at the dentist's, *cherie*,' said Marcel blowing a kiss to Anna.

Half an hour later, Evelyn arrived home from work just as Anna was leaving the apartment for her appointment.

'Good luck!' said Evelyn. 'I'll be here if you need me!'

'Thanks – I'm sure I'll be fine.'

As Anna crossed the street she was unaware that she was being followed, the only thing on her mind being relief from the pain that had troubled her since biting into one of Flora's ginger biscuits. She had no fear of the dentist but was known to sometimes react badly to the local anaesthetic and if that happened, she would phone Evelyn if she felt unwell afterwards.

The treatment went according to plan and Anna paid the bill at the desk.

'Are you okay?' the receptionist asked. 'You look rather faint.'

'Yes, I am a bit,' Anna admitted, but being aware that the dentist and his nurse were waiting to go home and get on with their weekend, she said she would be fine, and made her way to the exit.

'I will phone my sister,' she said. 'She will come and make sure I am okay.'

The nurse kindly phoned Evelyn, who said she would come straight away and meanwhile, Anna sat down to wait for her on the steps outside. It was quiet for a Saturday afternoon but that was probably a lot to do with the football match which, being a semi-final, was also being televised. The only person in sight was a man in a long raincoat, wearing a trilby hat. His collar was pulled up. He walked with a stoop, wore dark glasses and carried a white stick and yet, although having the appearance of being blind or partially sighted, strangely seemed to be searching the ground for something. Some building work was in progress quite near to the dental surgery and Anna thought he must be looking for scrap but she felt too groggy to give much thought to him at that moment.

Suddenly the man found what he was looking for, quickly picked it up, tucked it under his arm and disappeared up an alleyway three doors away from the dentist's.

Anna then spotted Evelyn in the distance, driving Marcel's distinctive pale blue Renault and breathed a sigh of relief; all she wanted to do was get home and lie down.

While Evelyn was stopped at the lights, the man emerged from the alleyway, looked around and, still clutching the object under his arm, approached Anna, now half lying across the steps. He swung the object at her head, making full contact and drawing blood. Anna cried out in pain and shock. Again he smashed the heavy length of jagged lead piping into Anna's skull, the violence of his second blow causing his dark glasses to slip to the ground. Blood splashed from the gaping wound in Anna's skull onto the steps and the man's raincoat. Evelyn, still held up at the traffic lights further up the street, witnessed the horror of the whole incident and without waiting for the lights to change and risking a collision, accelerated down the road, dodging the oncoming traffic to get to Anna. She saw the man running away and he vanished back up the alleyway but Evelyn had no idea where it led to. Her main concern was her sister and she left the car with the door open and the engine still running and rushed to her sister's aid, deaf to the cacophony of horns blasting from nearby traffic, now in chaos as the lights changed again.

Detecting a faint pulse, Evelyn was relieved that Anna was at least still alive, having feared the worst.

A passer-by, who had witnessed the man running off, immediately telephoned for both an ambulance and the police. Flashing blue lights and blaring sirens were quickly at the scene as both emergency services arrived simultaneously. Evelyn went with Anna in the ambulance, while the police sealed the area and requested that nobody leave without their permission. The length of lead pipe and the dark glasses were placed in sterile plastic bags while the forensics team carried out their usual thorough search, taking samples of the blood and photographing anything that could be relevant to the attack.

'Interesting footprint here,' one of the officers observed, pointing out a pattern left by a bloodied sole. 'And again here. Our witness said the man ran off in that direction,' he waved towards the alleyway, 'but did not actually see where he went.'

'Up the alleyway would be my guess,' his colleague replied. 'Description?'

'Tall, wearing a raincoat with the collar pulled up and a trilby hat. Dark glasses and white stick, obviously intended to give the impression he was blind or partially sighted.'

Robbie and Marcel were caught up in the throng leaving the football stadium. Robbie was elated, his team having beaten the Swiss giants in the closing minutes of the match with a spectacular goal by the Dutch player, 'Bolo' Zenden. Marcel was disgusted with Basel's performance.

'Man, they missed so many chances,' he complained, tossing his programme in the bin. 'They played like dummies… and in front of millions of television viewers!' He shook his head and groaned in despair.

Robbie grinned, recalling the moment when he had seen an image of himself and Marcel in the crowd flash up on one of the TV monitors. He wondered if his dad had seen that – he knew he would have been watching the match on TV at home if at all possible.

'Hah, they are no match for Middlesbrough. So many people underestimate them, but at their best they are a force to be reckoned with!'

'They certainly were today,' Marcel agreed. 'Let's go for a beer if we ever get out of here?'

'Best suggestion I have heard all day,' Robbie replied. 'Thirsty work, all that shouting!'

'Yeah, man, especially for nothing, uh?'

Robbie slid a comforting arm around his friend's shoulder, fully understanding his despondency at his team losing the semi-final of a trophy game.

'I wonder how Anna got on at the dentist's?'

'She will be fine,' Marcel assured him. 'I told Evie to use my car to take her home if necessary.'

Eventually they reached the exit gates and made their way to a bar a short distance away.

'I'll just go and phone to see how Anna is,' Robbie said and headed for the public telephone, leaving Marcel to get the drinks in.

When the phone just kept ringing out and no one answered, Robbie did not know what to think. Maybe he had misdialled. He tried again, but apparently there was nobody home.

'Girls!' Marcel said when Robbie told him. 'They will have gone shopping for the shoes and the handbags, uh? Come on, drink up, she will be fine.'

They had another drink and Robbie tried phoning once more. By now it was getting late to be out shopping and he was concerned that something had gone wrong.

'We should go straight home,' he told Marcel. 'I don't like it – they should be home by now.'

Marcel shrugged. 'Okay. But I am sure they are fine – probably on their way home, too.'

Outside the dental practice, Marcel's car had been moved to the side of the road and two forensic officers were examining both the interior and exterior of the Renault and dusting for fingerprints. A few yards away, a Detective Chief Inspector was questioning Anders Kleibel, the man who had witnessed Anna's attacker running away.

Where were you when you saw him, sir?'

'I just came around the corner there,' he pointed to his right, 'and saw a man get up and run off towards the alleyway just past the dentist's.'

'So you did not witness the actual attack?'

'No, but he obviously did it. No one else was near at the time.'

'You say the man got up? Was he on the ground?'

'No, he was bending over the young lady and as soon as he saw me coming, he ran.'

The detective nodded. 'Towards the alley? Did you actually see him enter the alleyway?'

'Towards the alley, yes,' Anders replied, 'er, but no, sorry, I did not actually see him go into the alley; I was more concerned about ringing for assistance.'

'Yes, of course—and quite rightly,' Chief Inspector Goehner replied. 'Walter, get up there will you and see if there's anything relevant—any more footprints or blood stains.'

'Yes, sir,' his sergeant replied.

'And make some enquiries. Somebody must have seen this character.' He turned back to his witness.

'Where were you coming from, sir?'

'I had been to the bookshop.' Anders held up a small carrier bag, indicating his recent purchase.

'May I?' The inspector took the bag, removed the book, examined the inside of the bag, made sure there was nothing hidden within the book's pages, and handed it back to the man. 'Thank you. And where were you going, sir?'

'To get a tram to go and visit my friend. It is his birthday—that is who I bought the book for.'

'I see. Thank you.' Goehner called an officer over. 'Well, if you would be good enough to give your friend's name and address to my officer here, and your own full contact details—'

'Am I a suspect then?'

'Mr Kleibel, a vicious and unprovoked attack has been made on a defenceless young lady. I am treating it as

269

attempted murder and everybody is a suspect at this moment. But you may go, for now.'

At the hospital, Anna's condition was critical. She was still unconscious and on life support following emergency surgery to stop the bleeding from the brain.

'It can go either way,' the doctor told Evelyn. 'I am very sorry to have to be blunt, but you should prepare yourself for the worst. She is very lucky to have survived at all and we are doing everything possible. However, we cannot assess the scale of any brain damage until she regains consciousness.'

Evelyn herself was in shock, having witnessed the attack from a distance. Highly strung and emotional at the best of times, interviewing her was not easy but the police had decided it should be done as soon as possible while the details were fresh in her mind. She told the detective that the man was wearing a long raincoat and hat. 'He also carried a white stick,' she added, but he clearly was not blind or even partially blind from the way he legged it up the alleyway.'

'How far away from the scene were you?'

'Oh… um, a hundred metres? Maybe a hundred and fifty… I was stopped at the lights just up the road.'

Evelyn's description of Anna's assailant matched that of the passing witness and it seemed that the man did indeed run off up the alleyway.

'So you had come to pick up your sister after emergency dental treatment?'

270

'Yes. The nurse telephoned to tell me that Anna was not feeling well—she sometimes reacts badly to the novocaine injection.'

'And why was she left sitting outside on the steps in such a condition? Don't you find that strange? That a dentist should leave his patient sitting on his doorstep, feeling unwell and unattended?'

Evelyn replied that she thought Anna would have needed some fresh air and also would not have wanted to inconvenience the dentist or his nurse any longer as it was a Saturday afternoon.

'And it was only a filling… my sister is not one to make a fuss; she knew I would be there within minutes.'

'I see. Nevertheless, you would agree that your sister was in a somewhat vulnerable situation?'

The inspector was still questioning Evelyn when Robbie and Marcel reached the hospital. A policeman had been waiting at their flat to give them the news that Anna had been attacked outside the dentist's and was seriously ill in hospital.

'My God!' Robbie exclaimed, clutching his chest as his heart lurched. 'I knew something was wrong when they did not answer the phone.' Distraught, he asked, 'Can I see her? She is my fiancée.'

A policeman on guard at the doorway raised his eyebrows questioningly to the doctor treating Anna.

'Fiancée?' she asked. 'Yes, you may sit with her. She is unconscious. But your presence will do no harm; it may help her if you are with her.'

Robbie thanked the doctor and sat on the cold grey plastic chair by Anna's bedside.

Marcel waited outside in the corridor, wondering where Evelyn was.

'Her ring!' Robbie suddenly said. 'Her engagement ring is missing!'

Anna loved the ring that had been especially made for her and had taken great pride in wearing it. Now her ring finger was naked.

The policeman stepped forward. 'You say her ring is missing? Might she have taken it off for any reason, do you think?'

Robbie shook his head. 'Absolutely not! She never took it off.'

'Can you describe the ring, sir?'

Robbie told the officer that the white gold ring had been custom made at Meister, describing in detail the diamonds surrounded by tiny crafted rose petals.

'Like all Meister jewellery, it is unique,' Robbie explained. 'Instantly recognisable.'

'So the motive could have been robbery,' the policeman murmured, more to himself than anyone else.

The tall detective inspector stood with her back to the window in the small waiting room just down the corridor from the intensive therapy suite where Anna was being treated. Her arms were folded in an aggressive manner as she continued to question Anna's sister.

'You were called by the dental nurse at what time?' she asked Evelyn.

272

'I told you, just after two o'clock,' Evelyn replied.

'How much after? Five minutes? Ten?'

'I do not know for sure—I think ten past, no later than that.'

'And you left straight away to go and collect your sister?'

'Yes.'

'How long did it take you to get there?'

Evelyn screwed up her face; her eyebrows twitching with tension. She sighed. 'I don't know, a few minutes— what is this? Why are you asking me all these questions? I have already told you all I know!'

'They are just routine,' the DI replied calmly. 'A serious crime has taken place and these questions have to be asked. I am sorry; I understand it is very distressing for you.'

'Can I see Anna now?'

'All in good time. Just a few more questions.'

Evelyn was eventually released from her ordeal and asked a doctor if she could spend some time with Anna.

'It would be nice for your sister to have someone at her bedside,' the doctor agreed. 'The police have taken her fiancé and the other young man in for questioning.'

Evelyn's eyes widened; her jaw dropped. She was horrified. 'Taken them in? To the police station, do you mean? But they would not… listen, they had nothing to do with it – they have been at a football match all afternoon!'

The doctor smiled sympathetically. 'Apparently they are having difficulty proving it!'

The interview room at the police station contained two basic tables and four chairs, all of which were bolted to the floor, and a recording device that slotted into a specially made recess. These were standard measures, taken to minimise violent attacks by suspects under interrogation. A clock was fixed high above the heavy duty door. The room, obviously reserved for interviewing suspects involved in serious crime, was windowless and Robbie felt like a convicted criminal as he sat fielding a barrage of questions from a rather arrogant French detective sergeant. Marcel was in a holding room with a police constable, awaiting his turn to be interrogated.

Robbie was angry. So much precious time was being wasted. The girl he loved was on a life support machine and it hurt him beyond words to think that anyone could carry out such a vicious attack on her. He should be at her bedside and here he was, with the Third Reich, being practically accused of trying to murder her. He also felt guilty that he had been at a football match enjoying the game with Marcel while his beloved Anna was being subjected to this vicious attack and was now fighting for her life.

I should have insisted on going with her, he thought, blaming himself.

'So,' the sergeant said, 'you were watching a football match with a few thousand other spectators and the only one who can vouch for you is the person you went with... your buddy? You do not even have a programme of the match and you admit you spoke to no one who would be likely to recognise you again. Not very convincing is it, *M'sieur Anglais*?'

'But what about CCTV?' Robbie asked, irritated at being addressed in such a manner. 'Surely that will have recorded everyone who entered the ground? And by the way, I do have a name!'

'We already have an officer checking that, *sir*, but so far it is not looking—'

'Wait a minute!' Robbie interrupted his interrogator who gave him a look of contempt.

'Well?'

'Sorry, but I've just remembered – Marcel and I were shown briefly on the TV monitor when the cameras panned the crowd during the match. I remember hoping my dad was watching at home in London and might have seen me.'

The detective's lip curled. 'Is that so?'

'I have just said so.'

The detective picked up the phone. 'Schmidt, get on to SRF,' he ordered. I want a complete tape of this afternoon's big match.'

There was a pause while Schmidt answered his boss.

'That, Schmidt, is your problem. Just get it here,' he growled, and slammed the receiver down. He nodded to the duty officer present in the interview room. 'Take this one back to the cells. We may as well have a go at his accomplice while we are waiting.'

'Acc... accomplice?' Robbie could not believe what he was hearing. This surely was a bad dream? He would

275

wake up in a minute, with Anna safe and well in his arms…

Marcel's account of the afternoon fitted exactly with what Robbie had already told the police. The videotape from the television company did indeed show that both were at the match and their alibis were confirmed. The police had no option but to release them and were left none the wiser and thus no nearer to finding Anna's attacker.

Chapter 19

Robbie was given a few days compassionate leave to visit Anna. It wounded him deeply to see her lying there hooked up to tubes and drips. Her eyes remained closed, her skin was pale and bandages took the place of her beautiful, let's-go-fly highlighted curls. He constantly asked himself the same questions... Who? Why? How could anyone do this to his lovely, vivacious Anna who loved life more than life itself? The only sign right now that she was still alive came from the monitor nearby that beeped constantly as it detected and reported the performance of her vital organs. Over the following few days, Robbie spent most of his time at her bedside, holding her hand, sometimes talking to her softly, and occasionally dozing. At times a nurse would persuade him to have a short break and he returned home to take a shower, have a meal and sleep for an hour or two.

Meanwhile, the police continued with their enquiries. Robbie kept in touch with his friend Kurt, hoping that there may be some news from Fritz. He drove to the company gates one afternoon on his way home from the hospital and asked him about Kristina's movements because he still suspected her of being involved in some way.

'She comes to work; she goes home at the end of the day. She is just the same as usual,' Kurt replied.

'And has Fritz been keeping an eye on her? Has he heard anything?'

'Fritz cannot talk too much about the case,' Kurt replied, 'but it is no secret that Kristina has been questioned like the rest of us and let go.'

'The rest of... what, you as well?' Robbie was surprised that all his work colleagues were being interrogated.

'Certainly me as well – in fact everybody here who has a link with you,' Kurt said. 'Even the professor—'

Robbie cut him off, astounded. 'Not the professor?'

'In this country, my friend, no stone is left unturned to find the guilty party when a vicious criminal act is being investigated.' He paused. 'There are many motives for trying to kill someone and it is not always the victim who is intended to suffer... Fritz did tell me that once.'

'Kurt, are you suggesting that someone could be getting at me?'

'Not necessarily, but the police have to consider every possibility.'

'Well, has Kristina been acting strangely, or looking suspicious?'

'As I said, the same as ever. Look, Robbie, leave it to the police; they are working flat out on this case. They will get their man,' Kurt reassured him.

'Or woman,' Robbie muttered as he shook hands with Kurt and thanked him.

'Robbie!' Evelyn ran to the door to meet him as he entered the flat. 'The hospital has just phoned. There has been a change and they ask if you will go back straight away?'

'A change?' Robbie made a grab for the doorpost to steady himself, feeling as if the ground was moving beneath him.

'A change for better or worse?'

'I did ask; they would not say, even though I am her sister.' Evelyn's voice broke with emotion.

'Was it the doctor?' Robbie asked.

'No, the ITU nurse.'

Robbie gently touched Evelyn's arm. 'Could you tell from her tone of voice?'

Evelyn, sniffling, took a tissue from her pocket. 'No. You know how buttoned up they are.' She began to sob. 'Sorry, Robbie, I...'

He gave her a hug. 'You'd better come with me, Evie – I know you're as worried as I am. Get your coat.'

Evelyn and Robbie hurried to the intensive therapy unit where Anna had been lying unconscious for three days. The charge nurse met them in the anteroom.

'There has been a change?' Robbie asked the nurse. 'We got here as soon as possible.'

The nurse smiled. 'Yes. Anna has regained consciousness—'

Evelyn gave a little whimper. 'Oh what a relief. My poor, poor sister...'

'That's fantastic news!' Robbie said. 'I knew she would make it!' He turned to go into Anna's room but the nurse gently caught his arm.

'One moment, please.' She spoke quietly. 'I do understand that you want to be with your fiancée, but I have to tell you that she is still very seriously ill and the slightest disturbance at this critical stage could cause a relapse.' She indicated the chairs in the anteroom and asked them to have a seat for a moment.

'Normally, with a patient in such a serious condition, we would not allow anyone to visit for another twenty-four hours at least,' she explained. 'We like to give them a chance to stabilise. However, Anna became very agitated and was asking for you. She insisted that we call you and I felt there was a risk of her suffering a relapse if she remained in such a state. She has been sedated to reduce the chances of that happening.'

'I see,' Robbie said, downhearted at being given this news. 'Do you think she will make a full recovery?'

The nurse shook her head. 'Impossible to say at this very early stage. I'm sorry I cannot be more positive.'

'At least she has regained consciousness,' Evelyn said. 'That is positive in itself.'

'You may go to her now,' the nurse said. 'I am sorry, only one at a time, and only for a few minutes, please.'

'You go in,' Evelyn told Robbie. 'I will wait here for you.'

Anna's voice was stronger than Robbie had expected and her words were clear.

280

'Robbie... oh Robbie, thank god you have come,' she said, becoming distressed and reaching out to him.

He took her hand and kissed it. 'I have been here most of the time, my love.'

'But you were not here when I woke up?'

'No, but apart from the times when I went home to shower and have a meal, I have been at your side all the time.'

'How long have I been here?'

'This is the third day. You were attacked outside the dentist's on Saturday. Do you remember?'

'I remember having a tooth filled and feeling faint afterwards. I was waiting for Evie to come for me but she did not arrive...' Anna's voice trailed off and she looked confused.

'Evie did come for you, but she was held up at the traffic lights. She actually saw the person attack you but she was too far away to do anything and although she jumped the lights and raced to your assistance, she was too late. Your attacker had disappeared.'

'And was Evie wearing my trench coat?' Anna asked. 'Before I blacked out I thought someone came to help me wearing a coat like mine.'

'No. Evelyn didn't even stop to put a coat on. What you saw was somebody wearing a long raincoat and a trilby hat – the person who attacked you.'

Anna was anxious and bewildered. The nurse stepped up to the bed and checked her pulse.

'I am sorry; Anna must rest now. We will also need to do some further tests now that she is conscious. Perhaps you would like to visit again a bit later this evening?'

The nurse saw Evelyn's worried face peering through the small glass panel of the door. She went to her.

'You may come in and see your sister briefly,' she said, 'and then she must rest. She is still very poorly.'

Robbie rose from the bedside and bent and kissed Anna's cheek.

'See you later, sweetheart,' he whispered as he moved aside to make room for Evelyn. 'I love you.'

Evelyn held her sister for a few moments. 'Me too,' she managed, choking back her tears.

'I hate leaving her like that,' Evelyn said as she and Robbie walked down the long hospital corridor towards the exit.

Robbie put an arm around Evelyn's shoulders. 'I know, but we have to stay positive for Anna's sake – at least she is conscious again, and they are doing everything they possibly can for her.'

The following day, Robbie went to visit Anna at lunch time. She was still being fed intravenously but was now free of most of the other wires and tubes apart from the heart and blood pressure monitors. Robbie thought she looked better, although she was still very pale, as well as drowsy from the cocktail of drugs designed to keep her calm and pain free. Conversation was limited and Robbie just sat quietly at her bedside, holding her hand as she rested, talking softly to her occasionally and responding if she spoke.

'Your mama is coming in to see you later this afternoon,' he told her.

Marianne had kept in constant touch with both Evelyn and the hospital and she had kept the rest of the family updated. The police had interviewed all family members as a routine part of their enquiries but all were eliminated and then left in peace.

'Ah, Mama! It will be good to see her. She will be worrying about me...'

'Naturally she is concerned, as we all are, but you are on the mend now. You will soon be out of all this.' With a hand movement he indicated the wall of highly technical, life-saving equipment.

Anna gripped his hand. 'Oh, Robbie, I have been very lucky...'

'Well, if you consider it lucky being viciously attacked and left for— '

'Dead? But I wasn't. Someone called an ambulance straight away, Evie was with me almost immediately and *all this*', she repeated his gesture, 'has saved my life. Yes, darling, I am very lucky!'

Robbie looked at her. Half lying, half sitting against a bank of sterile white pillows, her face was bruised beneath the bandages that protected her injuries. Her skull may be broken but her spirit certainly wasn't. A girl in a million. He was the lucky one. He leaned over and fleetingly touched her lips with his.

'I love you so much,' he whispered.

When Robbie returned to the hospital later that evening, Anna was sleeping soundly. He asked the duty nurse how she was.

'Her mother spent some time with her this afternoon,' the nurse replied, 'and Anna was talking quite a lot.'

'Tiring for her,' Robbie suggested.

'Yes, but a girl needs her mother at times like this and it has been good for her moral. However, you are right, it has also exhausted her!'

'Mm, they have always been very close. But she is all right? What I mean is there are no further complications?'

'No, she is as well as we can expect at this early stage and her vital signs are stabilising,' the nurse assured him.

'Okay, thanks for that. Well then I think I will leave her to rest. When she wakes would you tell her I said goodnight and I will see her in the morning?'

When he entered the room the following morning, Robbie noticed a glass half full of water on Anna's bedside table. The drip had been disconnected and moved to a corner of the room.

'Wow, are you able to drink again now?'

Anna smiled and nodded, her eyes focused on her vanity case that Robbie had brought at her request, together with a bag containing her own feminine nightwear – up to now she had been wearing what she called the hospital *smocks* that did nothing for a girl's image.

He put the case and nighties on the bed and kissed her.

She thanked him. 'Did Mama tell you what I wanted?'

'Oh yes, she was very specific.'

She smiled again. 'Yes,' she said in reply to his question, 'I have been drinking water. They are going to bring me soup and also some fruit drinks so that I can soon begin to feed myself.'

'That is terrific news. And are you feeling better today?'

'My head still throbs when the medication wears off, but not too bad otherwise. They might be moving me out of here soon. Robbie, I—'

'Good, that's great news!'

'Yes. I want to—'

Again Robbie cut her words off. 'I expect they will want you near the desk for a while to keep an eye on you, but that is fantastic, I am so pleased.'

'Well yes, I must be doing all right. I have...' she pushed her hand against his mouth as he opened it to speak again. 'Will you please listen for a moment? I have something important to tell you – something I remembered when I woke up in the night.'

'Oh, right. Sorry. Go on?'

'My attacker – I know who it was... it was Kristina!'

'Kris... Anna, are you sure?'

'Oh, I am sure – I had a very vivid recollection. Those eyes of hers. When she hit me for the last time her dark glasses slipped off and I saw those jealous green eyes glinting with evil. I have only been close enough to her once, but I have never forgotten those eyes.'

'But the police want to trace a man in a raincoat and trilby hat, possibly carrying a white stick.'

'Well she looked like a man! And you have always suspected that it was she who somehow entered our home and stole your property the first time and then came back and trashed the place!'

'Yes.' It was true. Robbie had always suspected Kristina of being involved and he remembered Kurt's warning – to be careful. And yet now that Anna was making an accusation he found himself struggling to believe it. It felt surreal.

'And Robbie, where is my ring?' She looked down at her naked ring finger and stroked it between her finger and thumb. 'Have you taken it for safekeeping?'

He wanted to tell a white lie to protect her from any further distress, but he had to tell her the bald truth, that it had been stolen, more than likely during the attack.

'Anna, listen to me. If you are serious about your attacker being Kristina, then I am pretty sure the ring will be found in her possession.'

'I am serious, Robbie, and certain.'

Although she was recovering from a near-fatal attack and was still weak, Anna's memory was returning and she was becoming more lucid.

'I am going to phone Fritz straight away,' Robbie told her. 'There is no time to waste.'

When he came back, Anna, helped by her nurse, had changed into one of her pretty nightdresses and applied some lipstick and blusher.

'Hey, look at you! Are you doing anything tonight?' he joked.

She gave him a crooked smile that gladdened his heart after all the worry and stress of the last few days.

'Fancy me, do you?' she teased.

Kristina faced her interrogator across the same table in the same interview room where Robbie and Marcel had been questioned. She was an attractive woman when she made the effort and was looking particularly glamorous today in a primrose yellow linen suit with its short skirt and fitted jacket that showed off her curves and long, shapely legs. She wore a low cut top that almost perfectly matched the colour of her eyes, and her shoes and bag were of the usual black patent that she favoured for accessories.

Her blonde curls bounced as she tossed her head in response to the DI's question about her movements last Saturday lunchtime.

'Inspector, I was at work last Saturday from eleven in the morning until well after three p.m.'

'Do you normally work on Saturdays? I thought office staff worked a five-day week?'

The curls bounced some more. 'I am not just office staff. I am also employed to meet, greet and look after visitors to Ciba Geigy and one of my responsibilities is showing potential new practicants around the factory and laboratories and providing them with food and entertainment, and that is what I was doing last Saturday.'

'How many practicants were with you?'

'Four; two male and two female.'

'Names?'

'Oh, I cannot remember their names now; there is a list in the office.'

'I shall want to see the list and I shall want their contact details.'

'Of course, Inspector.'

'What time did the new practicants arrive at Ciba-Geigy?'

'They had all assembled in reception by eleven o'clock.'

The inspector stared straight into Kristina's mesmerising eyes. 'At these times I believe it is usual for visitors to be issued with name badges.'

'Yes.'

'And yourself, of course?'

The interview continued in some detail; the inspector carefully wording his questions with the intention of unnerving Kristina. So far, she seemed to be perfectly composed and at ease.

The inspector's sidekick, Sergeant Francois Boulier spoke up.

'If we speak to these people they will confirm that you were with them between two p.m. and two-thirty?'

'I was indeed with them between two and two-thirty. We were in the bowling alley. We first had lunch in the cafeteria at about one o'clock and then went bowling.'

'What time did you leave?' the inspector asked.

'It was just after three p.m.... look, what is this? Why are you asking me all these questions?' Kristina spread out her arms as if to show that she had nothing to hide.

'Miss Gotti, we have an eye witness who places you at the scene of a serious assault last Saturday afternoon between two and two-thirty p.m. and,' the inspector raised his voice as Kristina opened her mouth to deny his accusation, 'furthermore, identified you as the person who carried out the attack.'

'But that is absurd,' Kristina replied. 'I have just explained my movements covering the time I was supposed to be somewhere else.' She leaned forward aggressively. 'And where am I supposed to have carried out this attack?'

The sergeant read out the exact address of the dental practice.

'The attacker also left behind some vital evidence,' he told her, 'which we are currently checking for DNA.'

'Checking for what?'

The inspector smiled to himself. 'Ask your bosses to explain,' he replied, 'they are scientists, are they not?'

Kristina gave the policemen a look of contempt. 'So can I go now?'

'No, I'm afraid you cannot. You will remain under police detention until we have checked out your story and are satisfied that you are telling us the truth.'

'You cannot keep me here; I have done nothing wrong!' she complained.

'We can hold you here for as long as necessary, miss,' the inspector replied. 'And if you have done nothing wrong, then you have nothing to worry about!'

Within a few hours, the investigating officers had traced three of the four practicants who corroborated her statement and she was also visible on the CCTV tape, entering the bowling alley with them around one p.m. and also leaving, a little after three pm. She was also seen to be going into the bowling alley again just before two-thirty but was accompanied by the two female guests. Kristina was released, leaving the police as baffled as before.

Robbie had always been convinced that Kristina was responsible for what had happened to Anna. He had no evidence, apart from her general behaviour, and the stalking – it was mostly a gut feeling. He decided to have a chat with his friend Kurt, who seemed to know more about Kristina than anyone.

'She was in police detention for several hours, you know,' Kurt told him.

'Yes, I heard on the news that they had made an arrest but she had been released. I really thought they were close to charging her.'

'She has a watertight alibi,' Kurt replied. 'The CCTV footage proves that she was in a bowling alley with four witnesses at the time of the attack on Anna.'

'Hm, I know. Martina told me, but I still have this nagging doubt that she is behind it.'

'Is she still stalking you?' Kurt asked.

'I haven't noticed her – she is either being more discreet or has given up.'

'Well, I wondered if she had found someone else.'

'Really?' Robbie's eyebrows shot up with surprise. 'That would be a relief – for me, anyway. Have you seen her with someone, then?'

'No, but she was wearing a ring on her engagement finger this morning.'

Robbie's pulse quickened. 'Kristina is wearing an engagement ring?' He took a step towards Kurt so that their faces were almost touching. 'What does it look like?'

Kurt backed away, putting more space between himself and Robbie, and folded his arms.

'Sorry, didn't mean to... you know.'

Kurt nodded. 'It's okay.'

'Can you describe the ring?'

Kurt thought for a moment. 'Well, I didn't, you know, get a very good look at it, but it is certainly very unusual—'

'Unusual? So is Anna's – yes, go on, go on...'

Trying not to show his irritation, Kurt continued, 'It looked like silver—'

'It's white gold—'

'If you would just give me a chance, Robbie? I know you are overwrought at the moment...'

'Sorry, Kurt. Please go on.'

'Okay, maybe white gold then, and I think... like a cluster of flowers with a diamond in the centre of each...'

As he paused, trying to recall the detail, Robbie again chimed in with, 'Roses, four roses with diamonds set in the middle of their petals.'

'Yes,' Kurt agreed. 'That's a fair description from what I remember.'

'It's Anna's ring. There isn't another like it in the world; we had it specially commissioned by Meister.'

Kurt frowned. 'How do you think she got hold of Anna's engagement ring?'

Robbie shook his head, not wanting to discuss what was on his mind but asked Kurt if he would get Fritz on to it.

'Of course, my friend. Fritz is a member of the investigative team and there should not be any problem with him visiting her at work to further their enquiries. He has anyway been working on the case day and night.'

However, the police did have something of a breakthrough the following day. A parcel was found dumped in a back garden, just a short distance from the alleyway near to the dental surgery. Wrapped in several pages of the *Basler Zeitung* newspaper and roughly secured with masking tape was a man's long raincoat along with a trilby hat, black wig, blood-stained trainers and a folding white stick, the handle of which poked out at an awkward angle. There were also extensive blood stains on the raincoat.

'Masses of DNA,' declared the investigating officer, who was keen to be involved with the then fairly new and almost infallible method of identification.

While the forensics team was engaged with the testing and comparing of blood and hair, Fritz took a telephone call from Kurt.

'Kristina has just turned up for work wearing the ring,' Kurt told him.

'All right,' Fritz replied. 'Well spotted. I'll be right over; see you in a few minutes.'

When Fritz burst into reception to confront her, Kristina was not wearing the ring and claimed to know nothing about it.

'I have a witness who saw you wearing a ring…' Fritz took a photograph out of his tunic pocket, '… this ring, to be precise, when you started work this morning.'

Kristina looked at the photograph. 'You are joking of course! Where would I get a ring like that? And if I had one do you seriously think I would wear it at work?'

'I presume you would if it was your engagement ring.' He watched her very closely for a reaction to the word engagement. A narrowing of the green eyes was sufficient.

'So you have not been wearing this ring?' Fritz asked.

She shrugged. 'Not even seen it.'

'Then you won't mind if I carry out a quick search?'

Another bored shrug. 'Be my guest; you won't find anything like an engagement ring.'

Fritz asked her to empty the contents of her oversized shoulder bag, which contained surprisingly little, and her pockets, including her coat. Nothing. He then searched her desk drawers and looked beneath papers and any crevices that could conceal the ring. Still nothing. He ought to have brought Martina, he thought; she could have done a full body search.

'Told you!' she crowed as he thanked her and left.

When he returned to the police station he was met with glum faces there too.

'What's wrong with everyone?' he asked Martina.

'DNA results have come through,' she replied. 'The blood stains on the raincoat and trainers are confirmed to be a match with Anna's.'

'Hm, no surprises then. And the black hairs; anything there to go on?'

293

Martina pulled a face. 'Nylon – from the wig.'

'No kidding... and no fingerprints?'

'No; he must have worn gloves. We haven't found any gloves though.'

As Anna began to regain her strength, Robbie spent less time at her bedside and visited only in the afternoons or evenings. He and Evelyn and Marianne worked out a rough schedule to ensure that Anna, now out of intensive care, was never alone during visiting hours. Robbie was planning to return to work in a few days but in the meantime, as the police were getting nowhere, he thought he would do a bit of sleuthing himself – time he did a bit of stalking for a change.

Knowing that Kristina regularly walked the short distance to the shops in her lunch hour, he centred his attentions on the cake shop. It was well known that she could never go near the place without going in to buy something smothered in chocolate which she would then consume during her mid-afternoon break.

On the first day she did not show up. Fair enough, he thought, Mondays were always busy. That made it all the more likely that she would be there tomorrow, then.

Tuesday lunchtime, at around one-thirty, Robbie, dressed in a dark hoodie and black jeans, positioned himself outside an electrical retailer's a few doors up from the cake shop and waited. As he had hoped, a tall woman, elegant in turquoise today, with springy blonde curls, entered the street from a side passage. Carrying her signature large shoulder bag, Kristina opened the cake shop door and went inside.

Pulling his hood closely around his face, he quickly reached the cake shop and, keeping his face hidden, looked at the range of cakes on display in the window. He glanced up a couple of times. Two chocolate éclairs went into her bag, she paid for them and was handed some change. She was coming out. Robbie kept his head down, the hood conveniently slipping down over his eyes. His heart skipped a beat. It was exactly what he had hoped and expected to see and yet it still didn't seem real.

As Kristina put the change away and zipped up her purse, he saw her hands clearly and there, on her third finger, was Anna's engagement ring. He so wanted to grab hold of her, force her to give the ring back and march her by the scruff of her neck to the police station but he knew that was the wrong approach and could make matters worse. He stood for a moment, making sure that she was heading the right way to be going back to work and crossed the road to a phone booth.

Robbie told Fritz what he had just witnessed. 'If you go now, you will be right behind her when she goes back to work,' he said.

'And she is definitely wearing Anna's ring?'

'Yes. Definitely.'

'Okay, on our way now.'

'And Fritz…'

'What?'

'For God's sake don't take the squad car this time or give her any hint that the cops are coming!'

'I am in uniform, man.'

'So wear a raincoat!'

The phone went dead, cutting off Fritz's expletive.

Chapter 20

Kristina was stowing her bag beneath her desk and looked up as the tall man entered reception. He was looking down, studying a photograph in his hand as he approached the desk.

'Good afternoon, sir.' She stood up to greet him. 'Welcome to Ciba-Geigy. How may I help?' she parroted, smoothing her skirt with perfectly manicured hands.

The ring was in evidence, much to Fritz's satisfaction. He slammed the photo down on the desk in front of her and pointed to it.

'You can help,' he replied, 'by explaining why you are wearing this ring and how you came by it!'

She looked at the image of the ring and immediately switched to her best bimbo routine.

'Oh,' she chirped, 'oh, will you just look at that – it's the same as my ring. Look!' She even held up her hand to show it to Fritz.

'*Your* ring, Miss Gotti? You have some nerve! You denied any knowledge of the ring when you were asked about it before.'

'Of course my ring,' she pouted now in mock indignation.

Humouring her, he then asked, 'Okay, so it is your ring after all. Do you mind telling me where you got it?'

'My Robbie gave it to me,' she replied. 'We are engaged.' The green eyes had a dreamy look as, crossing her upper arms, she hugged herself. 'He is such a romantic, you know – went down on one knee and everything – so *British*!'

'Really? Now look, I really do not have time for this – both you and I know that you are lying – that this ring was custom made for the occasion of the engagement of Robbie and Anna.

Kristina pushed the telephone towards him. 'Ring Robbie if you do not believe me. I have his number—' she spun around as Robbie's voice came from behind her. He had entered reception silently through the side door.

'That's the ring, officer. The ring we had especially made when Anna and I got engaged.'

Fritz nodded. 'Kristina Gotti, I am arresting you for theft.' He recited her rights, asked her to remove the ring, handcuffed her and led her away to his unmarked car in the visitors' car park, where Martina was waiting as back up.

Later that afternoon, while Kristina languished in police detention, Robbie told Evelyn and Marcel what had been happening and gave them the details of Fritz's latest update.

'After he'd arrested her for theft of the ring, he and Martina took her back to the police station and formally charged her but instead of letting her go, they held her in custody while they applied for a search warrant.'

298

'Well they could not let her go free, surely?' Evie said. 'Who knows what else she is capable of?'

'I don't understand how she expects the police to believe that she is engaged to Robbie,' Marcel said.

'Well, I told you from the start she was a nutcase,' Robbie replied. 'Anyhow, they searched her flat in her presence and found her trainers, covered in blood, a cheap black wig, a pair of wellingtons covered in dried on mud – remember when she got in here and vandalised the place, leaving mud everywhere?'

'I remember the mess we had to clear up,' Marcel said, pulling a face.'

'They also found my collection of gold sovereigns, as well as my grandfather's medals, so she had no option but to confess and she also admitted to stealing and duplicating my door key.'

Evelyn's eyebrows came together in a deep frown. 'She could have been here at other times that we don't know about,' she remarked, shivering at the thought.

'Yes, that's what I thought. And she admitted stalking me as well as Anna, and then apparently broke down and confessed that she had attacked Anna on the steps of the dental practice with a length of lead pipe she had picked up on the nearby building site.'

Both Evelyn and Marcel stared wide-eyed and open-mouthed at Robbie.

'So what happens next?' Evelyn asked.

'She has now been charged with the greater felony of attempted murder with multiple other offences to be taken into consideration and will appear before a magistrate as soon as possible and then held in custody to await trial.'

'Will there need to be a trial as she has confessed?' Marcel asked. 'She will plead guilty, surely?'

'I don't know Swiss law, but there will be a trial to determine the sentence, I imagine,' Robbie said. 'But knowing her, she's capable of changing her plea!'

'What, and try to say that all the evidence was planted in her flat?' Evelyn said.

'Exactly.'

'Should we tell Anna all this?' Evelyn asked.

'Anna knows it was Kristina who attacked her,' Robbie replied, 'so yes, I think we should tell her that she has now owned up to it. We don't need to go into every detail – she is bound to ask questions but we can keep the answers simple, for now at least. I don't want to cause her more stress than necessary.'

Marcel nodded. 'I agree. We must look ahead; think only of her recovery and try to bury the past.'

Robbie plumped up Anna's pillows and made sure she had fresh water and her magazines handy if she felt like reading. She was making steady progress and Robbie felt he could return to work. Her mother and Evelyn would visit during the daytime and keep him informed of her condition.

'You are sure about me going back to work, Anna?' he asked. I can take another week or two off if necessary.'

'Robbie don't worry so much,' she replied, smiling back into his anxious face. 'I am feeling much better.

There is no need for you to be spending every minute of your time at my bedside. I am sure I will be able to leave here soon now.'

He did not know whether Anna believed that to be true or was just saying it to make him feel better, but he had already been told by the neurologist that her recovery would be slow and although at the moment everything seemed to be going well, it was not unusual to suffer a relapse. So although Anna was out of intensive care she was by no means out of the woods.

He gave her a hug and kissed her goodbye. 'Okay, my darling, I'll try not to,' he said. 'See you later!'

Apart from the fact that Anna was in hospital, life slowly returned to something resembling normality. Robbie returned to his work at the lab and was welcomed back by his colleagues who had missed his cheerful, easy-going manner. Kurt was especially pleased to see him and they met for lunch at the canteen.

'Ingrid seems to fit in well,' Robbie said of the newly appointed receptionist, 'and is a damn sight easier to work with after Kristina.'

Kurt agreed. 'Yes, the company is well rid of that one. I still find it hard to believe that she could carry out such a violent attack on poor Anna – and all because of her jealousy.'

'Well you did warn me about her,' Robbie replied, 'but you know, the very first time I met her I thought she was mentally unstable.' He ran his fingers through his hair. 'Do you think they will take her mental state into account when passing sentence? I mean she's obviously a sandwich short of a picnic.'

'A what? Sandwich…?

Robbie grinned. 'Sorry – it's an expression we use in Britain to describe someone who is not quite all there.' He tapped his temple, clarifying the meaning.

Kurt said he thought she was more malicious than crazy. 'Her jealousy obviously drove her to do what she did,' he remarked, 'but it was not a spur of the moment thing. It was very definitely premeditated and meticulously planned.'

'Yes, but she took some risks.'

'She did,' Kurt agreed, 'but she is also the type of person who gets away with it. Very manipulative and deceitful.'

'Clever.'

'But not quite clever enough, my friend,' Kurt added with a slight shake of his head.

Kristina meanwhile made a brief court appearance and was then held in police custody while reports were compiled about her state of mind, pending her trial date when her fate would be decided by a judge.

Robbie felt a huge sense of freedom now that Kristina was no longer able to stalk him and interfere in his life. However, in spite of the fact that she had made an attempt on his beloved Anna's life, he was not a vindictive person and rather than feeling she deserved all she got, he was saddened that she could be so driven by jealousy as to plan and carry out such a violent attack. The fact that her victim was his precious Anna made it all the harder for him to deal with. But days passed and Anna regained some of her strength and it seemed that the couple's future suddenly was looking much brighter.

They began to make plans – the main topic for discussion being their wedding.

Marianne was organising the wedding dress and was having it especially designed and made for Anna – this was her personal gift to her daughter, marking the occasion of her marriage to Robbie. Once a design had been approved, the dressmaker visited Anna in hospital where she was growing stronger every day, taking measurements and discussing the finer details that would make up the finishing touches. Anna was feeling well; the wounds were healing and her hair was beginning to grow back. Two or three more weeks of therapy, the consultant said, and she could leave hospital and become an out-patient.

This was encouraging news and when Robbie visited with Evelyn and Marcel, they talked mostly about their wedding. He suggested they hold the service at the Church of St. Joseph, the largest Roman Catholic church in Basel with 1,400 seats. The Neo-Baroque building was influenced by the Einsiedeln Monastery Church; this style was unique for a church building in the traditionally reformed Basel and the interior had been completely renovated in 1983.

Anna shook her head. 'No, darling. Swiss law requires a civil ceremony,' she told him. 'It has to be held at an official civil register office venue.'

'Register Office?' Robbie repeated in dismay. 'I want our wedding to take place in church, Anna.' He looked earnestly into her eyes. 'I know how important it is for you to take your vows in the sight of God.'

Anna smiled and took hold of his hand. 'That does not mean we cannot arrange our own religious or private celebration in addition, but it can't replace the civil ceremony. It is the law.'

'I see,' Robbie replied, feeling disgruntled. 'But we can have our marriage blessed by a priest as well?'

'Of course and most couples do, but as I said, a marriage in Switzerland must take place in a civil ceremony held at a registry office,' she reiterated. 'You had better make enquiries because there are several administrative steps to be taken in order to apply for a civil wedding and have it approved by the registrar. As a British citizen, you will have to produce your birth certificate and passport, a declaration of marital status and also complete a marriage preparation form.'

'Oh. God, what a palaver,' Robbie replied. 'I would rather live in sin,' he muttered as Anna shot him a look of displeasure.

'So I should go to the registry office to sort all this out?'

'Yes, and it is not half as bad as it sounds,' Anna said.

'And we can still have our marriage blessed in church afterwards?' he repeated.

'Of course,' Anna nodded. 'I told you, most are.'

Reassured that this was not only possible but also quite normal, they then went on to discuss the venue for the reception and Anna expressed a wish to spend her honeymoon in Venice.

Evelyn had a dreamy look. 'You can't get much more romantic than Venice,' she had remarked when they were all together discussing arrangements.

Marcel came straight back with, 'Well, if you are going to marry me, *ma cherie*, we will most likely be spending our honeymoon here, in our apartment!'

Evelyn stuck her tongue out at him then, her left eyebrow dancing with anticipation, enquired, 'That is not a proposal by any chance is it, Marcel?'

The dark eyes twinkled devilishly and a smiled pulled at the corners of his lips.

'You want we should get married as well, uh? All this talk of matrimony is making you feel brooding, I think.'

'Broody,' she corrected him, 'and I assure you that is not my problem but while we are on the subject you should know I do not intend to remain a spinster all of my life.' She gave him a confirmatory nod of the head. 'So now you know!'

Marcel shrugged, his infamous pout more pronounced than ever, his eyes still brimming with amusement.

'One day I may make an honest woman of you,' he declared. 'But not just yet, *ma belle femme fatale…*'

Evelyn rolled her eyes while the other three smiled, enjoying the exchange between the two who were so obviously devoted to each other.

A modest guest list was drawn up and Marianne offered to arrange and organise the venue and catering. Giuseppe agreed to pay for the reception and also

305

suggested that the bride be transported to the registry office in the classic Daimler for which Robbie had obtained a replacement headlamp. He would take them to the airport for their flight to Venice in a red Ferrari.

Excitement mounted as the day approached and Robbie could not believe his luck. He had come so close to losing his precious Anna and now it had all turned around and the couple were about to celebrate the most important day of their lives – the beginning of a lifetime of love and happiness that Robbie, before meeting Anna, thought had most probably passed him by.

As he strode towards his apartment, casual, with hands in his trouser pockets, he whistled tunelessly to himself and kicked at a small apple that had strayed from someone's basket onto the pavement. As he let himself into the apartment he thought briefly of Kristina and the lengths she had gone to in her quest to take him from Anna. Thank God all that is behind us now, he thought.

As he closed the door behind him, the phone began to ring. Expecting it to be Evelyn or her mother, he picked up the receiver.

'Hello? Robbie here… just got in, what is it?'

His heart turned a double somersault when the caller answered.

'This is Sister Klein, Mr Munro. I am so sorry to tell you this,' her voice was low and sympathetic, 'but your fiancée – she appears to have suffered a stroke. She is asking for you.'

'Ho… how bad is she?' Robbie asked. His hand trembled and he felt the blood drain from his face; indeed he felt himself sway as if his whole body was drained of every ounce of strength.

'She is stable now, and conscious, but rather agitated. Are you able to come in and see her?'

'I am on my way,' Robbie said. 'Tell her I will be with her shortly.'

Chapter 21

Anna was wired up to various monitors, and drips delivered drugs and fluids directly into her veins as she lay back against the pillows, her face pallid and strained.

She began to cry when Robbie entered the room and tried to sit up, holding out her arms to him.

'Robbie… oh, Robbie, I am so sorry. I do not know what is happening to me. I am so frightened…'

Robbie choked back his emotion; her anguished expression such a contrast to the happy, smiling vision that had waved goodbye to him just a short time ago. He held her in his arms, doing his best to comfort and placate her.

'Ssh, darling, try not to upset yourself too much, it won't help,' he soothed. 'They are doing everything possible for you…' he turned to the nurse.

'Do we know what happened? She was so much better; so cheerful and looking forward to the future.'

'The neurologist will come and talk to you both,' the nurse told him. 'He will explain the situation.' She left them together to talk in private. 'I will just be in the anteroom if you need me,' she explained.

The neurologist showed up about thirty minutes later and read the notes at the foot of Anna's bed. He told the nurse to substitute one of the intravenous medications with another. He closely examined the scans carried out immediately after the episode, shone a bright light into both her eyes and, stroking his chin, observed Anna for a few moments before addressing her and Robbie together.

'I'm afraid there has been another bleed from the brain,' he began, 'which has caused this latest stroke.' He consulted his notes. 'The good news is that this in itself has not caused too much damage, although obviously it would have been better avoided.'

'So she will recover?' Robbie asked.

''Mr Munro, I'm afraid we do not have a crystal ball and no one knows what the chances of Anna's recovery are.'

'You said... the good news...' Robbie faltered, hardly able to meet the consultant's gaze. 'Does that mean there is also bad news?'

The neurologist studied him gravely for a moment. 'The bad news is that the damaged blood vessels are extremely fragile and there is nothing we can do about their condition. It is completely out of our control. We had hoped that everything had stabilised and was settling down in its natural way. However, to begin bleeding again at this stage is not a good sign and it is my duty to tell you that this could be the forerunner of other, more serious brain haemorrhages to follow.' He shook his head. 'I am sorry. As I said, we have no way of knowing.'

Robbie glanced at Anna who remained silent but looked fearful.

'Thank you, for your honesty,' Robbie said, 'We can only wait and keep the faith.'

'Ruptured brain aneurysms are fatal in about forty percent of cases. Of those who survive, about sixty-six percent suffer some permanent neurological deficit.'

So if they don't die, they are left with disabilities, Robbie thought, knowing full well that the same thing would be running through Anna's mind.

'I see. And are you able to treat her?'

'We are monitoring her. At the moment she is responding to various stabilising drugs and necessary fluids and we are of course, keeping her as comfortable as possible. But before you ask, what we cannot do is prevent or even foresee any further haemorrhaging, so that, I am afraid, is in the lap of the gods.'

'Thank you.' Anna's voice was very weak and quavery.

The consultant nodded. 'I am very sorry,' he replied, gently touching her arm that lay outside the bedcovers, 'but please be assured that we are doing everything possible.'

As he left the room, the nurse rearranged Anna's pillows.

'You must rest now,' she told her.

'Should I go?' Robbie asked.

The nurse smiled. 'Stay if she wants you to,' she replied. 'It will be a great comfort for her to have you with her, but please don't tire her.'

'Robbie, please don't leave me,' Anna begged. 'I need you.'

It was three hours later when Robbie left the hospital, his mood very different from that of a few hours ago when he was looking forward to his marriage to Anna.

Later, at home, he discussed the situation with Evelyn and Marcel. Marianne was with them as well.

'I feel we should get married as soon as possible,' Robbie declared.

'What? Even in hospital?' asked Marcel.

'Yes – and then when Anna is well enough we can have a proper wedding – the way that we had originally planned to.'

'Will the hospital agree to hold the service there?' Evelyn asked.

Marianne assured her that it was not uncommon for weddings to be arranged in such a way when a partner was not well enough to go through the traditional civil ceremony.

'And it will be a legal and proper wedding? In the Catholic tradition?' Robbie was anxious that Anna's beliefs should be respected and fully honoured.

Marianne suggested that they met, as a family, with their local priest, Father Claude, to discuss the possibilities. Father Claude knew the family very well and in the circumstances, was more than willing to help in any way he could. He visited Anna in hospital to prepare her for the ceremony and assured her that it would be a true and honourable marriage.

Within two days, Anna was presented with her beautiful wedding dress, made of white satin, overlaid with white tulle and exquisitely worked French lace. The veil was sensitively designed so that it could be arranged to conceal most of Anna's head wounds which had now become livid scars. The outfit was completed with white satin shoes and gloves and she carried a fragrant, very delicate bouquet of alpines that Marianne had crafted into an arrangement that displayed their entwined initials surrounded by a heart of edelweiss.

As in England, only two witnesses were strictly necessary to legalise the marriage but in this case there was a small gathering consisting of Marcel, who took the role of best man, Evelyn, bridesmaid, Marianne and special guests, Kurt and Anna's best friend, Martina. Fritz also was invited but he was on duty so Martina also doubled up for him.

Robbie pushed Anna in a wheelchair to the small hospital chapel and she was able to stand proudly next to Robbie to take her vows and exchange rings… again bought from the same jeweller, Meister, with both their names engraved on the inside of the white gold bands. She looked beautiful and everything was very dignified. This had not been the wedding that any of them had planned or even foreseen but it was exquisite in its simplicity and it was as special and as moving as any wedding… indeed, it could be said that it was extra special. A two-tier wedding cake accompanied a bottle of sparkling wine and some glasses on a small side table and after the cake was cut, the priest proposed a toast and said a brief prayer for Anna, that God willing, she would make a complete recovery and both she and Robbie would enjoy a long, happy and fruitful marriage.

Anna, understandably, felt weak and tired after the ceremony and her medical team advised that she retired for a few hours' rest. She was taken back to her room and the nurse made her comfortable. Robbie sat by her bedside holding her hand as she slept. Sleep, he felt, was what she needed now and after a good rest he felt sure she would soon be back to her happy, smiling self.

Unfortunately, it was just a few hours later when Robbie rang for the duty nurse. It may have been the excitement of the day; it may have been as the doctor indicated – a random anytime, anywhere attack, but Anna had suffered a massive brain haemorrhage that was beyond treatment. The medical staff discreetly stood back and Anna passed away in Robbie's arms.

She whispered, 'I love you, Robbie,' and took her last breath as he held her close. She felt warm and soft, something he would always remember. Right now, though, he was numb with shock, and unable to take in the events of the past few hours.

Farewell, gorgeous lady… my beautiful wife,' he murmured, kissing her forehead, unable to prevent a tear from escaping and falling onto her pale cheek.

Chapter 22

Kristina was already in custody. There was to be no trial as such as she had already confessed and intended to plead guilty to all the charges brought against her. Her brief had suggested the judge would be more lenient in his or her sentencing if she were to be truthful and co-operative. The court appearance would be to decide upon an appropriate sentence and whether she was of sound mind. Robbie of course had always believed her to be of unsound mind. But when she was told that the charge of attempted murder had now been changed to murder she knew that meant a full life sentence. It would also have to be determined whether the attack was premeditated or not. If so, which seemed most likely given all the evidence, she would be committed to spend the rest of her natural life in prison. She was in her early twenties...

Anna was buried at a private service a few days later in a grave next to her beloved grandmother. She was wearing her wedding dress and her veil had been raised slightly to reveal a half smile that seemed to say, 'I made it... I married the man I love.'

Evelyn was inconsolable and clung to Marcel and Robbie, merely going through the motions of prayer as the priest blessed Anna and committed her immortal soul to eternal life. Marianne held herself with dignity, grieving the daughter who filled her life with so much joy, whose infectious laughter she would never hear again, but who would live in her heart for ever.

Robbie felt as if he had been taken over by aliens. Mind and body seemed to be writhing with a mass of emotions – grief, loss, heartache, anger, disgust, self-pity, resentment and most of all a deep sense of being robbed… robbed of a loving marriage and all he had ever wished for. He would never build the love nest that the two of them had dreamed of; Anna would never bear his children; they would never be a family. He had lost everything. Bereft and desolate, he watched as she was lowered into her resting place. Casting a single red rose onto her coffin, he bowed his head and then walked away. For some reason, Bethany entered his thoughts; the young girl who had spoken so movingly following the death of her father at one his Sunday School meetings. Much had happened in his life since then, he reflected.

Supporting the family were Kurt, Fritz and Martina – all special friends of Anna and who had all played their part in bringing her killer to justice. They, too, had to come to terms with the loss of a wonderful friend and she left a large hole to fill. Fiona and Mike were unable to be present but sent their condolences and felt the loss of their daughter-in-law very deeply.

The family party had booked a table at a quiet restaurant to have a meal in Anna's honour and round off the day with a touch of normality.

'What I don't understand,' Marcel said, 'is how Kristina managed to get away with all the other things, like getting a spare key to our apartment... you know, when she gained entry and vandalised the place?'

'Yes, I know,' Evelyn said, 'and even left clues – patterns of her muddy wellington soles for heaven's sake!'

'Yes,' Martina replied, 'but remember the size of those boots – we all thought the intruder was a man!'

'Well that was actually the second time she had been in your apartment,' Fritz added. 'The first time was when Anna and Robbie were away on holiday, and you and Marcel had gone to your sister's for the weekend. She stole Robbie's collection of gold coins and his grandfather's medals, but of course they were not missed until sometime later.'

'That's right,' Evelyn said, 'and it was not until Marcel asked to see the war medals that Robbie realised they were missing!' She nodded, trying to take all the information in. 'So how did she get hold of the key?' she asked.

'I believe it was when I left my jacket in reception one lunchtime,' Robbie said. 'I was only away for a few minutes, but when I went to get it later, I noticed my key was missing from the pocket. I remember asking Kristina if she had seen my key and she immediately said no and then suddenly remembered a workman had slipped from his ladder or something like that and knocked my jacket off its hook. She made a show of scrambling around on the floor for a few minutes and lo and behold – suddenly, there was my key! I was suspicious of her from the beginning, but of course, without any proof…

'So she had already copied your key?' asked Kurt.

'Yes, she must have, but she would have to have been damn quick – I mean she certainly took a few chances!'

'What would she want with war medals and gold sovereigns?' Marcel asked, frowning as he struggled to understand her motive,

'The sovereigns were in mint condition and worth a bit,' Robbie replied, 'but not easy to dispose of, I would imagine. And the war medals—'

'To make her feel close to you,' put in Martina, 'something that meant a lot to you – after all she was totally infatuated with you!'

Robbie nodded. 'From the moment I stepped into reception at Ciba-Geigy, it was like she had me attached to some kind of invisible chains that enabled her to follow my movements, keep track of all my comings and goings and yet all the while she was leading the way… very peculiar.'

'Huh, yes and very determined, my friend,' Kurt said. 'She knew from the start what she wanted and she intended to get it!'

Marcel looked up from his profiterole. 'Not a crime *passionel*?' he posed.

Martina believed it could be classed as a crime of passion. 'The insane jealousy,' she said, spreading her hands; 'the fact that she was willing to take such risks to get what she wanted. They are all pointers and valid to a sentencing judge.'

'And so she could get away with less than a life sentence?'

Fritz did not think so. He shook his head. 'There are other offences to be considered in connection with the murder,' he pointed out, 'and although the attack was made to look very spur of the moment and unprovoked, she had actually been plotting and scheming Anna's demise for many weeks. No, no, it was cold and calculated, first degree murder. Nothing less.'

Kurt nodded, waving his knife in the air like a sword of justice. 'Like I said… the woman is too clever for her own good.'

'Ingenious,' Fritz added, 'to fix the ring to the underside of her desk when we searched the area.'

'Is that what she did?' asked Robbie.

'A chunk of Blu Tack™ was later found with the imprint of the ring in it. Unfortunately we missed it during our search. It must have been hidden right at the back in a corner.'

'Such a tricky person to deal with,' said Evelyn. 'And I understand her entry into the bowling alley with her guests, but not how she was able to leave unnoticed, to go and kill Anna, and then be seen a short while afterwards on CCTV re-entering with two of the guests. How did she manage to do that?'

Martina held Evelyn's hand, feeling her distress. 'She entered the bowling alley with that huge bag that she always carried – allegedly packed with 'goodies and freebies' for her students – it is clear to see on the monitor. When they were all assembled, she distributed the gifts

318

and then went to freshen up before the entertainment began. But she had a long raincoat and her trainers concealed in her bag as well as a black wig and a trilby hat. For added disguise, she wore shades and carried a white stick. So, in the ladies', she quickly slipped into disguise and at four minutes past two, nonchalantly walked out of the bowling alley with her tote bag neatly folded and then must have run to the dentist's surgery where she immediately found a length of lead pipe lying around, perfect for—'

'Amazing that, by chance, she found a weapon for her purpose,' Evelyn interjected.

'Had she not found the piping, then the stick was to have done the deed,' Fritz added. 'They are made of metal now, quite substantial, and believe me, in the wrong hands can be lethal. She had it all worked out, but luck also happened to be on her side.'

'And not on the side of my poor Anna,' Evelyn sniffed, her grief almost palpable.

Robbie bit his lip in an effort to master the emotion that was rapidly rising to the surface.

Martina continued. 'She then ran like hell up a nearby alleyway where she was quickly lost from sight. But she had already made a big mistake. She wanted to make sure of doing the job properly and took one more swipe. Sorry, my love,' she said, hugging Evelyn, who buried her face in her hands, 'perhaps we will leave the rest of the details for the court to…'

'No, please,' Evelyn insisted. It is important for me to know these things, horrific as they are to me.'

'If you're sure? Well, as you know, her dark glasses fell off at that moment and Anna, still just conscious at this stage, caught a glimpse of her eyes – those vivid green eyes with their jealous glint that once seen can never be unseen!'

Evelyn nodded, shuddering at the thought of her sister's ordeal.

Fritz took over as Martina comforted her friend.

'Well, she kept on running, even found a very conveniently placed bin in which to dump the raincoat, trainers, stick and wig. She replaced her shoes, tidied her hair, slowed down to a dignified walking pace and incredibly, with lady luck still on her side, met up with two of the practicants who had left the bowling alley briefly to get a breath of fresh air and they all walked back in together, the practicants unwittingly providing the murderess with her vital alibi… making it appear that she had been with them all afternoon. But such a chance she took – she risked everything and so nearly got away with it!'

'But then she had the stupidity to go around flaunting the ring,' Robbie said, 'and told Fritz that I had given it to her.'

Kurt shook his head. 'And thought everyone would believe her when she said she was engaged to you.' He thought for a moment and cocked his head to one side. 'Did I say she was clever? I take that back. I do not think clever so much as audacious – scheming and deceitful, and very dangerous. I never trusted her!'

'I always thought she was a head case,' Robbie replied. 'Right from the start.'

Kurt was very proud of Fritz. His partner was deemed by them all to have been the most vigilant and effective investigating officer on the case. In fact, he had been given a commendation by his superiors for his vigilance and all the extra hours he had worked, often staying on after a long night shift in an effort to obtain the firm evidence they needed to make an arrest. They all agreed that he went far beyond the call of duty and it was fitting that he had been the arresting officer. He would be awarded his commendation medal in due course.

Fritz and Martina, as well as being work colleagues, were good friends and worked extremely well together. Their relationship was like that of brother and sister. Martina was also very fond of Kurt.

'Not just the best looking cop for miles around,' Martina said, smiling at Fritz and trying to lighten the moment, 'but also the best looking cop with a brilliant career ahead of him... I bags polish your medal!'

Fritz, a quiet, modest character, although obviously delighted that his efforts had been instrumental in bringing Kristina to justice, felt a little embarrassed and looked down, trying to hide his blushes at the praise being heaped on him.

'I was simply doing my job,' he offered.

Martina winked at Kurt and turning to her colleague, playfully tweaked his already pink cheek.

'Aw, come on, Fairycakes, you needn't be shy with us!'

Epilogue

Kristina was formally charged with murder and transferred to a secure custodial unit. She was examined by two independent doctors – one a physician, the other a psychologist – and found to be neither physically nor mentally impaired. Because of the nature of her crime she was held in solitary confinement for her own protection and it was during these long, lonely hours that she realised the full consequences of her actions. She was overcome with remorse at what she had done and, unable to live with the overwhelming guilt of ruining the lives of an entire family, as well as the prospect of having to spend the rest of her life alone in prison, she decided there was only one course of action.

One morning, after breakfast, she found her way, passing the governor's office, to the laundry, and said she had been tasked with helping to fold and store the linen. Waiting her opportunity – the one thing she had learned to do well – she tightly folded a sheet, concealed it beneath her grey prison sweatshirt, folded her arms firmly across her chest and calmly walked back to her cell.

'I was called to the governor's office,' she told an orderly who stopped and questioned her.

By the time the orderly had checked, Kristina had torn the sheet into lengths and tightly knotted them together.

She was found half an hour later, hanging by the neck from one of the bars that secured the small, high window. The table she had climbed on to reach the required height, lay on its side near the door where it landed when she kicked it away. The prison doctor was called and the governor herself tried to resuscitate her, but they were too late.

Anna would always be loved by those who were privileged to have known her, and was now at peace; in time, Robbie's broken heart would heal and he would find love again.

As for Kristina, she had passed her own judgement on herself and in so doing would no longer be troubled by her passionate intention.